PAULA BYRNE

Look to Your Wife

WILLIAM COLLINS

William Collins
An imprint of HarperCollins*Publishers*
1 London Bridge Street
London SE1 9GF

www.WilliamCollinsBooks.com

First published in Great Britain by William Collins in 2018

1

A catalogue record for this book is
available from the British Library

ISBN 978-0-00-827058-2 (hardback)
ISBN 978-0-00-827875-5 (trade paperback)

Printed and bound in Great Britain by
CPI Group (UK) Ltd, Croydon, CR0 4YY

For Matthew

So will I turn her virtue into pitch,
And out of her own goodness make the net
That shall enmesh them all.

William Shakespeare, Othello

Without the Tweets, I wouldn't be here.

Donald J. Trump, 45th President of the
United States of America, interviewed
in the Oval Office

Twitter is an online social networking service that enables
users to send and read short 140-character messages called
'tweets.' Registered users can read and post tweets, but those
who are unregistered can only read them. Users are
identified by a 'handle,' indicated by an 'at' sign.

Lisa Blaize @Lisa_Blaize
Twitter may be my undoing!

PRELUDE

The Letter

June 17th

Dear Headmaster,

Please, please, please do something about Lisa. When you first came to Blagsford School, we were all thrilled to have a man of your calibre and academic excellence. Edward Chamberlain is a name that inspires awe and reverence in the educational world. I, amongst many others, was full of admiration when you took on that academy 'sink' school in the north of England. How brave and clever of you. Everyone knew that you would turn it around. But you surpassed all expectations, raising it from 'Unsatisfactory' to 'Outstanding' in such a short time, before coming here.

Naturally, some whispered that you would use it to your advantage, only to gain the coveted knighthood for services to education. Congratulations, by the way. Well deserved (though we all know that you only got it because of your background). We know how lucky we are to have you. I have been one of your most loyal supporters since you came to the school a year ago. It pains me to have to write this: I can barely believe that I am doing so.

But please, Edward, silence your wife. She is a liability, and she is damaging your reputation. Blagsford is a small world. The community of public schools is even smaller. Social media is a very useful tool, but Lisa's embarrassing and vulgar tweets are presenting a very bad image for the school. The woman is barely literate, for heaven's sake. She has no idea how to use French accents. Her grammar is appalling. I winced when she tweeted about meeting the opera singer 'Jesse Norman'.

To many of us, it beggars belief that Lisa Blaize has published a book. Still more that it got some very good reviews and was shortlisted for the Fashion History Book Prize. Did she flash her boobs at one of the judges? Many say you wrote it. At the very least, her copy-editor must be first rate. I'll wager the poor thing dreads the day when Lisa's next typescript comes in.

I was invited to your celebration party, but, like quite a few other people, couldn't face being subjected to another episode of The Lisa Show. Like many others, I was dreading what becoming Lady C would do to Lisa's already grossly inflated ego. I am pleased for you, Edward, and would have happily attended the party if all I had to do was talk to interesting, intelligent and perhaps even inspirational folk. But I simply don't have the time, let alone the inclination, to seek out 'glam' clothes to feed Lisa's attention-seeking fantasies.

It's clear from Lisa's Twitter account just how obsessed she is with designer clothes and shoes and skin potions, and how much time and money she devotes to her appearance, but it's naïve of her to expect the rest of us to do the same when we are extremely busy people, and, I might add, far less vain than Lisa.

I don't know how much attention you pay to Lisa's Twitter account, but if you have a look at her tweets over the past five or six months you will get a sense of what people are concerned about and why Lisa has become an object of ridicule, not just

at Blagsford, but across the public school network more widely.
You will be able to see that she comes across as almost
pathologically vain and egotistical …

* * *

'Lisa, I've had a poisonous letter. It's unbelievably cruel. And very funny. It claims to be from a member of staff. It's a vicious attack on you. Of course, I don't believe a word of it. These idiots know nothing about you.'

'Why do you say "about you", and not "about us"? Is the letter aiming to hurt you or me? Is it about who you are and where you've come from?'

'Probably me. First there was Airfaregate and now this. You're my Achilles' heel. They know that.'

'Does it mention Sean?'

'No. Would you like to see it?'

'No, Edward, certainly not. I make it a rule not to read anonymous letters. People who write things like that are rarely "well" people. And I don't want spiteful things sticking in my head. In fact, I'm surprised that you read it, knowing that it was unsigned. The person who did this wants to sow a seed of doubt in you. Please don't read it again. Throw it away and forget about it. In fact, just give it to me.'

'But they seem to know so much about you. I'm curious. It reads to me like a bitchy gay, you know the type who hates women. Well, there are lots of them in the world of teaching, so no clue there. Critical of your tweets, your grammar, your body. Digs at your Liverpool background. It even implies that I wrote your book for you.'

'Ah, Sir Edward Chamberlain, that purveyor of feminist fashion history. The man I met a year after my book was published.

But I hate to see you so upset. Don't let them get to you. It doesn't bother me one bit. Is it someone jealous of the knighthood? How petty and unkind. Anyway, I'm not ashamed of being a Scouser and not having had a posh education.'

'Darling, perhaps you had better stop tweeting for a bit. Just let the dust settle.'

PART ONE

Innocence

CHAPTER 1

Hamlet Cocks Up

Blagsford School for Boys was founded in 1552 under a law set out in the Charities Act of 1545, which had been passed by Henry VIII to put to use funds from the dissolution of the monasteries. For nearly four hundred years it stood opposite the Cornmarket in a quiet, pretty Midlands market town.

Between the wars, it moved to the edge of town. There was a need for more boarding houses, and an opportunity arose when death duties forced a local gentry family to sell their eighteenth-century mansion with its landscaped grounds – readily convertible to a sports field – and its small lake (or was it a large pond?). A few Old Blaggers objected, saying School wouldn't be School in a new location, but the move was a success.

Blagsford had twice made it to the top fifty of the *Sunday Times* Independent School Ratings. The *Good Schools Guide* described it as 'a comfortable mix of brains, brawn, and artistic flair, but demanding and challenging too'. Less good headlines were made after twenty-six pupils were taught the wrong Shakespeare play (*Hamlet* instead of *Much Ado about Nothing*) in preparation for an A level examination.

Every English teacher's worst nightmare, Edward had thought to himself, reading the story in the paper. As a Tudor historian with a particular interest in the cultural consequences of education policy, and a special fondness for *Hamlet*, he felt a real sympathy for Mr Camps, the poor man who was forced into early retirement by the governors after the *Hamlet* cock-up. Though he was also quietly grateful. Camps happened to be the head, who liked to lead from the front by taking one A level set himself. It was probably because he was overwhelmed by administrative duties, and didn't have time to attend departmental meetings, that he had taught the wrong play. The resultant vacancy had been Edward's opportunity to apply for the position of Headmaster of Blagsford.

*   *   *

Edward had won a scholarship to a famous public school himself, got into Oxford, and taken a first-class degree in history.

He had stayed on to complete his doctorate, which was then published as an academic monograph entitled *Gilded Lilies: Grammar School Education and Social Mobility in Tudor England.* He was pleased with the pun in the title, though he had to explain it whenever someone at a cocktail party asked him what his book was about.

In the early sixteenth century, a man named William Lily wrote the standard Latin grammar textbook for use in schools. In the middle of the century, the Tudor monarchs founded numerous new grammar schools in order to train up a kind of civil service for the nascent modern state. This gave lower middle-class boys ample opportunities for social mobility. By the end of the century, Lily's grandson John had benefited from this – he had become the most famous and popular writer in Elizabethan England, thanks to his clever (but admittedly unreadable) novel *Euphues*, and his court comedies that Queen Elizabeth absolutely adored. And, of course, this same process of education and social mobility was the key to the life and work of William Shakespeare, whose plays he adored. So you see, Edward would conclude, in best lecturer mode, it was the educational revolution that had made *Hamlet* possible.

Edward had wrestled with the idea of becoming an academic, but felt that he didn't quite have the killer touch. He knew from certain aspects of his postgraduate experience that he would never gain full institutional acceptance in the world of Oxbridge, and he saw too many fellow students exiled to junior lectureships in dreary, rainy places like Dundee and Belfast. He was more of a big fish in a small pond sort of guy, and felt that he would have more freedom (and certainly more money) as a teacher in a good public school. They were always on the lookout for bright young men who knew the tricks of the trade when it came to Oxbridge admissions, which was what the parents cared about. He soon had half a dozen offers to become a history teacher. He was relieved that the independent schools didn't bother with all the nonsense of having to do an additional teacher training degree, where all you learned was lesson planning and crowd control.

Well, he certainly had the money, thanks to the live-in accommodation arrangements when he became a housemaster. But not quite the freedom he might have expected to continue his writing career. In time, though, he was glad of that. He discovered that he was good at organization, and liked running meetings. There was something satisfying about the art of letting everyone have their say, while still pushing the business along. Before long, he was promoted to deputy head in a minor public school just outside Guildford, in the south of England. It was a place that aspired to imitate his own famous *alma mater*.

Then he had a kind of epiphany. He wasn't really sure whether it was out of idealism or ambition, but he suddenly decided to leave the private sector and venture away from the south. Was it

11

because he looked around the staffroom one day and saw old men with thinning hair who had never left the cocoon of public-school life? Or was it that he genuinely believed that, having made his case about education and social mobility in Tudor England, he could actually put it into practice in the real world? Was it his vocation to bring black kids out of the ghetto? Or maybe he knew that it would give him a certain edge, a fast track to greater things. So he had applied for the position of head teacher at St Joseph's Academy in Liverpool.

His friends had teased him mercilessly, saying he wouldn't last five minutes. 'Too posh, mate,' said Nick, his best friend from Oxford. He knew that there was an element of truth in this; he was Oxford through and through. Of course it was a risk applying for the Academy job, but, unlike most of the people he knew, he liked taking risks. St Joseph's was desperate for a turnaround, and in normal circumstances would not have even considered a man from the public-school sector.

At interview, the panel was impressed by Edward's CV, but more so by the man himself. He was told that he and another candidate were to be called back for a second interview. He had a hunch, from things he had overheard on the day of the first interview, that his rival was an internal candidate. I bet they'll go for the safe option, he said to himself. He had been impressed by the governors, and had liked the energy and grittiness of Liverpool. He really wanted the job.

He phoned Nick to talk it over.

'Ed, that's so weird that you called – I was about to email you. Did I ever tell you about my American cousin? Lives in Boston, filthy rich and on the board of a top school out there – I mean really top, Milton Academy. Just outside Boston, feeder for Harvard and Yale. Couple of the Kennedy boys went there. T. S.

Eliot, James Taylor, you name it. They're looking for a new head of history, and he asked me for advice. You said you wanted a change: how about the New World?'

Edward was an Englishman to his core. He had no desire to move to America, not even to Anglophile New England. But he saw his opportunity. He emailed the secretary to the governors of St Joseph's Academy and asked about their timetable for a final decision, mentioning in passing that he was also having to make a decision about an offer from a top American private school. He stressed that he was really passionate about the St Joseph's job, but that if it wasn't going to work out, he'd want to take the American opportunity.

This swung the decision. One of the St Joseph's governors was in PR. He persuaded his colleagues that this would be a great story for the school. The decision was made before the second interview, and the PR man made sure that there was a big splash: 'Ed the Head turns down $250k to come to Liverpool' screamed the headline in the *Echo*. It was the sort of story that Scousers loved, just like the rumours that long-lost son John Lennon was allegedly heading back to Liverpool – the day before he was brutally gunned down on a cold December day. No one had really believed it, but they all loved the story.

Ed was delighted, though he did wonder how the internal candidate had reacted at being brushed off before the second interview. Later, he learned that the newspaper story was the first that the internal candidate, Chuck Steadman – who, by a strange coincidence, was an American – had heard of the news. Black mark for the governors, Edward said to himself. Communication, communication, communication.

CHAPTER 2
Lisa

What Edward hadn't expected was to fall in love. Not just with that vibrant, exciting city, with its stunning architecture (built on slave money, he noted to himself, appreciating the irony) and its warm, friendly people, but with Lisa. She was a textiles teacher at the school. He noticed her at once, at his first assembly, because she was the only one not listening. She was whispering to a colleague. She was also the most beautiful woman in the room. Arguably the only beautiful one. She had shoulder-length dark hair, which flicked up at the bottom, huge grey eyes with sooty lashes, and a friendly dimpled smile. But it was her bone structure that mesmerized him most. She'd give Kate Moss a run for her money in that department, he thought. You could slice cheese with those cheekbones.

She annoyed him, though. He felt that he was being teased for something he hadn't yet done. Later, when they were formally introduced, she thrust out her hand and gave his a firm, confident shake. But he couldn't help noticing (with his devotion to Shakespeare) that her palm was slightly moist. So not *that* confident, he thought to himself. What did Iago have to say about sweaty palms and sexual desire? She could be trouble, he thought. Just as well he was happily married.

'You've always liked your Donnas and your Lisas,' his wife Moira joked.

'What's that supposed to mean?' said Edward.

'Well, you know. All those Felicities and Sophies in your previous school didn't really do it for you. I mean from a teaching perspective, not a dating one. You love the idea of educating those working-class girls, but you'd never fancy them. I know I'm safe on that score. What did Oswald Mosley once say, "Vote Labour, sleep Tory"? That's you through and through, Ed.'

'Well, look what happened to Mosley. Are you trying to tell me that I married up?' He laughed. 'Well, I did. And I'm not ashamed to admit it. But I do agree that I love being around these feisty girls, rather than teaching dull, posh Lucindas, always flicking their long, glossy hair and cultivating a look of studied indifference. I've seen enough of them to last me a lifetime. Yes, I like the St Joseph's girls, even though I only see them when they're naughty. I miss the teaching sometimes. That's the only downside of a leadership role. You don't see enough of the children. And they make me laugh. They really do. And I miss you too, Moira. And the bloody cat. You'd love the city, if you gave it a chance.'

Moira had not come north. She worked in publishing in London, and didn't want to give up her job. They had agreed to commute, meeting every other weekend in term time. Edward would return home during the school holidays.

'Well, I'll think about it, darling. Do you know what my mother had the cheek to say to me the other day? "You should live in Liverpool, Moira. Men have their needs." What a dinosaur! Well, I'm sorry that you raised a feminist, Mummy, I told her. Why should I pack up my great job, and leave our lovely little house in Surrey with its easy commute to London, when you probably won't stay five minutes in ghastly Toxteth. I tried to explain to her that this job was just a stepping stone. You could never live permanently there, and nor could I.'

'No, I think you're right, I don't think I could, much as I love the flat they found for me. But the commute is killing me. My hair is going grey. You've got to come north more often, Moira.'

Edward had gone straight in with a plan for St Joseph's, and it was working. On his first morning, an Inset day, he had walked slowly around the school grounds, taking in everything. He carried a small orange Post Office notebook. There were no markings in the playground for football or netball. The canteen stank of cabbage. The staffroom was painted corporation cream, with paper-thin brown carpet tiles, sticky underneath his hand-made Italian shoes. The buildings were as tired as the staff. There was no sense of dignity or care, for either the teachers or the children.

He called the governor who was in PR and arranged for paint-ers and decorators to come in overnight. The Scousers loved a challenge, especially on double overtime. When the children arrived for the first day of term, a five-a-side AstroTurf football pitch had been laid down, and a basketball court was marked out on the playground. The staffroom was freshly painted with a Dulux imitation of Farrow and Ball Cornford White, and there was even a new carpet. On the classroom walls there were large framed posters of aspirational heroes: Shakespeare, Einstein, Emmeline Pankhurst, Nelson Mandela (this was a detail he had arranged in advance). God knows how they had performed the makeover in one night or how much it had cost, thought Edward – but he had charmed the governor into picking up the bill.

He had been told that on the last day of term, the children smashed the fire alarm. It was a ritual. This interested him. He thought long and hard about why they did this. And then he got his answer. They wanted to make a mark. To end their schooldays with a statement and go out with a bang. So he came up with an idea. They would end their schooldays with a prom. There would be a survivors' breakfast. Suits for the boys, and prom gowns for the girls.

He instigated other rules too. Report cards. If you failed, you would be sent down a year. A strict dress code. The girls now wore below-the-knee checked kilts, with long socks. Black or brown shoes, or you were sent home. Boys' hair had to be no more than a number four cut. Ties were not to be tucked into shirts. Everyone must walk down the central aisle in silence into assembly. Students (no longer 'pupils') would stand when a teacher entered the room.

To create a sense of belonging, he instigated houses: Lennon, McCartney, Harrison, and Starr. The school was rebranded as SJA (St Joseph's Academy). The initials appeared everywhere.

'They deserve the same standards', was Edward's mantra. He brooked no dissent. 'You are free to enrol your child elsewhere,' he would tell the odd disaffected parent. But they never did. They all wanted their children to be part of a success story. He insisted that if ever he had children of his own, they would attend the school. He had no intention of having children, but this was a good way of putting pressure on the staff to set an example and do likewise with their own offspring.

One of Edward's best interventions was securing funding for a Literacy Support Dog called Waffles. The kids from Starr house were a bit dim, and he figured it would be a novel way of improving their reading skills. The students would take it in turns to read to Waffles, who lay patiently in his basket. When they had finished reading their two pages loudly and clearly to Waffles, he would raise his head in expectation of his doggy treat (his favourites were Arden Grange crunchy bites). It was another huge success of Edward's.

The GCSE results soared, as if by magic. When SJA won an award for Most Improved Academy in the North West, he organized cupcakes for the entire school and gave permission for lessons to be abandoned for the day. Again and again he emphasized that grades mattered.

The children, also, proved a doddle. From that first week when they returned to school after the summer holidays to find the playground marked out with football and basketball lines, they knew he was all right.

The staff were the problem. They were lazy, disaffected, gossipy, complacent. They loathed Oxbridge, and they probably loathed him, even though they were nice to his face. Januses. Except for Lisa. It was not so much that she disliked him; she just didn't notice him. Towards the end of his first year, he decided to throw a party for the staff. He tried to pretend that it was to improve staff morale, to show that he was, after all, one of the guys: that he cared about his staff as much as he cared about his students. But he knew none of this was true. He wanted to see Lisa. He wanted to take her in his arms.

*   *   *

'Will you come to the party?'

'Yes, of course darling. May I bring Tabitha?'

'Well as long as she doesn't pee all over the flat. Or sleep on the bed.'

'Fantastic. I'll take the train. Tabitha prefers it that way. Can't wait to see you, Ed. Guildford feels cold without you.'

*   *   *

'Will you come to the party?'

'Is it OK to bring my husband?'

'Oh – do you know, I wasn't aware that you were married. You've kept that quiet! But yes, of course it is. I'd love to meet him.'

'Then I'll come.'

CHAPTER 3
After the Party

The invitation asked everyone not to wear stiletto heels. This puzzled Lisa. What a curious detail. What on earth did the head-master and his wife have against high-heeled shoes? It was only when she arrived and saw the beautifully polished wooden floors that she understood. The pinprick of heels would not be a good look in such an immaculate flat, although, personally, she preferred a shabby chic look. She once shocked her husband when she took out a hammer and violently pummelled a brand-new butcher's block that had been delivered that morning from Ikea: 'It needs to look old,' Lisa explained, 'as if it's been around for centuries.' Later, she rubbed oil into the indentations. She liked to press her fingers into the holes that she had made. She loved the feel of wood.

The textures of natural materials; beauty. These were things that mattered to Lisa. She was a working-class girl from Bootle. But she had a love of beautiful clothes. It came from her father. He had been a postman, and he had a gambling habit. When he won on the 'gee-gees' he would bring her and her sisters posh clothes from George Henry Lee. The next day her mother would return them. Lisa never forgot the quality and cut of the garments. She bought her first beautiful dress with the first instalment of her student grant. It was black silk, cut on the bias, with embroidered dull-gold roses. It was the first time she truly understood how beautiful clothes bestowed confidence.

Lisa had been educated at an all-girls' convent school, run by the Sacred Heart Sisters. Sister Agnes, unintentionally, used to crack them up: 'Girls, please remember, do not eat your sandwiches up St Anthony's back passage.'

Lisa loved the school chapel, with its smell of polished wood and incense. The other girls were a nightmare, though. The height of their ambition was to get pregnant, so they could bag a council flat. But she also knew that these girls wanted a baby to love. She was sure about that. Sadly, the men they went for were such losers. She knew, with absolute clarity, that once she left, she would never go back.

On leaving school, she applied for a foundation course in textiles at the London School of Fashion. The long-term plan was Textiles in Practice, BA (Hons), at the Manchester School of Art, but first she had to complete a foundation course, and London was the natural choice. She adored London. It was her city, and always would be. She still remembered how naïve she had been when she first arrived. She blushed at the memory of seeing posters around the city saying 'Bill Stickers will be prosecuted'. Who was this man Bill Stickers? Why hadn't anyone caught him. Her new sophisticated southern friends cried with laughter when she asked them.

But she made it to Manchester, and after the BA came an MA for which she wrote a dissertation called *Lipstick and Lies: Reassessing Feminism and Fashion*. It was about third-wave feminism. How it was OK to embrace your femininity and still be a feminist. She traced the connection between fashion and female politics from 1781 to the present day. She began with the mother of feminism, Mary Wollstonecraft, arguing that her ideas about dress and women's liberation were paradoxically close to those of Marie Antoinette, a fashion icon from the other end of the

21

political spectrum. She ended with Alexander McQueen by way of Coco Chanel. She had always worshipped McQueen. She appreciated the wit and style of his final act of defiance: hanging himself with his best belt in a closet full of beautiful clothes.

She was passionate about her work. It was her solace, her consolation and her joy. But jobs teaching the history of fashion were as rare as hen's teeth, and before she stood any chance of getting one she would have to spend three years working on a PhD thesis, earning no money. Things had also gone a bit pear-shaped in the boyfriend department, so she had returned home to Bootle. The next thing she knew, she had a job teaching textiles at St Joseph's Academy, and a husband from New Brighton – a man who was never going to set the world alight, but who was dependable, and, it had to be said, incredibly handsome: he could have got a job as a Tom Cruise lookalike.

Lisa was just twenty-three, straight out of her MA, when she got the job. She was taken aside by a wise old teacher, Will Butler, who told her to go in hard. 'Be firm, don't give an inch. Show them who's boss, and you will never have to discipline them again.'

Lisa took the advice to heart. She strode in, wearing a red jacket, and took no nonsense. Within hours, the gossip around the school was that Miss Blaize was 'dead strict'. From then on, it was plain sailing. She had a laugh with the pupils, but with just one look she could command complete attention.

She learned another valuable lesson, early on, about school-children and loyalty. It was towards the end of the school day, and she was tired. A boy called Michael Turner was giving her cheek. He was a redhead, and a clown, and he was trying to show off. 'Miss, I can't do it. Miss, I don't understand. Miss, Tim's kicking me under the table.'

Finally she snapped and slapped him across the face. Total silence. Utter horror. What had she done? Everyone looked at her. Then the bell rang.

'Off you go. You're dismissed.'

That night she told Pete, her husband, what she had done. He was shocked. 'Lisa, you'll lose your job. He'll go straight home and tell his parents. You will have to resign. What on earth were you thinking?'

'That was the problem. I wasn't thinking. Well it's too late now. There's nothing I can do.'

All night she agonized over the slap. What *had* she been thinking? She planned on going to the head first thing in the morning and fessing up. Hold up your hand, *mea culpa* ...

As it happened, she bumped into Turner in the playground. 'Aright miss, see you later!' He gave her a wide grin.

He never said a word. Nor did the other children. Loyalty. Children always have the ability to surprise teachers. He never gave her cheek again. But she still had nightmares about the slap.

Then there was Jordan. He was fourteen and the most handsome boy she had ever seen. He had huge hands, like Michelangelo's statute of the boy/man David. She would catch Jordan's eye in the classroom and he would respond with an intense stare. God, the boy was so bloody sexy. He disconcerted her. Made her feel that he was undressing her with his eyes. Then she would feel wracked with shame for having such thoughts about a schoolboy. Now I know how Humbert Humbert felt when he confessed that it was Lolita who seduced *him*, she said to herself. These were thoughts that she could never have voiced to anyone. Especially not to Pete, for whom the phrase 'jealous guy' might have been coined.

One day, Jordan stayed late in the textile room to help her tidy. She was stacking scissors into metal containers. Jordan was picking up tiny dressmaking pins with his oversized fingers. They were working in silence, but he suddenly broke down and told her that his parents were divorcing. She hugged him and kissed his forehead softly. And that was it. Just a chaste, butterfly-wing kiss. But she felt worse about that kiss than she had about slapping Turner. God, if anyone found out. Perhaps she wasn't cut out for teaching.

She wanted to keep her options open. She was already thinking that she might not be cut out for marriage either. Pete had the most gorgeous body, but never said anything interesting.

She was a grafter, and always had been. At fourteen, she'd sold records in Woolworth's. During her foundation year in London, she had worked nights as a hospital cleaner. While an undergraduate in Manchester, she had been a barmaid. So when she came home in the evenings, tired as she was from the noise of the school and the strain of being a new teacher, she sat at her computer and worked *Lipstick and Lies* up into a book. A small publisher took it on, and there were a few enthusiastic reviews in some little-known magazines and periodicals. It was even short-listed for a prize so obscure that there couldn't have been many competitors. She began thinking about a subject for a second book; one that might get her out of teaching.

* * *

She had to admit that she was rather attracted to the new head, and just a little excited about the party. She had pretended not to listen to his address in that first assembly back in the autumn; in reality, she had been mesmerized by his quiet but charismatic basso profundo voice, and the way that he spoke in perfectly formed sentences. His words had been like silk, his soft phrases a drug, a charm, a conjuration.

The day before the party, she found herself alone in the staffroom with Chuck Steadman, who had also applied for the headship. He had quickly overcome his disappointment and was making himself indispensable to the new man.

'What do you really think of him?' Lisa asked, fixing Chuck with her blue-grey eyes and twisting her hair around her index finger. Men always listened when she did that.

'Edward is an only child,' Chuck replied, 'that says a lot about him. He told me he was once destined for the church. Don't you think he would have made a good bishop?'

'Oh, I see what you mean: Scott Fitzgerald's "spoiled priest". Yes, I see exactly what you mean. He speaks in a very reverential way. He's shy underneath all that intellect and brilliance. But he's certainly tough. He's made a great start in turning this place around. Not an easy feat.'

'Aha, you gotta hand it to him. He's Mr God round here. Did you ever meet Mrs God?'

'Not yet. She doesn't come here very often, does she? I'm hoping she'll be at the party tomorrow. I've heard she's very posh, what do they say, very Edinburgh. She's Scottish, isn't she? I overheard one of my indiscreet sixth-formers saying that one Sunday night he'd been passing that old block of flats where the head lives, and he'd seen him stuffing a busty blonde holding a cat basket into a car. That must have been her. Not what I'd imagined he'd go for.'

'Well, as a red-blooded Southerner, I approve of the *Baywatch* type. Why, look at my Milly!'

'Very funny. Your wife's the most gamine, chic Audrey Hepburn doppelgänger I've ever seen.'

'Moira's more of a Marilyn.'

'Whatever. God knows how you persuaded Milly to marry a deadbeat like you!'

'My American charm and charisma, no doubt. English women love American guys because they're forthright and honest. Not like your English gentlemen, still in love with Nanny.'

'Chuck, we are not living in *Brideshead Revisited*. You do make me laugh. Anyway, you seem to hero worship Edward. You're never away from him. You still after his job?'

'Of course I am! First I can be his wing man and then I can take his place. Seriously, though. I'm fed up teaching. I fancy a bit of admin responsibility. That's why I had a shot at the headship myself, even though I knew I didn't stand a chance. Look, I like him. He's a nice guy. A good leader. He makes you want to be part of his winning team. That's your trouble, Lisa. You don't want to be part of any club that might accept you.'

* * *

Pete had refused to come to the staff party, though Lisa hardly pressed the issue. She was too selfish to look after him at a party. So she was alone and slightly nervous. To be honest, a little out of her depth. She didn't usually mingle with the other staff, preferring to teach her classes, get into her Mini, and head home to work on ideas for her second book.

She looked around the room and saw a fascinating scenario unfolding. There were two beautiful, long-haired young women deep in conversation. One was a teacher at the school, the other a sixth-former. The teacher, Maia Riddell, filled the wine glass of the student. The student didn't thank her. Lisa saw with instant clarity that they were lovers. It was simply impossible that a student would not thank her teacher. Now the evening was getting interesting.

26

Edward was watching her. She could feel it. But his wife was in the room, so he was being careful. He was biding his time. During a lull in the music, he approached and asked her to dance. She felt for his wife. But she wanted to dance: Lisa loved to dance. She had an odd feeling that Edward had orchestrated the evening so that it would end like this. They danced to k. d. lang's 'Constant Craving'. His wife's eyes were boring into them, though she was pretending not to notice. Lisa told Edward about the lesbians.

'Please be careful, Edward. I think this could blow up.'

'No, no,' he protested, 'you've got this wrong. Maia Riddell is an exemplary teacher. She would never, ever hit on a student. But, Lisa, I thank you for your concern.'

'Well, don't say I didn't warn you,' she laughed.

*   *   *

There is always a green-light moment in every relationship, especially in a clandestine one. The moment when a couple can make a decision, stop what they're doing, or just go ahead anyway. Lisa was no strict moralist when it came to relationships; she'd always had a loose notion of fidelity, but she wouldn't go any further if there were children involved.

Edward and Lisa met for a drink in the local pub after work one day. He asked if she had children. 'No,' she said, 'had my bellyful looking after my siblings thank you, to ever romanticize the idea of raising a family. I'd rather concentrate on my career. How about you?'

'No. We've been married for seven years, and we have never wanted children. In fact, we left out the prayer for children in our marriage ceremony. We're happy with our cat, Tabitha. I think my mother is disappointed. I don't see Moira as the maternal type. And she's quite paranoid about needles and childbirth.'

27

'Well, who can blame her? My mother had six, and it was no picnic.'

'Six? Are you serious? Such a large family. Where are you in the pecking order?'

'Third daughter. Says a lot about my character. My parents were desperate for a boy. He came after me. Spoilt rotten, as you can imagine. But don't get me wrong, I love being part of a big family. You learn from a very early age that life is basically unfair. You also learn not to take yourself too seriously. How about you?'

'I'm an only child.'

'Ah.'

'And by the way, Lisa, you were right about the lesbian lovers. The school is facing a law suit.'

He paused, and then said, 'By the way, I've been sent a couple of free tickets for a play over in Manchester. You know my wife lives down south. Would you fancy coming? Sounds a bit experimental, but that might be your kind of thing.'

'Why not?' she replied.

It was only when they were halfway to Manchester, Edward driving his black BMW very distractedly, that he mentioned that the show in question was a production of *Richard III*. She knew that he loved Shakespeare, and so did she, so this was no surprise. 'Apparently it's got wolf and boar masks, and dancing, movement, physical theatre stuff – probably more your vibe than mine,' he said, then he paused. 'And it's in Romanian.'

Silence. 'I'm not sure whether there are surtitles.'

* * *

She loved the show. And she loved that he loved it. On the surface, he was so English, so Oxford, potentially a right stuffed shirt, but underneath, he was mischievous, a bit radical, full of surprises. Ever so slightly dangerous. Afterwards he offered her a drink in his flat.

She had parked her precious Mini at the school, and she didn't want to leave it there overnight – the radio would be sure to be nicked. 'Can we swing by the school, and I'll follow you in my car?'

Later, and for many years later, he would tell her how he had looked into his rear mirror only to glimpse her terrified eyes.

She *was* terrified, because she knew that she was going to kiss him. He put on *Tristan und Isolde* (corny, but effective, she thought). He lit a fire, and they talked. As she was leaving, he took her in his arms. She felt less guilty for that long, passionate kiss than she had for tenderly kissing Jordan.

CHAPTER 4

The Truth Will Set You Free

Lisa knew that she would bear Edward's children. And she knew that he knew it too. Parting with Pete was painful but necessary. Once she had slept with Edward, she knew that she could never sleep with her husband again. Strangely, she felt that to sleep with her husband would be a betrayal of Edward.

Moira was furious, chilly, vengeful. She threatened to ruin Ed's reputation in and around his old school in the south. It was she who had raised him from the gutter, supported him whilst he rose in his career, put her own career on hold. She stormed over to Liverpool to have it out with him, taking her beloved cat and some empty suitcases. Edward was on the phone when she arrived. He hastily hung up.

'Hello Tabitha, and where's your mistress?'

'She's here, and don't let me prevent you from chatting to yours.'

Ouch. She could be cutting, Moira, but she was also terribly witty. When she realized that he had made up his mind to leave, she told him that she would destroy him and take every penny. She told him that he and Lisa wouldn't last five minutes, that he was making a big mistake. Then she proposed an open marriage. Half-ironically, half-seriously, Edward put the proposition to Lisa: 'Gosh, that's too sophisticated for me,' she replied. 'I'm a simple, north-ern, working-class girl, we're all or nothing up here, I'm afraid.'

Moira begged him to go into marriage therapy. Then she tugged at his heartstrings, saying that she now wanted children.

He would give her the therapy. But he was cruel when he told her that even if he only lasted three months with Lisa, he would still want those months. The marriage was over. He loved Liverpool. He wanted to stay. He didn't want to return to that tiny house in boring Guildford.

Lisa was angry when she heard that he was going into marriage therapy. She felt it was a mistake, and cruel to Moira, when Edward had no intention of saving the marriage. But he was adamant. He owed it to Moira and the seven happy years they had spent together.

Then one night Edward phoned from Guildford. 'Darling, you will never believe what I have to tell you. Moira's admitted in our therapy session that she's been having an affair with one of my colleagues from the history department at my old school. I feel fantastic. Liberated. I no longer have to feel so guilty.'

'Why did she tell you, Edward? Did she want you to know that she was desirable and sexy in the eyes of other men? Was it a last-ditch gamble to save the marriage, to show another, dangerous, side that you didn't know existed? What's her agenda?'

'She said something rather noble. She said, "The truth will set you free".'

*　　*　　*

Lisa married Edward. He'd first proposed in the Puck Building in Manhattan on New Year's Eve at midnight, where he'd flown her for an old Oxford friend's wedding to some hedge fund manager. They were dancing together to the sounds of an all-girls jazz band. She turned down his first proposal. 'Edward, we're both still married to other people. It's too soon to think about another engagement.'

He tried again, this time in Paris, after they had both got the decree absolute. He gave her a box containing a beautiful gold lamé Vivienne Westwood dress, wrapped more exquisitely than any present she had ever received. Then he told her that he was taking her to a train station café for supper. When she got there, she saw that it was the fabulous art deco restaurant at the Gare de Lyon, Le Train Bleu.

Edward told her that this was the restaurant where Coco Chanel would have dined, and Scott and Zelda Fitzgerald, and then they would have caught the famous Blue Train to the French Riviera, and that was the kind of life he wanted with her. When he took out a small blue box, she grinned. It was a beautiful ring, in a style called *Moi et Toi*, which he had bought from Cartier. Two stones, a diamond and a sapphire, twisted around one another.

'So is this a Yes, this time?'

'OK then, Edward. Let's do it. But it must be a small and intimate wedding. No family. No fuss.'

So they married. Edward in a cream linen suit, Lisa wearing a simple, elegant second-hand Chanel dress, made of cream tweed and bought at a bargain price from a student friend who had started an online store buying and selling vintage couture. It was cut on the bias, and fell to just below her knees, nipped in at the waist. It showed her figure to perfection. Her measurements were exactly the same as Marilyn Monroe's (as she often reminded Edward, and anyone else who would listen). 36, 24, 34. The dress hugged her perfect breasts, and accentuated her tiny waist. She carried a handmade posy of white roses. She looked sensational. They told nobody that they were getting married, other than Chuck and Milly, who were the witnesses.

Edward and Lisa had their honeymoon in Venice. They stayed in a hotel on the Grand Canal opposite the Ca' d'Oro. Lisa loved the 'Golden House', which she could see from their bedroom window, so-called because of the gilt that adorned its façade. They woke in the morning to the cries of the gondolieri, and the splash of boats carrying their wares in the early morning sunshine. At that time of day, the sun was not yet shining on the Ca' d'Oro, so it was more putty-coloured than golden, but that would change with the afternoon sun, and then it would glow and shimmer, casting its gorgeous reflection on the glassy green waters below. Narcissus in love with its own dazzling, dizzying beauty.

Venice was the city that ignited Lisa's passion for food. After Edward, it was her most enduring love affair. It was early September, just before the start of term, and the restaurants were not so crowded. She made friends with the *cameriere* at Al Mascaron in Santa Maria Formosa. He recommended the stuffed pumpkin, then *risotto ai funghi* with rocket and warm bread. They drank chilled Prosecco and then Refosco from the demijohns that lined the wooden bar. The *cameriere* brought figs and pears in a bowl of iced water. When she asked him to point out the locals, he told her that Venetians mainly eat at home, but buy bread at the *panificio* and pudding at the *pasticceria*, where, he said, you can also buy biscotti *al vino*, tiny plum tarts, and almond *cornetti*.

The next morning, whilst Edward slept late, Lisa wandered to the Rialto, home to the famous food market. She failed to find Shylock, but she saw wreaths of onions, bunches of aromatic herbs, late-ripening *San Marzano* tomatoes and bulbous glossy purple *melanzane*. Then, next to the fresh market was the *pescheria*, fish pulled straight from the Adriatic, squid, soft-shelled crabs, writhing eels, swordfish and tuna. The *macellerie*, where rabbits hung from hooks, and steaks and chops lined the tables.

Lisa did not speak Italian, unlike Edward who was fluent and spoke the language like an ambassador, but she understood when the market farmers proffered shards of melon, and warm figs, 'Tasta, tasta bea mora.' She stopped off at a bar and ordered a cappuccino. Even in the morning, the local people swigged glasses of Prosecco and gulped down espresso in one go; the Italian way.

The next morning she headed to the market on the Lido, not to buy, but to look at the rolls of damask, cappuccino-coloured, bolts of creamy silk, embossed linen napkins.

When she got back, Edward was showered and ready to explore. He wanted to show Lisa the Carpaccios at the Scuola di San Giorgio degli Schiavoni.

'Main course, or starter?' she teased.

Edward laughed.

'Well, coming from the girl who's currently reading the high-brow, literary thriller *Gondola Girl*, nothing surprises me.'

'I'm also reading *The Wings of the Dove*,' Lisa protested.

Edward never read trash. He only read improving books.

'Shall we take the *vaporetto*, or walk?'

'Let's walk.'

Edward was happy showing Lisa his beloved Carpaccio painting of St George and the Dragon. Lisa was surprised by his choice. St George astride his stallion; his long, silky blond hair streaming behind him, his lance poised to strike. She didn't like the picture; it reeked of violence and destruction. He saw the patron saint of England valiantly fighting the dragon, she saw toads and snakes, vipers, lizards. Then the dead bodies, a woman's torso, still clad in a half-devoured dress, severed arms and legs. Why did he love this so much? She wondered about this side of Edward; a side she didn't really know.

'That spear's rather phallic,' she joked.

34

'The whole thing is beautiful, astonishing.'

Lisa was glad of the cool, a respite against the burning heat of the day. She lingered to buy a postcard. It was time to tell her parents that she had quietly remarried.

'Let's find a *bacari*. I'm desperate for a drink. Edward, it's my honeymoon.'

Edward disapproved of lunchtime drinking. He could be such a Puritan. He liked breakfast, lunch, afternoon tea, supper. Sometimes, when she offered him an early aperitif, he would say that he'd prefer a cup of tea. He would drink two glasses of wine over supper. He never liked to feel out of control.

As they walked along the Salizada Sant'Antonin, Lisa spotted a dress shop called Banco Lotto n. 10. In the tiny window was a beautifully cut cashmere coat. There was a notice pasted on the door saying that the clothes sold inside were made by the female prisoners of the Casa di Reclusione Femminile. Lisa pushed the door open and walked in. The woman behind the counter spoke English, and she explained that the Guidecca's Women's Prison was situated behind the walls of a former thirteenth-century convent. There were about eighty inmates who ran a tailor's workshop and then sold their goods in the little shop. Even Edward was intrigued.

There were rails of organza dresses and coats, hats and scarves. Lisa bought a couple of silk scarves and the cashmere coat. She vowed to herself that she would try to discover more about the prison workshop and the women who made these beautiful clothes. Maybe she could write an article about it for *Textiles* magazine.

That evening, Edward and Lisa went to the Teatro la Fenice. Chuck had made them promise to go to the theatre, as it was one of his favourite opera houses in Europe. They had smiled when they heard that Verdi's *Otello* was being performed. They decided to dress up for the occasion. Edward wore black tie, and Lisa a backless Helmut Lang maxi dress of black, draped jersey. As Chuck had predicted, the theatre was indeed fabulous, if baroque was your thing. The gilded private boxes and crimson velvet seats, and the painted ceiling were opulent, though it was not Lisa's aesthetic. Edward looked happy; he was glowing, and looked so handsome in his dinner jacket and bow tie.

The opening was spectacular. The Cypriot crowd anxiously waiting for Otello's ship to come in, singing the storm in a swell of percussion and brass. There was Desdemona, wearing a fishnet veil over her bright blonde hair, peering out looking for her husband, and then, there he is, the crowd are giving thanks and rejoicing. But something is wrong. Lisa sensed her husband stiffening beside her. His mouth was set in a hard line, his eyes angry.

'We're leaving,' he whispered.

Thank heavens they were sitting in the end seats. It was bad enough enduring the black looks of the audience as they left, without having to squash past a line of angry Venetians.

Once outside in the balmy air, Lisa learned what had upset Edward. He spoke quietly, calmly.

'He was blacked up. Can you believe it? I thought they'd put a stop to all that. It's fine for a white man to play Otello, but why cover his face in soot? We're supposed to be colour-blind.'

'Edward, I barely had time to notice before you dragged me out. I understand why you're upset, but shouldn't the best singers have the best roles?'

'Yes, of course, but, for God's sake, it looked like shoe polish on his face. He looked absurd. And Verdi's *Otello* is not particularly interested in race. Otello is the archetypal jealous Italian husband.'

At that very moment, a gorgeous black man in a sharp suit walked past them, looking every inch as if he'd just walked out of Shakespeare's imagination. He gave a barely perceptible nod in Edward's direction, and an appreciative glance at Lisa. She was mesmerized.

'Crikey, look at him, why didn't they drag him off the streets and into the theatre!'

They both burst out laughing, and the tension dissipated. Edward smiled and enveloped her in his arms. He gently kissed the top of her head. They walked home to bed.

CHAPTER 5

'I'm Going to Rescind that Ticket, Sir'

The postcard of St Augustine in his study with his little dog, sent from Venice, was signed Mr and Mrs Chamberlain. Lisa waited for the storm to break. Her mother wanted the details. She tried not to feel disappointed that her daughter had married in a register office. Lisa told her that she didn't want a fuss. She told her mother that after the ceremony, they ate thin slices of veal, sipped champagne, and gorged on confectionary from a corner shop. It was exactly how she wanted it. Her mother forgave her, even though she knew that the Pope wouldn't. She had always worried that there weren't going to be grandchildren with Pete, and she had a mother's instinct that it would be different this time around.

Lisa was pregnant when they returned from the honeymoon. They called their daughter Emma.

Lisa loved her with a visceral passion and ferocity. She herself was born in August, a Leo, and although she didn't hold much faith in astrology, she was a lioness through and through. She had flaws aplenty, but she also had loyalty and courage in spades. Her revered Coco Chanel was a Leo too, and collected lions, and used them again and again in her work. Lions embroidered onto bags, costume jewellery, even jackets.

It had been a tricky start to motherhood, however. Emma was premature and tiny. Her lungs were not developed, so she was whipped away into intensive care before Lisa could bond with her. There was a terrible moment when she experienced a fleeting desire to grab the baby and smash its tender skull on the hard hospital floor. The feeling went as quickly as it came, but it horrified Lisa. Is this how an animal feels when confronted with the runt of the litter? It was a Lady Macbeth moment. She dared not tell a soul, not even Edward, who understood her so well, and would never judge. She felt a deep sense of shame.

The love for baby Emma came later, but, when it did, it was all-encompassing. It was the truest, purest, love of her life. Emma was her Achilles' Heel. She would die for her. The difficult first few months – Emma in an incubator, with the only possible contact through a tiny finger-hole in the Perspex casing – brought her close to Chuck, who had by now been promoted to deputy head. He had become Edward's trusted confidant.

Chuck had lost a baby. A boy. The baby had been three weeks old when he and Milly found him lifeless in his cot. Cold as any stone. Chuck – smart-talking Chuck, the coolest dude to come out of South Carolina – still cried when the boy was mentioned. His marriage to Milly had foundered under the strain, though they would always remain the best of friends. Milly ran a small local charity for battered wives. Edward arranged for it to be the school charity, supported by cake-sale days, and sponsored walks along the banks of the Mersey.

Some of Lisa's colleagues disliked Chuck: he was too American, too forthright, too clever. But she knew what he had suffered. She sympathized, and he in turn revealed a tender side as baby Emma struggled to pull through those first weeks.

Despite this, Lisa was never entirely sure that Chuck could be trusted. Soon after arriving at St Joseph's, she had been warned by a colleague to be wary of him.

39

'Do you know what he said about you?'

'No, Jan, and I'm not sure I want to. I'm insecure enough as it is.'

'Well, I'm going to tell you because he's no friend to you. He doesn't like women, Lisa.'

'What do you mean? He's not gay. No one has a better gaydar than me. Go on then, what did he say?'

'Well, it was at your book launch party. Someone asked for you and he piped up, "You can't mistake her. She'll be the one with her tits hanging out of her designer dress".'

Lisa chuckled. 'Oh come on, Jan. That's the way he speaks. He means no harm. He's just joking. You know he's got a thing about breasts, because his wife is so flat-chested.'

'Well, look at the way he dressed for your party, in all that combat gear and muddy boots. Why would anyone turn up to a party celebrating a book about *fashion* looking like that? It was a deliberate slap in the face. He doesn't like you, Lisa. I see the way he watches you all the time.'

*   *   *

Emma wasn't very lucky with her health. The under-developed lungs had consequences. Apnoea episodes in the night. Parental panic. More than one 999 call. The hospital became a familiar place.

Clinics, scans, tests. And then, during what was supposed to be a merely precautionary ultrasound, the radiographer said, 'Something's not quite as it should be here. Can you wait a minute while I consult a colleague?'

A more senior-looking figure came in, holding the printout of the ultrasound. 'Nothing to worry about, but just to make sure, we're going to admit Emma to hospital down in Birmingham

where they specialize in this area.' They refused to say exactly
what was wrong, only that when a young child's lungs struggle,
it was important to keep an eye on the heart. 'Let's leave it to the
experts in Birmingham.'

'How do we get there?' asked Lisa. 'On the train?'

'No, we'll take her in an ambulance – just to be on the
safe side. Maybe call your husband and get him to drive down
and meet you? Nothing will happen before he gets there. It'll
probably be a day or two before they complete the necessary
tests.'

'You're one of the Heart Kids now,' one nurse joked, as little
Emma was admitted onto the ward. A Heart Kid, thought Lisa,
as if that were a good thing. You had to laugh or you'd go mad.
Soon, Emma was hooked up to an array of machines, and a whole
team of doctors was standing over the bed. And then Lisa heard
words that no parent should ever hear: 'Your daughter is in serious danger of heart failure. We are going to have to perform
bypass surgery. Immediately.' A 'nil by mouth' sign was hung up
in preparation for surgery.

Broken hearts, Lisa thought. Men and women whine on about
broken hearts. Narcissists. Know what it's like to have a consultant tell you that your child needs bypass surgery. The kind of
thing you associate with old men whose arteries are clogged. A
child in intensive care. That's a broken heart.

Edward fell apart when she telephoned him. He cried and he
cried. No time for tears, thought Lisa. Get this girl through the
operation. She sat at Emma's side, holding her hand, as she waited
and waited for her to be taken into theatre, willing her to survive.
I can be the mother of a sick child, she thought, but God please
spare her. She was reassured when the surgeon came to speak to
them. He told her that heart bypass surgery, even for children,

41

was a routine procedure these days. 'No different from having your tonsils out in the old days when you were young,' he grinned, slightly flirtatiously. She didn't believe him, but she liked his style. He looked alarmingly young to be performing heart surgery. He had blond, floppy hair, and was wearing DM boots. He's OK, Lisa thought. A surgeon in DM boots is going to save my child. And he did. She never doubted him.

On coming round from the anaesthetic Emma cried silent tears and tried to mouth the word 'Mummy'. From that moment on, Lisa knew she was going to be all right. She was strong, like her mother. No one likes a child who screams and throws a tantrum, but a child who is trying not to cry, when she has had major heart surgery … well, that was courage.

Edward had only just made it down from Liverpool to Birmingham in time for the operation. When Lisa had called him, he had been in a tricky meeting, and he'd seen it through to the finish before setting off. He was always the professional. When he arrived, Lisa shouted at him, accusing him of caring more about the bloody school than his own daughter. 'Don't worry,' he said, 'I'm here now.' Though he'd only made it in time by virtue of driving the wrong way down the one-way street outside the hospital and parking in a direction that revealed his transgression.

When he emerged into daylight, after the long night waiting in the parents' room while the surgery was taking place, then the relief of stroking Emma's hair in the recovery room, he found a yellow ticket on the windscreen of the BMW. His head throbbing with fury, he stalked into the police station that happened to be opposite the children's hospital. He had a thing about the police. He had been incandescent on the occasion that he had been pulled over in Toxteth, just because he was driving a black BMW.

He demanded to see Officer 354, who had issued the ticket, explaining through gritted teeth that his young daughter had just gone through open-heart surgery.

The constable looked visibly taken aback, and said, 'I'm so sorry to hear that, and in the circumstances I'm going to *rescind* that ticket, sir. And I do hope your daughter makes a full recovery.' She did, and somehow his faith in human nature, even in God, was restored by the policeman's evident delight in the opportunity to use the word *rescind*.

Having come close to it, Lisa knew that there could be no pain in the world like losing a child. Once it was clear that Emma had got through the operation without infection or complication, she was moved from isolation to a ward. One evening, Lisa saw a tiny premature baby boy in a side room. The door was ajar, and she overheard family members saying platitudes to the mother like 'he's a little fighter', 'he looks stronger today', 'you'll be home before you know it'. But when Lisa looked at the father's pale, pitiful face, she knew that he knew the truth. At least her daughter was still alive. She thought of Chuck that day, and the hell that he had endured.

In the months following Emma's recovery, Lisa became desperate for another baby. Edward had always insisted that he only wanted one child. That was his own experience. 'Have two and it will soon be three,' he said. 'And then you lose your man-to-man marking capability.' And again, 'If there are three, one child will always feel left out – and then you'd have to buy a people carrier, get an extra bedroom on holidays.' His other worry was Emma's health. What would happen if she needed another heart operation, if there were a new baby in the family?

'I'm not talking about six children, like in my family, darling. Not even about three. Just one more.' Lisa was not to be deterred, and Edward believed her when she said that she could cope just fine. Her strongest argument was her concern that their home life would be dominated by Emma's poor health. What could be more distracting, more lovely, than a baby in the house? The milky, yeasty smell of a new baby. Then, as Emma began at school, a toddler making them all laugh.

Edward never really had a choice. When a woman wants a baby, nothing or no one will stand in her way. Emma told her colleague Jan about her plan to become pregnant. She had conceived easily the first time. She had no worries on that score. 'Tonight's the night,' she said. 'The champagne's in the fridge, and I'm going to seduce my husband.' Three months later, she told Jan that she was having a baby, a boy. They both giggled conspiratorially. 'I always knew you were a determined woman,' said Jan, admiringly.

Emma was delighted to know that her mother was having a boy baby. Lisa told her, 'He's yours. I had him for you.' She wanted something good to come out of the sadness of Emma's health problems. She had secretly longed for another daughter, but little Emma much preferred the idea of a brother.

Emma was special. One day when Lisa was heavily pregnant and climbing the stairs, she felt two little hands underneath her belly, lifting up the weight. The support felt fantastic. During the early part of the labour, Emma came into the hospital ward and encouraged Lisa to walk around and work through the pain. Much to Lisa's amusement, Emma found a large pink plastic ball in the maternity suite and rolled it towards her.

'Em, how on earth do you think that exercise ball is going to help?'

'Sit on it, Mummy. Then your back won't hurt.'

It worked like magic.

44

Because Emma had been premature, Lisa had been told to have an epidural. There had then followed a messy forceps delivery. This time, she wanted a natural birth. She wanted to know whether physical pain could be as bad as her mental anguish over Emma's heart condition. Nothing could be worse than almost losing her daughter. Physical pain is physical pain and could be endured. Perhaps she was punishing herself. She wasn't entirely sure about her motives, and the pain was excruciating. It was Edward who got her through it.

'You can do it. You can do it. I know you can.'

That was all she needed to hear. Afterwards, she was too exhausted to take the baby in her arms. She told the nurse to give the baby straight to Emma. Job done, she told herself, as she saw Emma's happy, excited face. Lisa fell asleep.

Emma was only five when he was born, but she carried George around the house as if he were a doll. Lisa's girlfriends were amazed that she let Emma carry the baby in her arms over the flagstone floors of their farmhouse – having married, recovered from the financial clean-out of their respective divorces, and had a family, they had moved out of the city to a village in Cheshire. After the trauma of Emma's first few months of life, Lisa had decided that she would only go back to her textiles GCSE class part-time. With the arrival of George, she decided to give up teaching altogether. She might finally have some time for that second book.

'Aren't you scared that she'll drop him? She's only a child herself.'

'She won't drop him. There's more chance that I would drop him than that Emma would. He's too precious.' And she never did.

*   *   *

Over the years, Chuck always offered support through the difficult times. Once, when Edward and Lisa had returned home after several days and nights in hospital with Emma, who had come down with a serious infection, they had found, waiting on the kitchen table, a Fortnum and Mason hamper of goodies and a huge vase of blue cornflowers. A stew in a brand new Le Creuset casserole dish was warming in the Aga, and the lawn was freshly mown in neater stripes than Edward had ever achieved. Chuck had arranged it all, liaising with one of their neighbours, who had a spare key to their house.

Touched by such gestures, Lisa and Edward asked him to be George's godfather. Lisa also hoped that it would help him to have a child in his life. Chuck took his godparenting duties seriously. He gave generous and thoughtful Christmas presents, and said that he would lay down a bottle of the best Californian red wine every year so that George would have his very own cellar when he was eighteen.

CHAPTER 6

Missy

Lisa kept saying that she had had enough of teaching. Apart from Jan, she didn't get on with the other women in the staff room. Especially not with Ms Robinson. There was history between them.

Misan Robinson was formidable. Most people at SJA were terrified of her. She was so right-on, with her dreadlocks and her Adidas trainers. The students respected Missy. There was no messing about in her classes. She taught religious studies (even though she was an atheist). Her special interest was in feminist theology. She worshipped Rosemary Radford Ruether. Her dream in life was to teach at Howard University, and, to that end, she had enrolled on an MA programme at the Open University. Missy had a dream.

Lisa could not stand Ms Robinson. She was so pretentious, so achingly cool. What a phoney. Edward, of course, loved Missy. This was one of the rare instances when he and Lisa did not agree.

'She's exactly what this school needs. Know your privilege, Lisa.'

'What's that supposed to mean?'

'You know exactly what I mean.'

'Do you fancy her?'

'Don't be absurd. She's a first-class teacher, and a team player. You don't make any effort to win her over.'

'I don't intend to. She patronizes me about our relationship. She's a cow. And I'm not going to be nice to her because she's black. Because that's racist.'

'Lisa!'

'What?'

Edward shook his head as he unlaced his shoes. Sometimes, Lisa was utterly impossible.

'She likes you, Edward. A bit too much, in my view. I've seen her, with her velvet doe-eyes giving you the look.'

'Lisa, she's gay. I've met her partner.'

'Don't believe that for a minute. She told me she's gender fluid. As if! I could float a canoe in her gender stream. You mark my words; she'll be married by Michaelmas.'

Edward burst out laughing. God, Lisa was funny, even when she was being ridiculous.

Missy was sexy, though. He wondered if she did swing both ways. It was true, she loathed Lisa, and she did give him the eye. He quite liked those feminist types. At least she had an opinion about something. Maybe he should promote her to deputy head. Let's face it, she deserved a break. What was it they said about religious studies teachers? 'Can't do: teach.' 'Can't teach: Teach RS.' Besides, Chuck was starting to drive him mad. He was getting a bit too big for his boots. It would teach him a lesson to announce that the duties had to be shared and a second deputy head would be appointed.

Edward decided to sound Missy out. No matter how tough they all behaved in staff meetings, the mob usually crumpled when he called them individually to come to his office for a little chat. He kept her waiting outside his door for a good ten minutes, pretending he was making a phone call. It helped to exacerbate their anxiety. They always thought that they'd done something

48

wrong; that they were in trouble. It gave him the psychological edge.

The meeting did not go well. Edward asked Missy what she thought about extra-curricular activities. It was his belief that SJA was not doing enough. It was that sort of thing that created a sense of belonging and camaraderie. He went on a bit too much about improving standards. Missy was looking bored. When she finally spoke, she was bolshy. She was a prominent member of the Union, and this was exactly the sort of thing that the Union feared and loathed. The teachers were under great strain, too much red tape, and time spent on the phone speaking to stroppy parents. Edward insisted that books should always be marked promptly and handed back – no excuses. The staff were at breaking point. No, Missy certainly did not support the idea of extra-curricular work.

Later, he spoke to Lisa, when they were in the black BMW heading back to towards the Birkenhead tunnel.

'She was a nightmare. I forgot that she was a powerful voice in the Union.'

'So what will you do? Did you mention the deputy post?'

'Well, I dropped the hint. I told her that her CV would benefit from a leadership role, that she was highly respected by the students and staff, blah blah blah, but then she blew it by banging on about the Union. I need her to be onside. I'm not sure that I trust her.'

'But if you don't promote her now, she'll be really pissed off. You've dangled the carrot.'

'No, it's fine. I'll find a way to give her something. Keep her quiet.'

'Well you know my feelings about her, and I never change my mind: *about clothes or men.*'

'That's a quote from Jane Austen, isn't it?'

'Wow, Edward, you're really learning. But it's true. I don't trust her one bit. Do you know what she said to me today? I saw her chatting with the girls in the loo, and as I walked in she said, "Oh don't come in, we're having a good gossip about you." She's a spiteful cow.'

'Ignore her. She's trying to rattle you. She's jealous. I think she's OK, deep down. What she needs is a good seeing-to by a real man.'

It was Lisa's turn to be shocked.

'You can't say things like that. You'd be sacked, if anyone heard you.'

Edward chuckled; that wonderful, throaty laughter (as infectious as herpes, as Chuck once described it).

'Don't worry, sweetheart, it won't be me; she's not my type.'

A police car's siren wailed as they drove past the docks, and a slight look of anxiety flickered across Edward's face. He watched as the car passed, and then he descended into silence. Lisa put her hand over his as he switched gear. Her man, her love.

*   *   *

Missy waited to see what would happen about the promotion. She guessed that Edward was sounding her out for the deputy headship. She knew she had it all; she was mixed-race, gay, female, clever, and young. God, if she only had a disability she'd be running the world! Missy was all for positive discrimination. Diversity was one of her things. She loved playing that game with all her white friends: 'How many black friends do you have?' That usually shut them up.

Missy's mother was Liverpool–African. Her father was white, and from a working-class Catholic family. He was a boxer, and the gentlest man she had ever met. Her mother had died of cancer when she was thirteen, so it was always just Missy and her dad, Tony. Tony's father was a racist, so they had very little to do with his extended family. Her father was insistent that she should be proud of her roots and in touch with her African heritage. He took her to the Maritime Museum at the Albert Dock, where she read about the eighteenth-century slave trade that had made her city rich on the blood and tears of African slaves. Tarleton Street, Tony explained, was named after one of the richest slave merchants. They owned plantations in the West Indies. They got rich on sugar and slaves.

Her father told her the story of the Zong massacre, where healthy slaves, including women and children, were thrown overboard, for an insurance claim, when the ship ran out of water. He told her about Lord Mansfield and Wilberforce, and Thomas Clarkson, the man who wrote the first history of the slave trade. Tony had inspired in Missy a love of history, but she had read religion and ethics at university. Tony was so proud of Missy. Time and time again, he told her to live her own life, get a boyfriend, and a flat, but she would never leave her dad. She hadn't told him, either, that she was attracted to women. That could wait.

To begin with, Missy had quite liked the new head. He was a great appointment and he was really turning the place around. He set a very good example, but she didn't like it when Lisa became his girlfriend. It was a bit of a scandal when the news broke that they were an item, and that he was leaving Moira. It was the talk of the staffroom. No one thought it would last. They were so unsuited, so different. She felt he was letting the side down, again. Though she had to admit, that working-class Lisa wasn't quite such a sell-out as posh, blonde Moira. No matter, he would come to his senses once the sex wore off. He was too ambitious to be stuck with someone as gobby as Lisa.

Missy was annoyed when Lisa started getting into feminism. Far too close for comfort for Missy. Lisa was writing some tripe about fashion and feminism. Disguising her frivolity and shallow nature and obsession with clothes and lingerie by transforming it into something political. Well, she, Missy Robinson, wasn't having any of it. She despised clothes and fashion. Gay men designing expensive clothes for stick-thin women starving themselves to death. She was waiting for Lisa to bring up the subject in the staffroom, so she could confront her. But she would do it cleverly: attack her with words, with considered argument. Missy did not buy into third-wave feminism.

She had been secretly flattered by the head's attention. Promotion would be a great opportunity. She was glad that she had mentioned her interest in the Union. He was impressed by that, she could tell. He was right-on, Edward. She had a feeling that he wanted to get rid of Chuck. The power had gone to his head, and he was becoming insufferable. Since Edward had married Lisa and they had had the baby and moved to the country, the Head had become rather less visible around the school. Chuck, picking up the slack, was strutting around and giving orders as if he were the top man. When Edward was around, everyone mocked Chuck for running around him like a bitch on heat. Chuck was all right with Missy, but he kept his distance, too. He knew a rival when he saw one.

But then the weeks passed and no word was forthcoming. Edward was avoiding her, and then an announcement was made that Chuck would be carrying on as sole deputy head for another year. Bastard. Leading her on like that and then discarding her like orange peel. I bet that Lisa had something to do with it.

52

She'd always been so thick with Chuck. She needed male adoration, that one. Well, you just wait. I'll have my day with you. You'll make a slip and I'll be there to see it. To bear witness.

CHAPTER 7

The Fashion Mistress

They were both prone to itchy feet. Edward – as she always called him, though to the other staff he was Ed – began to worry that he had gone to the ends of the earth, fallen off the radar. His applications for deputy head positions at some of the great public schools went nowhere.

'If it gets past ten years, I'm stuck,' he said. 'I've achieved everything I can here. From the brink of Special Measures to Outstanding, and North-West Region School of the Year. But once the turnaround is complete, it's boring – and still bloody hard work. And you need a change as well. If I got a good position in the private sector, we'd have a house, and I'd have a bigger salary, and you wouldn't have to teach any more. That's what you keep saying you want. You could get on and finish that second book. You've been stuck on it for years.'

He saw no alternative but to look further down the public school pecking order. A respectable but dull, middle-ranking 'minor public school'. He could make an impact there. Move them into the big league. Improve the Oxbridge acceptance rate while also starting a programme of scholarships for deprived inner-city kids. That would hit all the buttons.

Blagsford came up, and he walked it. His unusual background – street cred combined with Oxford – would give the school edge over all its rivals. The chairman of governors rubbed his hands with glee at the thought of Edward Chamberlain's first appearance at the Headmasters' Conference. But Lisa wasn't at all sure she wanted to move away from her big family. Nan was such a great babysitter, and Emma loved her cousins. Edward always had an answer.

'Come on, in your heart you've made the move already. You hardly see them now we're out in Cheshire. When did your mum last babysit for us?'

'And what about work? It really kept me sane, going back part-time once we knew Emma was OK. I was going to start again now that George is a bit older.' This wasn't true, but she had a point to make.

Edward was exasperated. Lisa was always changing her mind about whether or not she wanted to carry on teaching. 'You won't have to work – Blagsford are offering a big salary and a free house.'

'Great, so we'll be homeless when you get bored and leave.'

'We'll sort something out on that front – a holiday home by the sea, maybe, or a London flat.'

Lisa liked the sound of a London flat.

Then Edward played his trump card.

'Look, you don't really want to go back to teaching.'

This was the truth. She'd crack open the champagne if she knew for sure that she'd never have to spend another hour in a classroom in her entire life. She knew what Edward was going to say next. They always read each other's minds.

'All you want is a little bit of money that you can say is your own. That you've earned, and that you can spend on whatever you want. Which is mainly designer dresses. And shoes. And make-up. And more shoes.'

Lisa laughed. He was so right. That was why there had been no regrets when she left her brief starter marriage. Pete had been a control freak. He had insisted that she close down her bank account and get her teacher's salary paid into their joint account. The account in her married name. She should always use her married name, he insisted. The only compromise he allowed, and even that had been a battle, was that she could be Miss Blaize at St Joseph's.

Then, one afternoon towards the end of the summer holidays, when she was bored at home because Pete was out playing cricket all day, as he did every Saturday, she took a DVD case off the bookshelf. Out fell a folded bank statement. She glanced at it and saw that it came from an unfamiliar bank. So Pete had kept his own personal account, despite making her giving up hers. She looked down the row of figures. Every month, there was a payment for a few hundred pounds, marked 'Dividend'. It took a while for her to work it out. But there could be no question. He had some sort of family trust fund that he'd never told her about. The sums weren't huge, but that wasn't the point. It was the principle. She took the statement and found her own hiding place for it.

She said nothing to Pete that night, though she did refuse to make love to him – on the grounds that he had come in late from drinking with his cricketing mates. The folded statement was her get-out-of-jail-free card.

Edward knew all this. They had talked over the circumstances of their respective divorces a thousand times. When they married, he insisted that she should keep her own name and her own bank account, and that he had no interest in how she spent her teacher's salary and any other earnings. 'You won't find me snooping around your private account for Ladies' Nice Things,' he assured her.

'Listen, though,' he now said, 'you've got your magazine column, and that could be the beginning of a career as a proper freelance fashion writer. One thing leads to another. That's what I've found with my articles about education policy. Soon you'll be getting all sorts of commissions – but that'll only happen if you're near enough to London to go to parties and openings, and to start meeting the editors. It's such a trek from Cheshire. Blagsford has a really fast link to Marylebone on the Chiltern Line. Most reliable network in the country.' With all his London meetings, Edward had become a bit of a railway timetable nerd.

This was the clincher. Lisa had always rather regretted how she had scuttled home after her MA and fallen into teaching textiles. She should have gone back to London and tried to make it in the fashion world. She had hoped that publication of *Lipstick and Lies* would lead to other opportunities, but it hadn't happened, mainly because she was stuck in Liverpool. Now she'd just had her first real break.

A friend from her Manchester Art School days had become features editor at *City & County*, an upmarket monthly glossy magazine. She'd asked Lisa to start writing a regular column answering readers' requests for fashion tips, with a spin that offered nuggets of information from fashion history. It was a neat idea, and Lisa's first couple of columns – for which they'd made up the readers' questions – had gone down well. Edward was right – working out of Blagsford would give her many more opportunities to go to London and build on this success.

*   *   *

Jane (by EMAIL) to The Fashion Mistress: *I am getting married this summer in a marquee in the country. I have my wedding dress, but am struggling to find something for a breakfast party we are hosting the following day. I want a more relaxed look that's still a bit bridal, which I can wear again. I am 25, 5' 6" and a size 12. I have good arms. My budget is £350.*

A touch of lace will help to carry through a romantic wedding theme into the day after. As it's a summer wedding, you can pep things up with a pop of colour. Mango has a lace, sleeveless dress in acid yellow, or for something slightly more 'fash' and floaty, you could go for a two-piece silver set from Hobbs. Tuck the cute cami into the culottes' grosgrain waistband, and keep heels fuss-free – or wear with white brogues.

What kind of lace? Duchess point (*Point Duchesse*) is the term for a Belgian lace that does not have a *réseau*. It was named after the Duchess of Brabant, Marie-Henriette of Austria, who was a supporter of lace production. It is made entirely on the pillow, with a pattern where the leaves and flowers naturally join, so there is rarely a bar thrown across to connect them. As there is no *réseau*, the designs are more continuous. It's that elegance which makes it my favourite lace.

TFM

*   *   *

In order to promote the new column, Lisa's editor friend asked her to write a regular feature for the magazine's website.

MEET OUR NEW COLUMNIST FOR FREE: LISA BLAIZE IS THE FASHION MISTRESS

It's Lisa, The Fashion Mistress here.

First Up: How do you make a miniskirt less 'Hello, Vicar'? Wear a long-line knit for a grungy take and add tights. New Look has a Contrast-trim sweater (£50), and check out Topshop's vinyl miniskirt (£45) in orange or emerald for a pop of colour.

Tweed is everywhere right now, and the High Street is all over the Chanel look. Topshop and Reiss have some great wool-blend, very wearable jackets. Complement your jacket with jeans to nail the new louche. Opt for ripped, skinny ones (my denim of choice), though bell-bottomed jeans are also making a big splash this season. Check out Zara for great jeans at great prices.

Finally, for that kick-ass look, add MIRA shine boots (£280) and some rose-tinted specs. Try Bodoozle gold-mirrored sunglasses £55, LE SPECS.

As Chanel said, 'A girl should be two things: classy and fabulous!'

TFM

Read Lisa's column in the magazine, available from all good newsagents.

TELL US WHAT YOU THINK:

Jessla

Hi Lisa. Love your column and fashion advice. CC also said 'Dress like you are going to meet your worst enemy today'. I try to follow that rule, and just want to say that you look so stylish in your pic. I'm going to try out that knit.

Littlepurpleme

TFM Lisa Blaize does not know what she's talking about. She's a fashion snob, and self-obsessed. Can't stand her or her pointless column.

> **REPLY TO: Littlepurpleme**
> **Jessla**
> So why are you reading it?

Michelle Turner

Spot on, Lisa. I love the way you promote High Street shops like Zara and Topshop. I bought the leather mini you recommended.

194602

You can make a million pounds a day if you follow this link.

Ijustwanttosay

Anyone who spends this much time on fashion is completely shallow. That's the problem with this world. It's all style and no substance. I'm voting Trump.

Amodernwoman

Love you Lisa.

* * *

Edward's leaving do at St Joseph's was a big moment. Lisa chose her outfit carefully. She wore a classic above the knee LBD. Her dark hair was cut shorter than usual, accentuating her high cheekbones.

When Edward gave his leaving speech, he paid tribute to Lisa. He told his staff of his love for Liverpool, its people and architecture. Above all, he confessed, he had found Lisa, the love of his life. 'My gobby Scouser,' he called her. That was what Tony Blair had affectionately called Cherie. He thanked the governors for taking a chance on a 'soft Southerner'. More laughter. He thanked the staff, picking out a few names, including Jan's. He was about to thank Chuck when he was distracted by the sight of Lisa stretching out an affectionate arm to Jan and in so doing creating an opening in the top of her dress, through which he could see a gossamer-thin bra over the curve of her breast. Stopping his mind from wandering, and remembering his reputation for not wasting time in meetings or boring colleagues with long speeches, he went straight to the anecdote that he had been saving for the end.

A taxi driver had once taken him home from Lime Street Station to his flat. Edward had noticed that he was reading a book and asked him about it. It was a John Buchan novel. But the driver said that his favourite author was Sir Walter Scott. 'He takes his time, old Sir Walter, and you have a lot of waiting time in this job.' He then asked Edward whether he was a reader. 'Well, I've been a history teacher, so books are a big part of my life.'

'History, eh? Then you'll know all about Sir Walter, inventor of the historical novel and all that. Tell me something, though: why do you think that *The Fortunes of Nigel* is Scott's only failure?'

Edward had not even *heard* of *The Fortunes of Nigel*. Dramatic pause. Then he did what all teachers do when confronted with their own lack of knowledge: 'Hmmm, why do YOU think that *The Fortunes of Nigel* is a failure?' This brought the house down. Edward didn't notice that Missy wasn't laughing.

CHAPTER 8

Drugs Chat

Blagsford was a return to what Edward knew. It wasn't exactly Eton or Westminster, but it was still familiar territory. Lisa teased him that he was truly happy in a scholar's gown, flapping around like a crow. She suddenly saw a new side to her husband. He suited the gown and the school. In Liverpool, she had sometimes felt that he was trying too hard to fit in. Here, he simply belonged. He walked differently, talked differently. He was a round peg in a round hole. The staff always called him 'headmaster', which was somehow so much more satisfying than 'the head' or, worse, 'head teacher'. On his study door was a bronze plaque inscribed 'Edward Chamberlain, MA DPhil (Oxon)'. Inside his book-lined room were squashy sofas, kilim rugs and tasteful lamps. In winter, a fire burned in the grate.

The turning point of his past life had been the winning of the coveted scholarship that gave him the free place at the great public school on the edge of London where teachers were 'beaks', a term was a 'half', and lessons were 'hashes'. Soon after he and Lisa had become lovers, he had explained to her about the sixth-formers' blazer, with one button on the cuff for normal boys, two for prefects, three for house captains, four for the head of school and the captains of sport, and five for a boy who was both head boy and a captain of sport. As elected head boy and captain of the cricket team – he was a mean fast bowler – Edward had been the first founder's scholar in history to have five buttons.

Lisa saw his delight in learning about Blagsford traditions and turns of phrase. The deputy head was called the 'usher', the matrons of the boarding houses were all called 'ma', the head of sixth form was called the 'ancient', said to be a variant of the Elizabethan term ensign, meaning the commander's right-hand man. The chapel bell was called the 'bong', the hatch through which the Indian takeaway deliveryman passed in his wares was called the 'Black Hole of Calcutta'. That was the one name that Edward swiftly abolished, on pain of detention. One evening, soon after their arrival, Edward told Lisa that she was expected to give out the Supreme Bosh Cup.

'What the hell's that?'

'It's the inter-house competition. There's a competition for everything – rugby, hockey, cricket, drama, musical recitals, chess, even Jenga. You're going to have to give a silver cup and a kiss to the captain of the house that wins the largest number of competitions.'

In honour of the school's Tudor origins, each boarding house was named after an Elizabethan hero. The arty boys were concentrated in Shakespeare and Marlowe, Tallis and Byrd (Balls and Turd, as the Marlovians put it). The hearties were allocated to Drake, Raleigh, and Essex – one of which was always the winner of the Rugby Bosh. Boys with potential for a future in politics or public service were allocated to Burghley, who always won the Debating Bosh.

'Nobody knows what "bosh" stands for. The Marlovians think it means Bugger Off Shakespeare House, their great rivals. Others think it's a variant of "bash". The Blagsford creed is that everyone should have a bash at everything, however lacking in talent they are. But some people think that it's really a reference to the First World War – fighting the Boche.'

Lisa loved to wind her husband up.

'Edward, I can't believe you take this crap seriously.'

'I know I have mixed feelings about the British Empire, but a lot of Blagsford boys lost their lives in the Great War. That's not crap, it's history. I'm going to have to read the Roll of Honour on Remembrance Sunday, and I'll expect you to be there, dressed in a suitably dignified style. No cleavage.'

'You don't have to tell me *that's* a moving thing, darling – you know how I love First World War poetry. I meant the slang. Bongs, Blacks Holes and Bosh.'

'The slang's a form of bonding. It creates a sense of community, of people not being left out.'

She had to admit, though, that Blagsford was beautiful, with its mock Oxbridge quad, its cloister, and the Arts and Crafts chapel with its frescoed walls, triptych of pale oak, and metal furnishings of bronze, hand-beaten to the patina of pockmarked skin. Lisa loved to run her hands over the bronze. Edward insisted that the whole family attend chapel during term time. 'So they can all have a good nose,' she muttered to herself.

The Headmaster's House had a large garden, with mature deciduous trees. Best of all was the sunken White Garden, which was laid out immediately behind the house. It was inspired by the famous example at nearby Hidcote Manor, also designed in the Arts and Crafts style. A bronze statue reproducing Michelangelo's *David*, no less, overlooked beds of scented old English white roses, white lavender, aquilegia, and penstemon. The roses flowered for just five weeks in June – a riotous, exuberant and blowsy show, fading all too fast from white cream to curling brown. Their own private White Garden. She didn't know it then, but one day that garden would save her sanity.

She got on well with most of the staff, with the exception of the housekeeper. She was dumpy and lazy, and she began by telling Lisa all the duties that she refused to undertake, such as making the beds and doing the laundry. 'Mr Camps was a very particular gentleman, didn't like me going into his bedroom, and insisted on washing and ironing his own shirts. We're set in our ways here at Blagsford, Mrs Chamberlain. I had my list of duties for Mr Camps, and them's what I'll do for Mr Chamberlain.'

'Dr Chamberlain,' said Lisa curtly. She listened patiently as Doris rambled on about her bad back and the good old days when the masters wore gowns all the time, not just for special occasions. Then she fired her.

'We mustn't be accused of victimizing the loyal retainers,' said Edward. To avoid any fuss, he moved Doris over to fill a cleaning vacancy in one of the boarding houses. Lisa brought in a lovely young Polish girl called Bianka, who worked tirelessly, didn't speak too much English so didn't want to chat, and moved gracefully around the house like a blonde, ethereal house sprite. And she could drive, unlike Doris. So morning and evening she ran Emma and George into St Gregory's, Blagsford's Catholic primary school. Lisa did not want to get into yummy mummy school-gate gossip.

The pupils at Blagsford were hard-working, and, on the whole, polite. Edward soon found that the parents were the problem. They were paying the school fees, and, by God, they wanted their money's worth. They really believed that they were giving away their little darlings to come back at the age of eighteen as fully formed, charming, and intelligent human beings. The parents didn't know about the drugs, the feral behaviour in the dorms, the vomiting into the lake, and the escapes into town for supplies of cider. Some things were best left unsaid.

*　　*　　*

66

Back at SJA, Chuck became acting head until a new one was appointed. Edward wrote a judiciously worded reference on behalf of his old deputy. But once again Chuck was thwarted. Another outsider was appointed, a safe pair of hands with a solid track record in Lancashire.

When the news was announced, Edward called to commiserate. Chuck clearly didn't want to talk about it, so Edward turned the conversation to Blagsford.

'So was I right in guessing that they'd be spoilt and over-privileged brats?' Chuck asked him.

Edward – he had decided to dispense with 'Ed' – replied, somewhat testily, 'Well, that depends on how you define privilege.'

'Come on, Ed, you can't pretend your new toffs can be compared with the SJA kids. They wouldn't know their kale from their cabbage.'

'They told me that last Christmas one of our boarders was put into a taxi at the end of term. As soon as he arrived at his Hampstead home, his mother put him straight back into the taxi and sent him back to school. We then sent him to his father's penthouse flat in Clerkenwell, but he didn't want him either. Finally located a grandparent who agreed to take him in.'

'Aww, my heart just bleeds. I'm sure he cheered up when he was flown to St Moritz by his folks for the holidays.'

'They're not all wealthy, Chuck. Some of our parents really make sacrifices to send their children here, because they believe in the importance of a good education, with the best teachers.'

'Bullshit, Edward. They want their kids to have social connections. To mix with the right sort of people. The good old British school tie, old boys' network – it's still alive and kicking. Nothing like that in the States.'

'Hmmm, but you can't buy your way into the best universities like you can in the Ivy League Schools. Anyway, Chuck, Lisa's longing to see you, so you should come down and see us some time.'

'And I'm dying to see Lovely Lisa, too. She doing OK?'

'Yes, and no. She misses the warmth and friendliness of the north. And her family, of course. But she's a chameleon. She can settle anywhere and make it home. She's bought six chickens, playing at being a real countrywoman. Anyway, as long as Emma's health remains stable, she's happy. Some of the staff don't know what to make of her, but she seems to be adapting well. Enough about us. How are *you*, Chuck? You sound a bit strained.'

'Oh, nothing really. I've got to go into hospital for something. Just a routine test. A sore throat I can't seem to shift. I'm fine. We all miss you guys so much.'

As when he had first arrived at St Joseph's Academy, Edward was determined to hit the ground running. One of his friends who had got a headship had announced his intention to spend the first year just watching and waiting, seeing how things worked, getting his feet under the table before making any changes. By the time it got to the second year, it was too late to do anything about a staffroom full of teachers stuck in their ways. Within another year, the governors had persuaded him to move on. Edward wasn't going to make that kind of mistake.

Drugs, he thought, that's where I begin. He announced in his first assembly that in his previous school he had instituted a zero-tolerance drug policy and that he was going to do the same at Blagsford, with immediate effect. He was well aware that most public schools were hiding their problems with drugs, and he was determined that he would shine a spotlight on the great modern blight of the independent school system. Somewhere along the way, he would need a sacrificial lamb: enter Bertie Cole. Bertie was handsome and charming, an only child of wealthy parents. His father, Max, a hedge fund manager, had donated significant sums of money to build a new sports hall at the school.

Bertie's mother, an attractive, thin blonde, always dressed head to foot in Boden, had run off with another woman (though somehow she had still managed to keep the family home, an old vicarage in a beautiful village just outside Blagsford). The affair had been the talk of the common room.

Bertie had always had a penchant for drugs. He had been dealing cannabis (not skunk, he had some morals, he said), and then moved on to MDMA. It was small-time stuff, and he was careful not to get caught, until he got caught. He was the ringleader of a group of five, and Edward caught them online halfway through his first term there as head. The fools had set up a Facebook page called 'Drugs Chat'. Why would you do something if you couldn't boast about it online?

Edward saw his opportunity to make his mark. He called in all five sets of parents and told them that he had no choice but permanent exclusion. It was an ugly scene, but Edward was determined. It was his first challenge at Blagsford, and he knew that he had to maintain his tough line. Of all the boys, Bertie was the one he was sorry for, he really was. He always felt a kinship for lonely, only children, like himself, and the boy had suffered. But there it was. The exclusion letters were sent out, though with the standard provision that an appeal could be lodged with the governors.

Bertie's mother Frederica (Freddie to her friends) was not going to give in that easily. While her husband instructed his lawyer to prepare the appeal letter, she adopted another strategy. She had read the school's announcement about the appointment of the new headmaster, and pored over the photograph of Edward Chamberlain and his pretty wife, 'the well-known fashion historian Lisa Blaize', and their two sweet-looking children. Freddie had female intuition. She could immediately tell that this was a man who was still in love with his wife. Probably too much in love. Get to the wife and that will get to him, she thought.

She went online to Amazon and bought Lisa Blaize's *Lipstick and Lies: Reassessing Feminism and Fashion*. The jargon was impenetrable, but she liked the illustrations, and read enough to see that Lisa was not some dull academic. Freddie was also a fan of Lisa's new column in *City & County*.

She emailed Lisa, saying how much she admired her writing, and how she wondered if Lisa could possibly give her some advice about enrolling as a mature student for a fashion degree, since her life had been through a lot of upheaval and she needed a new start.

Edward shared everything with Lisa – that was one of their rules – so she knew all about the 'Drugs Chat' group, and Bertie was one of the boys she had got to know and rather liked. She was also curious about Freddie and her late-flowering lesbianism. She agreed to the meeting, which took place in The Coffee Bean, a cosy, independent coffee house in Blagsford town.

Freddie, who had driven her Range Rover in from her village home at breakneck speed, came in wearing dark, oversized shades. It was a bitterly cold late November day. Lisa, being a clothes snob, despised the Blagsford Boden-wearing yummy mummies. She also hated the way that these women lived off their husband's earnings. Yes, marriage is, and has always been, a form of legal prostitution, but these skinny cows didn't even put out to their chinless husbands. That's why the husbands took mistresses. Who could blame them?

And they were all such snobs, so entitled. Soon after arriving at Blagsford, Lisa had agreed to join Edward and the braying parents on the touchline for a rugby match. He took every opportunity to show off his pretty young wife. She had got into conversation with one of the posh mummies, who had asked about her accent. She told her she was from a two-up two-down in Bootle. 'What's that?' she had asked. Lisa had laughed it off, determined not to sound chippy: 'Do the maths, two rooms upstairs, two rooms down.' But she had not gone to any more matches.

She was determined to dislike Freddie, but there was something about the way she wore her zebra-printed coat with hot pink lining that suggested a mischievousness and sense of irony that the other mothers lacked. Not the Mumsnet type. Freddie had short blonde hair, and an elfin face: she looked like a boy-girl.

They ordered their coffees, and Freddie got straight to it. They both knew that they could dispense with the fiction about advice on a fashion course.

'Mrs Chamberlain, or should I say Ms Blaize –'

Lisa interrupted, 'Please call me Lisa.'

'Lisa, I know that you are a mother, and I am appealing to you as a mother, to try to persuade your husband to think again about Bertie's exclusion. He's just a boy. This will ruin his life. He's made a mistake. A big mistake, but everyone deserves a second chance.'

'I'm sorry, but there's nothing I can do to help. Edward has always been adamant about his zero-drugs policy. He'd exclude his own children if they were caught using drugs.'

Freddie smiled. 'I understand. But Bertie has been through so much, lately.' She blushed, 'It hasn't been easy for him ... my situation.'

Lisa was intrigued that Freddie had introduced her 'situation' so quickly. She's obviously out and proud, Lisa thought. She smiled warmly to show her support.

'Walking out on my husband was the best thing I've ever done. I'm deliriously happy with my new ... partner. Marriage is so hard for women, don't you think? How many of us are really, truly happy?'

Crikey, Lisa thought to herself. She doesn't pull any punches.

'Well, I'm happy with Edward. And I love being a mother.'

'But are you, really, really happy?'

'Well, I'm not sure how to answer you. I think I am.'

'*Think?*'

'Yes, think.'

'Anyhow, Mrs Cole, this is about you and Bertie, not about me. And I just don't think that I can be of help. I'm so sorry. Edward is a stubborn man, and he has the bit between his teeth on this one. I will try to speak to him, but I can't promise anything.'

'Thank you, Lisa. I trust you. You're not like the other mothers I meet. You're very warm. I can see that you are a woman's woman. And please, do call me Freddie.'

They chatted about other things, Lisa's writing, and her children. Freddie's phone pinged and her eyes lit up as the name flashed across the screen.

'I'll call you back in five, sweetie. Thanks for meeting me, Lisa. And, by the way, I really enjoy your column. Didn't understand your book, but there are some really good jokes when you write for that magazine. You're hilarious. You should share your talents with the world on Twitter.'

'I've never seen the point of social media – Facebook and all that.'

'You really should try Twitter – you'll meet some interesting people there, have some fun, and promote your writing.'

'Thanks, but it's just not my bag.'

As Lisa walked back to the school, she reflected on the meeting. Freddie was something else. Utterly charming, but there was iron there too. She was a strong woman and her situation was certainly unusual. I wouldn't want to cross her, Lisa thought. Strange that she should mention Twitter – I guess she tweets herself.

It was obvious that Freddie had been trying to charm her. Good job I don't swing that way, Lisa smiled. She wondered about the new woman in Freddie's life. It took a lot of guts to leave a marriage and child. She must be something special. And who was on the phone? Bertie or the new woman? From the smile that had played across her mouth, and the light in her eyes, Lisa suspected the latter. Freddie was still in the first flush of romance. Those butterflies in the tummy, that all-consuming madness she had once felt for Edward. She had a tiny pang of regret that she would never have that feeling again. Marriage and motherhood were hard work, especially with a monthly column to write. It did not help that Edward had become entirely absorbed in his new job.

PART TWO

Guilt

CHAPTER 9

DMs

She was queuing in The Coffee Bean when she glanced down and saw a somehow familiar-looking pair of DM boots.

'Hi, I don't know if you remember me, but you saved my daughter's life. May I buy you a coffee?'

He smiled at her. It was a strange smile, she thought. A professional, practised doctor's smile, but there was someone else: as if he knew that he had a wonderful mouth and sensuous lips, and there was a hint of playfulness in the smile, too.

'I remember you. I really do. I think you're exaggerating my role. It was my boss who performed the actual surgery. I was only the registrar, the number two in theatre, though I'm a consultant now. I remember telling you that bypass surgery is now routine, even for children. I know that your daughter came through just fine. How's she doing now?'

'Emma's doing great.' Lisa whipped out her phone and showed him a photo.

'She looks so much like you, and look how tall she is.'

'She has her father's long legs. Not that I'm jealous,' she laughed. 'So what are you doing in Blagsford?'

'I live here. Lots of doctors and surgeons live here and commute to Birmingham. It's a nice town, with good schools, as I'm … I'm, I'm sure you appreciate.' He had a very slight stammer. She liked that. It made him seem vulnerable.

77

He ordered a flat white, and she again offered to pay, but he wouldn't hear of it.

'I'm an old-fashioned boy. I'm not letting you pay. If I'd seen you first, I'd have paid for yours.'

As a feminist, Lisa should have felt offended. But she didn't. She liked it. It made her feel special. Edward had no such scruples. He often let her pay for supper and lunch out of the money in her own bank account (the 'Ladies' Nice Things' account, as they had taken to calling it, with more than a touch of irony).

'If you insist, doctor.'

'Mister for a surgeon, but call me Sean. Sean O'Connor.'

'And I'm Lisa Blaize.'

'Well, come on let's have a quick coffee together then,' he said. 'You go on upstairs, find a space, and I'll bring up your coffee. How do you like it?'

'Strong and black, like my men.'

He chortled.

'Seriously – double espresso, extra hot. Thank you. That's really kind of you.'

They chatted for half an hour or so. She talked about her book, and how, now that Emma and George were both at primary school, she'd finally be able to get on with her second one. Though she admitted that she wasn't finding it easy being the headmaster's wife. That wasn't the kind of role that existed in state schools.

Sean enthused about the National Health Service – he was amazingly positive, considering how overworked he and his colleagues must have been – and about his newfound passion for Twitter. 'It's a great way of keeping in touch with things you're interested in, getting a quick fix of the world outside when you don't have time to read newspapers or watch the TV. And, as a surgeon, you *never* have time.'

*   *   *

That is how it started. A chance meeting in a coffee shop in the town where they both lived. They exchanged email addresses, more for politeness than for anything else. Lisa was grateful to him, but she had no intention of contacting him again. She was happily married, and Sean simply wasn't her type. She wasn't attracted to blond men with green eyes. She loved dark men with brown eyes. Eyes that you could trust. Sean was married with children, so that was another no-go area. She would never hurt a child. She could tell that Sean fancied her. She could feel it. Best not to stay in contact. It was gratitude that had moved her to flirt a little with him. Nothing else.

Twitter, though. Funny that two people in quick succession, first Freddie and now Sean, had suggested that it might be a medium for her. But then again, everyone was talking about Twitter that autumn because it was the favoured mode of communication of @realDonaldTrump, President-elect of the United States of America (Edward's words on this subject were unrepeatable).

Pregnancy and motherhood, Emma's illness, then the move – Lisa had never had any time for social media. She wasn't really sure what Twitter was. Something like Facebook, but limited to a hundred and eighty characters – was that the gimmick?

That night, when Edward was buried beneath a deluge of paperwork in his study, the children were asleep, and she was bored as there was nothing on TV, she clicked on Twitter.com.

*It's what's happening. From breaking news and
entertainment to sports and politics, get the
full story with all the live commentary.
Sign up for Twitter.*

No harm in giving it a go, even if she never used it.

@Lisa_Blaize

A profile was needed.

I like the idea of a profile, she thought. I need a new profile.
Something other than The Headmaster's Wife. This is good. It
could really help me to focus on the bloody second book, and to
promote it when it comes out.

Profile

Fashion historian & author of *Lipstick and Lies:
Reassessing Feminism and Fashion*. Married with
two fantabulous children. Special interest in
textiles & lingerie.

Twitter then asked her to post her first tweet. She deleted the
boring suggestion of 'Hullo, this is my first tweet' and typed
something of her own:

 Lisa Blaize @Lisa_Blaize
Twitter may be my undoing!

80

Twitter asked her to start 'following' people. She clicked on a few suggestions that came up under the categories of Fashion and Entertainment. Then she noticed a 'Search' box. She typed in 'Frederica Cole' and found that she tweeted with the handle 'FreddieSwings'. Should she follow her? Better not, it would look a bit stalkerish.

She was just about to type Sean's name into the search box – no harm in seeing what he had to say, especially as there might be some interesting links to stories about new research on paediatric heart conditions – when, to her astonishment, a number one appeared on a menu item marked 'Notifications'. They were apparently tweets in which your name was mentioned.

Mr Sean O'Connor @MrOCon

Hi @Lisa_Blaize! So you took my advice and signed up for Twitter? Lovely to see you today. You're looking so well.

Then, within seconds, before she could even register her surprise:

Mr Sean O'Connor @MrOCon

@Lisa_Blaize … I just ordered your book on Amazon. Can't wait to read it.

Lisa Blaize @Lisa_Blaize

Well hullo you @MrOCon. Guess I should thank you for the follow? So, thank you. And thanks for the coffee.

Mr Sean O'Connor @MrOCon

Great Twitter pic @Lisa_Blaize. Love the gorgeous backless dress. Very clever not to show your face. Very nice back, by the way.

Lisa Blaize @Lisa_Blaize

Stop flirting, Doctor @MrOCon. Helmut Lang. One of my favourite designers.

Mr Sean O'Connor @MrOCon

Mr not Dr for a surgeon. Stop flirting back @Lisa_Blaize. God, you'll have me struck off. If you're not careful, I'll unfollow you! DM me.

What's 'DM'? wondered Lisa.

Twitter told her.

About Direct Messages: Direct Messages are the private side of Twitter. You can use Direct Messages to have private conversations with people about Tweets and other content.

Like an email, Lisa thought. Apparently you could only exchange DMs if you followed each other.

She liked the sound of Private.

She added @MrOCon to her list of followers.

Within a minute, a number one appeared in the menu item that said 'Messages' beside a little picture of a sealed envelope.

DM from @MrOCon: Let me know when you're next in town and we can have another coffee?

DM from @Lisa_Blaize: Do you always follow chance encounters in The Coffee Bean with this kind of conversation on Twitter?

DM from @MrOCon: Never. Not once in my life. Hand on heart, I haven't looked at another woman in nearly ten years of marriage.

DM from @Lisa_Blaize: I don't know whether to be flattered or alarmed.

DM from @MrOCon: You're dangerous. I've been stalking you on the Internet. God, you're rewarding to stalk. BTW, best delete those first tweets and stick to DMs.

CHAPTER 10

Meaningful Coincidences

Twitter was a chain where one thing led to another. You'd see an interesting or funny tweet, click on the name of the tweeter (was that the correct term? Lisa still had a lot to learn) and then see the thread of their other tweets. Then you'd link through to someone else. A thread of fashion-related observations and pictures would lead, before you knew it, to a jokey exchange about ecclesiastical vestments. That was what led her to reconnect with a dear friend from her student days. She had been out of touch for ages, ever since marrying Edward. She was never quite sure whether her Father Confessor, as she jokingly called him, approved of her divorce, or, for that matter, her new husband. But it was one of those precious friendships that, the moment you picked it up again, it was as if you'd seen each other yesterday.

She had met John Misty in a London pub when she was doing her foundation course. He was training for the church. Misty was the funniest man she had ever encountered. She knew that they would be friends for life.

When she complained about the bitchiness of the fashion world, Misty smiled, wryly. 'Darling Blaize, you have not the first idea about bitchiness until you have been on intimate terms with members of the clergy. Most of whom bat for the other side, naturally.'

'Oh come on, I don't think that's true.'

'Darling, go for a drink in Old Compton Street any evening of the week and call out "Hello Father" – hundreds of men will turn around.'

I wonder if Father John tweets, she asked herself a few days into her new life trying out her Twitter persona, something she was enjoying very much indeed. She could see how easy it was to get hooked.

Yes, there he was, @FrJohnMisty.

Lisa Blaize @Lisa_Blaize
Hullo stranger. Bet @FrJohnMisty didn't expect to find *me* here.

REPLY TO @Lisa_Blaize
Vicar of Leicester @FrJohnMisty
Good God, Blaize, you couldn't even send an email when we last spoke. Would never have had you pegged for one of the Twitterati.

It was true that she was hopeless at email. The junk piled up in her inbox day after day, so she would often miss the occasional message that really mattered. Then Edward would patiently go through the backlog for her, tutting and moving dozens of emails to Trash. She had more or less given up using her email account. If something was important, people would phone. Or write an old-fashioned letter. Now, though, she could see that she would be much more suited to Twitter dialogue. It was immediate, and the backlog was invisible.

She told him all about Emma's heart operation and about Blagsford. She complained that she was stuck on the second book, but still writing articles about fashion. He told her about life in his Leicester parish. A television producer who had been to university in the city, had had the idea of a sitcom called 'Priest' about the vicar of a parish in an inner city populated almost entirely by Muslims. He had befriended Father John and got him talking about some of the more bizarre incidents in his daily life. Father John embroidered them all with his usual colour. Before long, he found himself in the role of consultant to the scriptwriter. It was a shame that the project was stuck in 'development hell'. Lisa was amused to hear an Anglo-Catholic priest using the language of the entertainment industry.

She could exchange banter with Father John all night. She loved the wit and economy afforded by this new medium. She would trust him with her life. And she knew that he never judged her. And he didn't. Lisa knew that she was Marmite. You loved her, or you hated her. Father John Misty loved her.

So she hit 'Send' on a Direct Message that read:

DM from @Lisa_Blaize: I've started a Twitter flirtation with a consultant heart surgeon.

The reply came straight back:

DM from @FrJohnMisty: I'm your consultant on matters of the heart. Take care, Blaize. No sexting.

*   *   *

Over the next couple of weeks Lisa's virtual affair with Sean progressed at a rapidly increasing pace. A few tweets here, then an exchange of phone numbers and a few texts there. Each day a few more. Then something happened that shook her. It was almost Christmas, and they met for a morning coffee in the Bean. Sean arrived with a silver cardboard box. They chatted, flirted, and laughed. God, he made her laugh. He was telling her a story about one of his son's drunken escapades. He was wonderfully self-deprecating. She loved that he didn't buy into the whole middle-class helicopter parenting shit.

In one of their text exchanges, Sean had mentioned that his favourite author was Laurie Lee. Lisa had read *Cider with Rosie* when she was a teenager, and vaguely remembered a scene with, what was it, a first kiss under an apple cart at harvest time? Sean had told her that his favourite book was not *Rosie*, but Laurie Lee's memoir, *As I Walked Out One Midsummer Morning*. 'That's a mouthful for a title,' she had texted back, 'I prefer one-word titles like *Othello*, *Lolita*, and *Emma*.' And then, in another message a moment later, 'Or two words at most. *Emma Bovary*. *Anna Karenina*.' Sean had seemed rather crestfallen. The scientist dipping his toe in arty waters and being slapped down. She clocked his disappointment and felt penitent, so followed up with a more encouraging text: 'My role models??!! …'

Bending forward over the table in The Coffee Bean, Sean started telling her about Laurie Lee's life. He had had a blazing – Sean raised an eyebrow as he uttered that word – affair with a woman called Lorna Garman. Apparently there were these wild Garman sisters. Beautiful and wild. They were from Irish Gypsy descent on their mother's side. They were amoral, too. One of the sisters, Mary, had an affair with Vita Sackville-West. She slept with her whilst her little boy lay on a bed only a few feet away.

Lisa objected to this. Why was it that the upper classes got away with infidelity? 'If that happened on a sink estate, there would be uproar, and social services would take away the child – but somehow the aristocracy and the Bloomsbury set got away with it and made it look cool and sexy and free.'

'Well, yes, but don't you think monogamy is very overrated? You strike me as a bit of a wild gypsy soul yourself. I'm not sure you could be tamed, Lisa. There's more than a bit of Lorna Garman in you. You look like her too.'

'Well, I don't swing both ways, like her sister. I'm more prudish than you think. I've had very few lovers, Sean. I'm quite an old-fashioned Catholic girl.'

'Well, I'm not going to tell you how many lovers I've had or you'll drop me. Men do that sort of thing, you know. Notch up the numbers.'

When she left, he gave her the silver box and wished her Happy Christmas. Just a few tokens, he said. Nothing to feel too excited about. She told him that she had a present for him too. She handed over a small parcel packaged in brown paper. Lisa, mortified at the put-down over book titles, had planned the perfect Christmas present for Sean. It had taken hours, but she had been lucky. On principle she never used Amazon, but websites for rare books were another matter. She had gone online and found what she desired, thanks to a book dealer in Milwaukee who was willing (for a price) to dispatch by express courier. It was a signed, first edition of *As I Walked Out One Midsummer Morning*. In pristine condition.

When she got home, she opened the box. It contained a hand-written love letter, a book about chickens, two CDs, and an old battered Penguin paperback. She smiled when she saw it. She could hardly believe it. Then her phone pinged:

L, You naughty girl. That is quite simply the most wonderful present I have ever received. I can't begin to imagine the time and trouble you took to find it. Let alone the expense. There is something in your box which is very personal to me, part of me, that I have had with me (all over the world!) for 25 years, but I really wanted to give it to you. This is perfect symmetry. I'm a man of science. I don't believe in magic, but there is something magical in this exchange of books that makes me question my belief in empirical, evidence-based knowledge. I gave you my most precious book, and I got it straight back. I will honour it, treasure it, take it everywhere I go, & it will always remind me of you. It means so much to me. Thank you so much. S. x

She texted back:

I'm sure, Mr C, that you're familiar with Jung's theory of synchronicity: Do you know the story of the Scarab Beetle?

Nope. Though I do know about Synchronicity: title of an album by The Police …

LOL. One of Jung's patients had a dream about a costly item of jewellery, a golden scarab. She was telling Jung about this dream when he became aware of a gentle tapping on the window. He saw that it was a large, flying insect trying to get in. He opened the window and in it flew. It was a scarab beetle, gold-green. Jung handed the beetle to his patient and said 'Here is your scarab.'

Meaningful Coincidences?

Exactly.

CHAPTER 11

All My Pretty Chickens

The spring term – or Lent Term, as they called it at Blagsford –
began, and the final decision about Bertie was pending. Lisa took
her chance to put in a plea on Freddie's behalf. Edward was
furious at this act of interference. The school was his territory.
This matter with Bertie was most delicate. His father was an
important figure, and a generous donor. It had not been easy to
tell Max that his son and heir was a drug dealer. The bust had
happened just before the Christmas holidays, so talks had been
suspended until the beginning of the new term. But Edward had
made it clear to the parents that Bertie's exclusion was likely to
be permanent. Bertie had not returned to school at the beginning of the new term. Arrangements were still being made.
Don't speak to her again, Edward warned Lisa. It's an ongoing
issue.

It was no surprise to Lisa that Edward was not to be swayed.
Though she hated the way that he had shouted at her – some-
thing he never, ever did – she quietly respected the smack of firm
of leadership that he was revealing once again. The shockwaves
rippled across the school as the news spread. Lisa felt bad for
Freddie. Felt that she had, somehow, let her down. Max and
Freddie came to the school, frostily together, to be told the news.
As they left Edward's study, Lisa was waiting.

'I'm sorry,' she whispered to Freddie, 'I did my best.'

Freddie ignored her, and walked out with tears in her eyes, and head bowed. Max stalked out, furious. Lisa could hear him yelling in the car park. I'm glad she got away from him, she thought. He's a bully and a coward. He hadn't shouted like that at Edward. He saved his wrath for his estranged wife. But her final thoughts were for Bertie, whom no one really wanted.

*   *   *

Lisa was sure that she would never have had an affair without the easy compliance of social media. She was using Twitter to communicate with her lover. But she was doing it for *all the world to see*. Except that she knew that only she and Sean would be aware of this. So it didn't really matter. Did it?

They could have emailed, but Lisa didn't like email, and Sean didn't think it was safe. They texted. But somehow Twitter was their medium. It had brought them together. The obvious thing would have been to confine themselves to Direct Messages, but Lisa didn't want this. Crazily, she wanted the world to know her secret, her guilt. Sean, cannier, and far more conscious of the professional cost of any false move, set up a secret Twitter account. In homage to Laurie Lee, and his Christmas present from Lisa, he chose the handle @AsIWalkedOut. In it, he poured out thoughts, memories and feelings in a stream of consciousness that made her think he was really speaking to himself.

LoveLaurieLee @AsIWalkedOut
Make me not want you so much. I can't get any peace always thinking about you – I want to be able to live in peace again.

LoveLaurieLee @AsIWalkedOut

A young man was playing a fiddle on a Cornish beach. He looked up to see a glamorous woman gazing at him.

LoveLaurieLee @AsIWalkedOut

She had shoulder-length dark hair, red-painted lips & blue, blue eyes.

LoveLaurieLee @AsIWalkedOut

She spoke to him: 'Boy, come and play for me.'

LoveLaurieLee @AsIWalkedOut

He was a writer called Laurie Lee. She was Lorna Garman, the youngest of the seven famously beautiful Garman sisters.

LoveLaurieLee @AsIWalkedOut

They began an intense love affair. She was married, but serially unfaithful. She gave birth to Lee's daughter.

LoveLaurieLee @AsIWalkedOut

Later she became the lover of Lucien Freud.

LoveLaurieLee @AsIWalkedOut

One day, Lorna and Freud were walking down Piccadilly. They bumped into Laurie Lee at a bus stop and a fight broke out.

LoveLaurieLee @AsIWalkedOut

Freud won the fight, but Lorna went home with Lee.

LoveLaurieLee @AsIWalkedOut

Lee, knowing he would lose her, put a razor blade to his throat, but couldn't go through with it.

LoveLaurieLee @AsIWalkedOut

Freud threatened to shoot her and shoot myself, but in the end he fired his gun into a cabbage patch.

REPLY TO @AsIWalkedOut

Lisa Blaize @Lisa_Blaize

Myself? HIMself. Freudian slip!

LoveLaurieLee @AsIWalkedOut

Lorna tired of both men and went home to her husband.

LoveLaurieLee @AsIWalkedOut

Freud never got over Lorna, and vowed 'I will never love a woman more than she loves me.'

LoveLaurieLee @AsIWalkedOut

Lucien Freud and Laurie Lee married Lorna's nieces. They never forgot her. She was a hard woman to get over.

*   *   *

Crikey, Lisa thought to herself. What a story. Could it be true that Laurie Lee and Lucien Freud got into a street brawl over a woman? She googled it. It was all true. Lorna Garman was Muse to both men, who became obsessed by her. Laurie Lee dedicated a book of poems to her. Freud painted her. Over and over again, *Girl with Daffodil, Girl with a Tulip.*

Lisa was surprised that this man of science was so romantic. He certainly wasn't your typical doctor. Their meetings were innocent enough; coffee at the Bean, lunch in the café at the Blagsford Heritage Centre. His every little act made her feel happy. He would never let her buy her own coffee. If she arrived early, he would text her to go upstairs and he would bring her an extra hot double espresso. As a feminist, she was appalled by her own double standards. But she allowed him to do it. In every other romantic relationship, Lisa had always had the upper hand. She feared that, for once, this time she might not.

Sean's best feature was his blond floppy hair. She wanted to kiss him on the mouth and run her hands through that hair. She also saw that he had a tiny black fleck in his right eye. She loved this little flaw, because she had always loved flawed things.

Sean was not especially handsome or distinguished looking, like Edward. He was becoming middle-aged, was developing a slight paunch and the lovely hair was thinning. Though his job was extraordinary, his appearance was not out of the ordinary. Her love for him crept up on her, stealthily, and then it hit her with the force of a train. She saw the boy in him. There was a vulnerability lurking behind the 'good doctor' persona. He told her that he had wanted to be a surgeon from the age of five, just as she had known at that age that she would be a writer. Sean was naughty, too. He told her stories of sexual encounters in linen cupboards on hospital wards that made her blush. He was deliciously indiscreet. And he made her laugh. Uncontrollably.

He teased her, calling her Lady C, a reference to Lady Chatterley. Lisa told him that she liked preppie men, not Mellors. Arthur Miller, not Jo DiMaggio. Mr Darcy, not Mr Wickham. 'Ah, you just haven't met the right Mellors,' he said.

Later, he texted her:

Thanks for having coffee with me, Lady C. You were looking so beautiful. Lovely dress. I have a confession to make …

OK, doc, so make it …

When you leaned over to check your phone, I peeped at your cleavage: magnificent.

Please behave Dr O'Connor.

Mr. Not on your life.

*   *   *

Love makes you cruel. Lisa was lying on her blue chaise, listening to her vinyl, and reading her lover's texts. She glimpsed Edward walking towards her.

'You have a very beatific smile on your face.'

'Do I? Maybe I'm pleased to see you.'

'Who's on the phone?'

'Oh, I was just speaking to my mum.'

'Send her my love.'

'Will do.'

Though she was the author of a book called *Lipstick and Lies*, Lisa hated lying. Lying to anybody. She hadn't lied to Freddie when telling her about what she could or couldn't do for Bertie. And she had never, ever lied to Edward. She did not feel good.

Then something happened that convinced her she should call it all off.

One evening in February, when Edward was away at a meeting of the Headmasters' Conference, Sean texted her to ask if they could meet for a cocktail. They had never been out together in the evening before. Lisa texted back to say that she could pop over for an hour. She hurriedly put on a chic black dress, black evening jacket, and twisted her hair into a messy bun.

'You look pretty, Mummy,' said Emma. 'Where are you going?'

'I'm just popping out to see a friend. Matron from School House is going to come over and keep an eye on you.'

'It's Ma, mummy, not Matron,' said Emma.

Lisa raised her eyebrows. 'I won't be long. And children, don't forget to put the chickens to bed.'

'OK,' said little George.

She loved those chickens, the five Cotswold Legbar hens and the handsome cockerel they'd christened Colin. She didn't mind that they provoked some teasing. 'Excuse me, Ms Blaize,' a particularly handsome tousled lower-sixth boarder said to her one day (Edward had announced that out of respect for 'her autonomy and her professional status' his wife was always to be called Ms Blaize, not Mrs Chamberlain).

'What is it?' she said, kindly.

'Is it true that you're woken up very early every morning by the headmaster's cock?'

She blushed.

He paused, then risked the unmentionable subject: 'It's a big one, isn't it?'

She blushed more deeply, then got it. She smiled and waited.

'The cockerel – we can hear it as far away as School House.'

She admired his spunk, and didn't report him. Edward would not have seen the funny side.

*   *   *

It was raining. They were meeting in a deconsecrated church that was now a cocktail bar. Sean, who was an atheist, joked that it was the only church you would ever find him in. He had a present for her. It was a first edition of *The Great Gatsby*, which Lisa had told him was her favourite novel. Those shirts of Jay Gatsby's, Daisy's cool dresses. The hemlines of the Jazz Age.

That was why he had called her. He couldn't wait to see her delight when he handed it over.

She didn't know what to say. Tears pricked her eyes. The present moved her beyond words.

'You do like it?'

She nodded.

When she got home, she hid the book in one of her shelves. She tucked George in, kissed his thick black curls, and then fell asleep on his bed next to him. In the early hours, she stole back into her own bed, and cuddled into Edward's warm body. In the morning, he woke first, as always, and pulled back the curtains.

'Christ Almighty!'

'What, what?'

'Shush, I don't want George to see. The fox has killed the chickens. I can see three on the lawn. I need to bury the bodies before he wakes up.'

Lisa jumped up.

'But where are the others? What about Colin?'

'The bloody fox will have taken them. The school gardener said he saw a vixen and a cub at the bottom of the lawn. I forgot to warn you. So much on at the moment, you know.'

'All of them. All six of them. Now I know the meaning of Macduff's words: *at one fell swoop.*'

'That's what foxes do, Lisa. They do it for fun. Did you lock them in the coop last night?'

'Emma and George did. But they mustn't have locked the door tightly enough.'

Emma was a careful girl, and George loved those chickens. What had gone wrong? Lisa felt a stab of guilt. She should have put the hens away herself, not been out having a cocktail with a married man. But what if someone else had let them out? Had someone from the school seen her dashing out in the rain? She felt sick to her stomach. Between them, she and Sean had five children. This was a bad omen. A warning. It was time to call it off before anyone else got hurt.

CHAPTER 12

What's Happening?

The compulsion was too great. Lisa could not stop herself tweeting. Their meetings were arranged by text, and there was the occasional intimate DM, but most of the time she kept in touch with Sean by posting tweets. Often about the most trivial things. When she had first discovered Twitter back in December she had been amused by the question that appeared in the box that popped up when you hit the Tweet button that was inscribed with a little icon of a quill (I must mention that Shakespearean quill to Edward some time, she said to herself).

Twitter: *what's happening?*

She took this literally. Twitter was her way of telling Sean what was happening in her life. What was happening to her, day by day, minute by minute. It was their way of connecting. Physical presence didn't seem to matter because every time she posted a tweet she knew that he would have read it on his phone within seconds, whenever he wasn't in the operating theatre, and that the moment he read it she would be in his head. It was a connection of the most intimate kind, unique to them, secretive without being sleazy, because it was also entirely innocent – I have no secrets, I am confiding in the whole world. That was the meaning of Twitter.

Photos, too. She didn't dare text them to Sean's phone, in case someone saw them. But selfies posted on Twitter were another matter.

Lisa Blaize @Lisa_Blaize
Duty calls. Dinner for important parents tonight. Designer dress de rigeur. Will this one do?

DM from @MrOCon: Christ, you're gorgeous girl.

Lisa didn't care what anybody else might think. She didn't have many followers, just a few fashion history nerds who had read her book, and a handful of acquaintances such as Bertie's mum Freddie. Nobody would dwell on her words. It was such an ephemeral medium, with hundreds of messages scrolling across each user's screen every minute, all mingled together so that nine out of ten posts would be missed. Except by Sean, who had @ Lisa_Blaize permanently in his 'Search Twitter' box (the one with the little icon of a Sherlock Holmes magnifying glass). Besides, she was enjoying the freedom Twitter gave her to develop a persona that was the antithesis of the received image of a public-school headmaster's wife. A mix of the literary and the ditzy, quoting lines of poetry in one post and making silly jokes in the next. She loved to laugh at her own expense, because she knew that Sean loved that too – and, though she didn't like to admit it – because she also knew that Edward would disapprove. She made lots of references to designer clothes and beauty regimes. This, she thought, would help to establish her 'brand' as a fashion professional. But it would also put the image of her body, her curves, her skin, into Sean's head.

Twitter: *what's happening?*

Lisa Blaize @Lisa_Blaize
I've lost my reading glasses.

DM from @MrOCon: Try looking on your head.

Twitter: *what's happening?*

Lisa Blaize @Lisa_Blaize
I've found my reading glasses. They were on my
head.

*   *   *

To her surprise, her Twitter account started picking up more
followers.

HokeyCokey @charlieboy
heyy @Lisa_Blaize I really like ur tweets.

Lisa Blaize @Lisa_Blaize
Hey @charlieboy Many thanks.

HokeyCokey @charlieboy
Can you follow me back @Lisa_Blaize.

Lisa Blaize @Lisa_Blaize
No problem. What you doing on here?

HokeyCokey @charlieboy

nothing really just bored cus off school.

*   *   *

Over the following weeks, @charlieboy, whoever he was (a pupil at the school?), kept making brief reappearances in her Twitter stream.

HokeyCokey @charlieboy

Heyy @Lisa_Blaize its me again u haven't been active in a while.

HokeyCokey @charlieboy

@Lisa_Blaize U still haven't followed me back.

HokeyCokey @charlieboy

@Lisa_Blaize well I'm transfixed by ur profile pics eyes.

HokeyCokey @charlieboy

@Lisa_Blaize what u wearing atm?

HokeyCokey @charlieboy

@Lisa_Blaize random question for u though what is your bra size lol.

Lisa Blaize @Lisa_Blaize

Who are you @charlieboy? Do your parents know you're doing this?

HokeyCokey @charlieboy

@Lisa_Blaize that's why i aint dumb enough to give u my name lol.

CHAPTER 13

Sandflies

There was an arms race between the independent schools. The famous ones – Eton, Harrow, Rugby, Winchester, Westminster, Radley – would always have the sharp-elbowed middle-classes jostling for places, bombarding admissions registrars, hiring tutors and interview coaches, pulling strings. But those outside the premier league, 'minor public schools' such as Blagsford, competed fiercely with each other. A rival school's new AstroTurf all-weather hockey pitch would require a response in the form of an indoor tennis court, an Olympic-sized swimming pool would be trumped by an offer of flying lessons. None of this came cheap, so the fees went up and up each year, far ahead of inflation.

Filling the boarding places was the biggest challenge of all. The margin was greatest there, with the fee twice that of a day place. But to most British people, boarding was neither desirable nor affordable. What was the point of having children if you were going to pack them off to school? There were city types knowing the lifetime advantage bestowed by the contacts made at boarding school. And the old county families determined that their offspring should endure the regime of loneliness and cold showers that they had endured themselves (and their parents before them), even if this meant taking out a second mortgage, driving an old banger, and taking holidays in Scotland instead of Tuscany.

But for clientele of this kind, the second division was no use. It was one of the 'great public schools' or nothing.

In order to fill the boarding places, schools like Blagsford had to look further afield. In the Far East they could play on the historic reputation of British private education, pepping it up with hints of Hogwarts' delights.

So it was that the headmaster was required to make an annual recruitment trip during the Easter holidays. Edward's predecessor had gone to Hong Kong and Singapore in alternating years. A bachelor, he travelled alone, insisting on business class so that on arrival in the sweaty tropics he was fresh for his meetings with prospective new parents. 'Did you find any boys?' the admissions registrar would ask on his return. 'I met some boys,' he would habitually say, 'but I don't think we'll be recruiting them.' One of the reasons why Edward had got the job was that he had persuaded the governors he would be much more successful in this area. The bursar was pinning everything on his results.

Edward had a plan. Blagsford's problem was that it was not a big enough hitter in Hong Kong and Singapore, where the top players in the independent school network were all fishing the pool. There just weren't enough wealthy families to go around. Now it happened that Nick, his undergraduate contemporary from Oxford – an adventurer who had never settled in any part of the world for more than a few years – had become head of the prestigious (he claimed) Pasar Minggu Academy in Jakarta. Indonesia: that was a new market. There was plenty of oil money. Its version of Islam was liberal, so there would be no worries about the provision of religious education, no demand for the construction of a school mosque (which would have been very off-putting to the more traditional British parents). Nick had promised him some excellent prospects, and they could have a jolly while they were about it.

Edward insisted on taking Lisa with him. She was such good company. She would be an adornment to the small dinner parties with Indonesian plutocrats that Nick was lining up. If he was honest with himself, he would have to admit that he was using his wife as eye candy. 'And what about her airfare?' the bursar asked. 'I'm sure you are aware that Mr Camps always travelled alone, though of course we allowed him to book a suite in his hotels, in case he was doing any entertaining there.'

'My wife will be an indispensable asset to the recruitment drive, I assure you,' said Edward, mustering the most pompous voice he could find. 'There is no question. The school should pay her airfare.'

'Well, we'll have to see what the governors say,' replied the bursar, sniffily.

The governors agreed without demur – it was crucial to give the new man a chance. But there were mutterings in the staffroom, orchestrated by a disgruntled physicist called Schrodinger, who seemed to have taken a particular dislike to the new headmaster, and his wife. Soon after arriving, Edward had walked into the staffroom and overheard Schrodinger saying '… only because of his background, and as for the wife …' He had looked at him, square on, and Schrodinger had muttered something about David Cameron.

Lisa told Edward that she was uncomfortable about leaving the children and spending a week on the other side of the world. If there was going to be a fuss – 'Airfaregate', they jokingly called it – he could go on his own. She was dreaming of a week of seeing Sean without constantly having to cover her tracks. But Edward was insistent.

107

'It's a point of principle that has to be laid down in the first year. We're a team. You're coming. There's no question. And it'll be good for you. George isn't a baby any more, and Emma's heart is doing just fine. There's got to be a first time away from them, and now is the best possible moment. Your parents will love having them back in Bootle. They'll be spoilt rotten and have the time of their lives. It'll make up for us moving away – you know how your mother hated us going, taking the children away from the extended family.'

Lisa knew that there were times when Edward was not to be budged, and this was one of them. Besides, she felt guilty at her desire to have him out of the way on the other side of the world, and she didn't want to raise any suspicions. She would go.

She'd never travelled business class before. Luxuriating in the space, she spread out her beauty products and occupied herself with a self-administered facial and manicure, taking a photo on her phone. She tweeted it when she landed, to make Sean laugh and reassure him that she had conquered her fear of flying.

Overcome by the humidity and the crowds every time she went outside, she was bored senseless in her Jakarta hotel room, waiting around while Nick paraded Edward before a selection of prospective parents. There was nothing to do but tweet. Things looked up when she was taken shopping by Nick's pretty and very Westernized girlfriend, Annisa: 'He has a different beauty in every continent,' remarked Edward.

Lisa loved the richly-coloured fabrics in the markets, and then, after lunch with two bottles of wine, they somehow found themselves in Melawai Plaza, Jakarta Selatan, famous for its jewellers. And, before she knew it, probably because she was angry with Edward for having dragged her away from the children (and

Sean), only to dump her in a hotel room while he schmoozed the millionaire parents, she was walking out with a beautiful sapphire necklace, the glassy blue of her own eyes.

She didn't tell Edward about the sapphires, paid for from her Ladies' Nice Things Account. But he had noticed that she was feeling neglected, so he had arranged a little treat for her. Nick had told him of a service whereby one of the best – and best-priced – dressmakers in Jakarta would come to a hotel room, measure up a customer for a bespoke garment, then make it up and post it to England.

> **Lisa Blaize** @Lisa_Blaize
> My dressmaker has just left (Yes, I did just say that!) and says he loves my 36, 24, 34 measurements. Yay.

> **DM from @MrOCon:** My Marilyn. Miss you. Xxxxxx

*   *   *

At the end of the trip, with Edward having bagged ten new pupils (more than Mr Camps managed in all his trips put together), Nick and Annisa took them on a boat to Pulau Macan, one of the Thousand Islands, just north of Jakarta. The sand was white, the palm trees out of a picture postcard, the indigo sea dazzling. They sunbathed and went scuba diving among darting, brightly striped Siamese tiger and lizard fish. Lisa had packed a white Elizabeth Hurley bikini with gold buckles. She asked Annisa to take a photo of her, standing sideways, on the edge of the ocean, the white sand between her toes. For Sean. But then, so as not to seem vain, she took a selfie of the unsightly red raw sand-fly bites that had appeared all over her legs.

Edward noticed them. 'I haven't had any bites. You're so hot-blooded that even the sandflies find you irresistible.'

Hot was the word. She and Sean hadn't texted much during the week, for fear that once they started they would not be able to stop, and that might result in a suspiciously large bill for international messages. But there had been one text that she cherished: 'You have the rare combination of being both warm and hot.'

Lisa Blaize @Lisa_Blaize
In the tropics! I'm so hot. Yay.

Then with the photograph taken by Annisa:

Lisa Blaize @Lisa_Blaize
Me in my Liz Hurley bikini.

Quickly followed by the selfie:

Lisa Blaize @Lisa_Blaize
#Uglyme. My husband says even the sandflies find me irresistible. LOL.

*   *   *

As soon as they got back from Indonesia, she returned full time to Twitter and to text exchanges with Sean, furiously checking the phone, which was glued to her hand all day, the first thing she looked at in the morning and the last at night.

Lisa and Father John used Direct Messages. He knew that privacy mattered.

DM from @FrJohnMisty: Hey sweetie. You online?

DM from @FrJohnMisty: Writing a sermon. Not really feeling it.

DM from @Lisa_Blaize: Why?

DM from @FrJohnMisty: Bored. I've started running. Trying to lose some weight. So there I was running around the park, thinking that I wasn't doing too bad and, I swear, this random guy walks past me and whispers 'Fat Cunt'.

DM from @Lisa_Blaize: LOL. There's a tramp by the river where I run. On good days he says 'Morning, miss.' When I'm looking old and gaunt he says 'Morning, madam.'

DM from @FrJohnMisty: I know. The bloody cheek. Anyway, how are things in Blagsford? How's the affair?

DM from @Lisa_Blaize: It's more of a virtual affair than a real one. I barely see him. It's really harmless. No one will get hurt. I'm in control. He loves his wife, and I love Edward. It's just a bit of fun. I do feel a connection with him, though. I feel like I've known him all my life. Like he's my Shakespearean twin.

DM from @FrJohnMisty: Well don't fuck him, because that = incest.

111

DM from @Lisa_Blaize: Ha ha.

 DM from @FrJohnMisty: Say 3 Hail Marys and 1 Our Father.

 DM from @Lisa_Blaize: Think it's a bit late for confession, Misty

 DM from @FrJohnMisty: You do tweet some risky things, darling. Some of those photos are a bit dodge. Not that I'm complaining. You look great. What did I say to you when we were students?

 DM from @Lisa_Blaize: You said I'd be OK if I lost weight and bought some decent clothes. LOL.

 DM from @FrJohnMisty: A writer of your calibre should not be tweeting LOL.

 DM from @Lisa_Blaize: Do you know HAK or PAL?

 DM from @FrJohnMisty: WOT?

 DM from @Lisa_Blaize: Hugs & Kisses and Parent Are Listening. So funny.

 DM from @FrJohnMisty: Got to dash. HAK.

She always listened to Misty, even though she pretended to him that she never did. Heeding his warning, she stopped posting so many selfies. She found another way of putting images into Sean's head, an innocent kind of sexting. She was the Fashion Mistress, an expert in lingerie. So it was part of her job to keep abreast of the latest trends. She began retweeting pictures of lingerie, always classy, never erotic. Just the perfect combination of sexy and innocent.

Her favourite company was Fleur of England, which specialized in luxury British design. Lingerie of the softest gossamer silk, and hand-made French lace, with names like *Belle de Nuit*, *Delphine*, and *Golden Hour*, in oyster, champagne, powder blue. Lisa tweeted a sensuous picture of the Delphine set, which boasted a delicate eyelash edge, allowing for an alluring glimpse of skin. The cheeky derrière peephole design on the briefs, and the silk side ties added the perfect touch of erotica, without being vulgar.

The Venetian-based designer Rosamosario was another favourite. Her designs seemed to belong to another world; of Old Hollywood. Robes in antique-rose silk georgette panelled with shimmering silver Venetian lace, lavender crêpe de Chine, cream and white meringue satin. Lisa tweeted them all.

The only trouble was, @charlieboy retweeted them, adding his own comment.

Ⴒ **HokeyCokey** @charlieboy
PHWOAR!

CHAPTER 14

The Cabinet of Curiosities

There was a difficult start to the summer term, known in Blagsford as the Corpus Christi Term, or CCT for short.

'The Bertie story has hit the press. Well, I guess it was bound to happen.'

'The *Blagsford Times?*'

'Yes, have a look. It's only a matter of time before the *Daily Mail* picks it up. Any excuse to have a go at over-privileged public-school kids.'

'I'm sorry. Have you made a statement?'

'Yes, the usual spiel: "The school conducted proper investigations in accordance with its policies and legal obligations. We have a clear substance abuse policy which leaves pupils in no doubt that anyone found to be supplying, possessing, or using drugs must expect to be permanently excluded with immediate effect".'

'Well, you've shown a hard line, which is the important thing. It's a shame, though. I rather adored Bertie. Can't believe the gang of five boasted about it on social media. Some of the comments on the article in the *Blagsford Times* are hilarious. "The parents are in shock? Have they not got a clue about the culture today?" And listen to this one: "Talking about A-class drugs on social media? Shocking! Worse still, their parents have NO CLUE."'

'Lisa, stop sounding like you're enjoying this. No parent wants to hear this about their child. Especially when they're spending 35k a year.'

'I know, but everyone scrolls down to the comments. Just to test the temperature, so to speak.'

'Well, frankly, I don't approve of anyone who takes this rag seriously.'

'There's no harm in knowing what middle England is thinking, Edward. You've got to live in the real world. Don't you always say that you need to apply the *Daily Mail* test when making any decision that might affect the public reputation of a school?'

'Social media is not the real world. Which reminds me, have you gone easy on Twitter?'

'On Twitter? I didn't know you knew I had started tweeting.'

'I didn't, until someone in the staffroom mentioned it.'

'Do you have a problem with that, Edward?'

'No.'

'So why should I go easy on my tweets? I'm enjoying letting myself go there, which I certainly can't here.'

'It's just that I had a glance at your followers. There's all sorts of people – everyone from that Freddie, Bertie's mother, to a surgeon in Birmingham. I think it might even be the one who operated on Emma all those years ago. God knows how he stumbled on your tweets. Wouldn't have imagined a surgeon to be a dedicated follower of fashion. And look, half the staff are following you, and those that aren't are probably snooping at your tweets. I don't like the way Twitter allows anyone to see anyone, even if they're not registered themselves. Apparently there's a setting that lets you "protect" your tweets, so you can screen out unwanted followers. Maybe you should try that. I really think you should be a bit more circumspect.'

'Oh, so now you're stalking me on Twitter? For God's sake. Why are you doing that? I thought you hated social media.'

'Well, having looked at Twitter for the first time, after I was told you were using it, I'm beginning to see the point of it. People retweet some very interesting articles that one would not otherwise see. I've set up an account for myself. It could be a good PR vehicle for the school. In fact, I'm following you.'

Lisa could not help laughing. Dr Edward Chamberlain, Tudor historian and distinguished headmaster, tweeting. It was just so incongruous. But she would have to be careful with Twitter from now on. Especially as he had mentioned Emma's surgeon.

Maybe Edward was right, she needed to embrace a bit of 'Twilence'. But then, how would Sean know that she was all right? The only reason she tweeted was to tell him what she was doing, what she was feeling, how she was. And she wasn't having anyone, especially not her husband, telling her to protect her tweets.

*   *   *

 LoveLaurieLee @AsIWalkedOut
Others may need a War, you've got one here (Lorna Garman to Laurie Lee).

*   *   *

'Does your wife use social media, Sean?'

'No! She loathes Twitter. Posts the occasional Facebook photo, but that's about it.'

'Sensible woman. Good for her. Does she ever check your Twitter account?'

'Don't think so. And if so, it would only be boring medical stuff. She doesn't know about my fantasy secret account, obviously.'

'Are you on Facebook?'

'No.'

'Nor me. I can't get on with it. I can just about cope with Twitter, but not Facebook. I leave that to the teens in the school, or to the sad adults who feel the need to post photographs of their holidays in Mauritius just to advertise how wonderful their lives are.'

She paused, and looked around The Coffee Bean. She was always afraid that a teacher might drift in, or a parent, or even a sixth-former with a free period. Just once, the matron of School House had seen them together, hunched over their coffees. 'Hullo, doctor – remember me? I brought that Blagsford boy in to hospital when he'd had a rugby injury, and you had to do emergency surgery to remove a blood clot. What are you doing here with Mrs Head?' Sean had explained that he had been one of the team who had dealt with Emma's heart problem, and he always tried to keep in touch with the families of special patients. 'Sweet,' Matron had said. Without suspicion, Lisa thought. Or hoped.

In her heart, she knew that the affair was escalating. She had joked on Twitter that spring was coming and the temperature was getting higher and higher. But now was the moment to pull back. That was the sign from above, communicated via the fox and the chickens.

'I've got something to say. You're not going to like hearing it. But I think we need to let the temperature cool a little, doctor.'

'Mister,' Sean corrected her. Their standing joke. But he agreed. He saw the danger. Though she wasn't a patient, she was the parent of a former patient, and that would be enough to get him struck off, or at the very least reprimanded. They made a pact. No Twitter, no texting. No contact. Sean was concerned that one of his sons was going off the rails. That was his sign. They decided to cool things down. It was for the best. Radio silence from now on.

As soon as she got home, she checked her phone. Nothing. He was keeping to his word. She cooked chicken and pesto, and then switched on her laptop. Don't go on Twitter, she told herself. Don't go on Twitter.

 LoveLaurieLee @AsIWalkedOut
I lay with my face in the grass, or with my mouth to hers.

 LoveLaurieLee @AsIWalkedOut
The act of kissing in public seemed to increase our pleasure. I know she is mine by the smell of her mouth …
1/2

 LoveLaurieLee @AsIWalkedOut
2/2 … the shape of her arms, and that intangible, free flow of her soft body when she embraces me.

 LoveLaurieLee @AsIWalkedOut
I want to feed amongst the lilies … I am my beloved's, and my beloved is mine.

He had lasted all of forty minutes.

*   *   *

She texted:

> O'Connor. Stop tweeting. Whatever happened to Radio Silence?

> I've done really well, Lady C. I left it at least one hour.

> LOL. Forty minutes by my reckoning. It's lovely to be in touch again ... I love the Laurie Lee quotes.

*　　*　　*

Before bed, she took a selfie in front of her bedroom mirror. She uploaded it to Twitter.

Lisa Blaize @Lisa_Blaize
Just taking off my hot pink dress before bed. Love that colour: must find out which designer invented it.

DM from @MrOCon: I wish it was me undoing the zip that goes all the way down the back.

*　　*　　*

Things went quieter as the CCT progressed, with the boys knuckling down to exams, and the teachers growing less uptight as the weather became warmer. The *Daily Mail* didn't pick up the Bertie story. No more publicity about drugs and exclusions. To her delight, Lisa was asked to write a review for a national newspaper of an Alexander McQueen retrospective in London. She was sent two tickets for the private viewing.

'Edward, I've got to review this fashion thing in London. You'd hate it. You OK for me to go alone?'

'Of course, I've got to prepare the papers for the next governors' meeting.'

She asked Sean to be her plus one.

It was a stunning exhibition. Lisa had wandered around in tears. Room after room after room of exquisitely tailored clothes, from eighteenth-century frock coats in satin silk, lined with human hair, to dresses made of the finest chiffon, shells, feathers, plywood, and flowers. The oyster dress was a confection of mille-feuille – endless circles of silk organza. She felt like Alice stepping into a wonderland of unimaginable pleasure and delight. *Grace* was the word that she kept repeating in her head. It was the embodiment of grace, combined with pain.

At the centre of the exhibition was the Mad Hatter's Tea Party, in the room entitled 'The Cabinet of Curiosities'. It was like seeing the inside of McQueen's tortured, troubled, but always extraordinary mind. Shoes, dresses, and accessories were arranged in floor-to-ceiling cabinets, accompanied by the sound of slashing scissors. There was a fetishistic quality to the accessories: gimp masks, leather harnesses, headdresses with impala horns, a cuirass made of glass, a corset of coiled aluminium. And feathers: peacock, pheasant, ostrich, and duck. There was a lacquered coat of gold feathers: Icarus. McQueen loved birds, especially birds of prey. That was the distinctive shape of his cut, known in the trade as his silhouette. Why his clothes moved, swooped and took flight.

Afterwards, in a nearby bar, she tried to explain her love for McQueen.

'He's like Chanel. Kindred spirits. They were both from humble backgrounds and understood the importance of hidden beauty. It was their aesthetic. Chanel said, "Luxury is the coat a woman throws inside out over an armchair, and the underside is more valuable than the exterior." Did you know what McQueen had tattooed on his upper right bicep? Shakespeare: "Love looks not with the eyes, but with the mind".'

Sean gazed at her.

'And, as with Chanel, his unique talent was in moulage (that's draping, to us), cutting, moulding, pinning, and slashing fabric on the live body. They often didn't bother with cutting patterns. True genius. Just slashing the fabric.'

Sean watched, listened, wide-eyed, mouth dropping in adoration. He loved to hear her talk with such animation, twisting her strands of dark hair with her long, tapered fingers as she rhapsodized.

'Sorry to bore on.'

'You're many things, Lisa, but you're not a bore.'

'Oh, well, as McQueen often said, "It's only clothes".'

As they left the bar, he grabbed her and pushed her violently against the wall, kissing her with such an intensity that she felt frightened. She wanted to call a halt, but she couldn't. She had to finish what she had started.

CHAPTER 15

Queenie

On the way back to the station, Sean put his arm around her shoulder. Oak, she thought. He's an oak tree. She had before never felt so safe in all her life. It was that simple. He was a healer. He would take care of her and Emma. She just knew that. She was ready for the next step.

He kissed her again as they said goodbye at the station – he was staying in London for the evening. He had told his wife that he was seeing an old friend from medical school. On the train journey home, Lisa took out her phone, went online, and bought some very sexy lingerie.

As soon as she got out of the taxi in front of the Headmaster's House, she saw that Edward and the children were waiting, expectantly, for her. She knew from their guilty faces that something was up. She was the one who should have felt guilty, not them.

It was George who couldn't contain himself.

'Mama, look what Daddy's done! It's a puppy. A real-life puppy.'

It was true. Edward handed her a tiny, white ball of fur. It snuggled into her arms, lifting its small, compact head over her hands, and then snuggling back underneath. For Lisa, this was utter love at first sight. This tiny creature was so soft, so vulnerable.

'Mum,' said Emma, 'she's called Queenie. You know, for Alexander McQueen. It's been our secret. She's a Pomeranian. We wanted to surprise you. It won't be more work for you. We'll take her out, every day.'

Lisa put her down. Queenie made a puddle on the floor.

'And Emma will train her. So you don't have to worry about that, either. Are you happy, darling?' said Edward.

'Yes, yes. I am very happy.' Lisa burst into tears.

*   *   *

But she couldn't stop herself.

LoveLaurieLee @AsIWalkedOut
She takes off some of her clothes and slips into the bed beside me.

LoveLaurieLee @AsIWalkedOut
My brain drowsy but my body fresh and awake. It's been cold under those scant blankets but now I feel I am standing naked in front of a fire.

LoveLaurieLee @AsIWalkedOut
A dark one, her panther tread, voice full of musky secrets, her limbs uncoiling on beds of moonlight.

LoveLaurieLee @AsIWalkedOut
I remember the flowers on the piano, the white sheets on her bed, her deep mouth, and love without honour.

LoveLaurieLee @AsIWalkedOut

L puts on her nightdress with such a soft, slow twist to her body that I think of salmon & the play of rivers & the gentle gestures of smoke.

LoveLaurieLee @AsIWalkedOut

I sit hunched in bed, watching her silent grace, a woman, alive, adoring the hour, the closed door, my eyes and the promise of sleep.

LoveLaurieLee @AsIWalkedOut

I cannot think why lovers leave their beds.

RETWEET

Lisa Blaize @Lisa_Blaize

I cannot thInk why lovers leave their beds.

DM from @FrJohnMisty: How many times do I have to tell you?

DM from @Lisa_Blaize: What?

DM from @FrJohnMisty: Ammunition?

DM from @Lisa_Blaize: Just an innocent quote from Laurie Lee about his passionate love affair with Lorna Garman. Did you know about this?

DM from @FrJohnMisty: Don't know and don't care. Please be careful. What's going on?

No reply.

 DM from @FrJohnMisty: Have you crossed the line?

 DM from @Lisa_Blaize: No I haven't. And even if I had, it's none of your business!

 DM from @FrJohnMisty: OK then. Be careful. I love you.

 DM from @Lisa_Blaize: I know you do!

 DM from @FrJohnMisty: Then get off Twitter!

 DM from @Lisa_Blaize: You must have been on it to see my RT. Pot, Kettle, Black!!!

 DM from @FrJohnMisty: Stop overusing exclamation marks. I feel like you're shouting at me.

 DM from @Lisa_Blaize: !!!!!!!!!!!!!!!!!!!!

DM from @FrJohnMisty: I liked your Grauniad article, but don't read the below the line comments.

*   *   *

Lisa was proud of her review. It was the first time she had written for a national newspaper. She hoped it would be a platform for more commissions – nothing had yet come on the back of her monthly column – and a spur to herself for the second book. Maybe a literary agent would see it, and sign her up. That would make it so much easier to sell the book, when she finally wrote it.

On one of her rare excursions into her email account, she found that her old tutor from the Manchester School of Fashion had written to say that her review was as witty and provocative as McQueen himself, and a tribute to his artistry and truly unique vision.

She couldn't stop herself from going below the line and reading the comments on the review, something she had made a point of never doing with her *City & County* blogs.

Zellie

I will go and just look at them for what they are, beautiful objects. Since McQueen is dead, unless you have any quotes by him to 'explain' anything, best not bother.

BingoTango

Unless you've got it from the horse's mouth, keep quiet.

Igglybuff

I thought the armour like and/or fear inspiring qualities came from his desire to protect women. He spoke of seeing his sisters go out to work, and what they encountered at work (hostility from colleagues, lasciviousness from men) and wanting to protect them. He would help his sisters put together outfits to protect them, make them appear invincible, make it easier for them to go out into the world. I've always thought some of his designs were an extension of that mentality.

CharlesRyder

You should visit the Balenciaga museum in Getaria. It is a stunning homage to the designer's artistry and innovative talent, referencing historical and social contexts, artistic influences with visual examples (e.g., a gown displayed beside a painting or photograph), and in relation to the work of contemporaries. The visit begins with a short film about his life, and I find that this helps to ground the pieces as items of clothing created for a particular woman, and, in some cases, occasion, rather than viewed in a vacuum, merely beautiful objects behind glass. The McQueen pieces look magnificent, shame about the lack of biographical information. It is disappointing if visitors need to purchase a £45 catalogue to fully appreciate the experience.

Yoda

I don't think you get it.

REPLY TO Yoda
CharlesRyder

DO explain then, master Yoda. I am sure we would all be interested to know your special insights. Ms Blaize seems to know what she is talking about.

42BrickBats

This comment was removed by a moderator because it didn't abide by our community standards. Replies may also be deleted. For more detail see our FAQs.

Spencer Ramsey

What, for instance, was going on in Britain when he launched his 'bumster' trousers, his moulded leather bodices, his crippling 'armadillo' shoes? What do these designs tell us, if anything, about ourselves? 'Ourselves' being a vanishingly-small clique, of course.

Midlands Man

Would love to see you, Lisa, in one of his corsets.

ZarkDenie

This so-called fashion historian clearly does not understand 'fashion'. What a dreadful article. Waste of time reading it.

God, what saddos, thought Lisa. Who has the time and energy to post comments online?

*   *   *

Lisa Blaize @Lisa_Blaize
There is no way back for me now – Alexander McQueen.

LoveLaurieLee @AsIWalkedOut
I want you to grow old and repulsive, so no one will look at you.

LoveLaurieLee @AsIWalkedOut
Her nipples were dark berries.

Tu si 'na cosa grande pe' me.

Altrettanto. Sx

CHAPTER 16

The End of the Affair

It was the anniversary of their first date. Edward had arranged a special dinner, but that morning he called Lisa to the drawing room.

'Lisa, I've got something to ask you.'

'What is it, darling?'

'You tell me. I've cancelled the dinner. I know what's going on. Please tell me the truth. You've never lied to me in your life.'

'I haven't. So, go ahead.'

'Are you having an affair?'

'No. I'm not having an affair.'

'Lisa, you're on the edge of a precipice.'

'No, I'm not. I'm at a crossroads. They're very different.'

'Do you love him?'

'Yes, I do.'

'Do you love me?'

'Yes, I do.'

'Are you going to Amsterdam?'

'I don't know, Edward. I'm very tired. Probably. How did you know?'

Sean had been making the arrangements for Amsterdam. Infuriatingly, there was no mobile phone signal in his wing of the hospital. He had needed to confirm flight times, so he had resorted to Twitter, contacting Lisa via a Direct Message. Lisa, meanwhile, had realized that, following the success of the review of the McQueen exhibition, she might receive email requests to do other work. So she had asked Edward to clear the junk mail from her inbox. Because she had stopped going on email herself, she hadn't realized that Twitter sent notifications of DMs to the email account with which one had registered for the service. In sorting through Lisa's inbox, Edward had gone cold upon seeing a message headed 'Mr Sean O'Connor (via Twitter)'. It read: 'Mr Sean O'Connor has sent you a Direct Message', and then '19.35 on the Friday night, Heathrow to Amsterdam, BA0444, pack that lingerie. Xx.'

'Edward, please don't tell anyone.'

*　　*　　*

Edward had made his discovery the previous night. He had remained eerily calm. Come on, he said to himself, you handled many a crisis at SJA. The key was not to react hastily. There had been times when he had spent an entire night thinking about how to deal with a delicate staffing problem. How to make the best of a bad situation. A knee-jerk reaction was the worst possible response. It was a million times harder to apply this to his private life, to quell the anger and agony of the thought of being betrayed by the Lisa he loved more than all the world, the woman for whom he had left his first wife, and with whom he had endured the anguish of Emma's heart condition. But he had stayed calm when Moira was using every trick in the book to keep him in the first marriage, and he damn well wasn't going to give up on the second one without a fight. Especially as this time his children were involved.

He thought about his strategy. He had no ideas. That's a first for me, he thought, wryly. He idly googled the phrase 'what to do when you discover that your wife is having an affair'. The first site that came up was called goodmenproject.com. The advice was surprisingly simple, and, it seemed to Edward, exactly right:

Give it Time

Though it may not seem possible, the affair will likely run its course. If you love your wife and see a future where you're able to forgive, hang in there. Affairs are founded on lies and deceit and tend not to grow into a deeper connection. If you're willing to put effort into saving your marriage, part of what that requires is biding your time and waiting to see how it plays out.

He lay awake all night. Yes, he would give it time. He would give Lisa the freedom to make her own decision.

* * *

'Of course I won't tell anyone, Lisa. You must do what you must do. I know you'll be discreet. Just remember that I love you and that I am always here for you.'

Lisa and Sean had known that the day would come. Sooner or later they would be found out. Lisa prided herself on her discretion. She had always thought that it would be Sean's wife – she'd see a text on his phone or something. They had arranged what they would do if it happened. A coded message via Twitter. If it were sent, they would lie low. No texts. And Twilence.

Lisa Blaize @Lisa_Blaize
Hi tweeps, let's play best novels. Graham Greene's best? I nominate The End of the Affair.

* * *

134

She cried in Edward's arms and told him that her chest hurt.

'Lisa, your problem is that you've never had your heart broken. That's not a good thing. You will never truly empathize with your fellow human beings if you are the one who always leaves.'

'I hate the word empathize. Why don't people just say sympathize? When did empathy become trendy, like synergy and blue-sky thinking? It's all bollocks, Edward. And yes, I haven't had my heart broken, except when Emma fell ill. That's heartbreak enough. Well, now I know how it feels for everyone else, and I'm a bit old for it, frankly. This should happen when you're a teenager. Not when you're a happily married mother of two, getting on for forty.'

That night, Lisa thought hard about heartbreak. She consulted Dr Google and found that there was a condition called Takotsubo syndrome. She went straight to Wikipedia:

Takotsubo cardiomyopathy, also known as transient apical ballooning syndrome, apical ballooning cardiomyopathy, stress-induced cardiomyopathy, Gebrochenes-Herz-Syndrom, and stress cardiomyopathy is a type of non-ischemic cardiomyopathy in which there is a sudden temporary weakening of the muscular portion of the heart. Because this weakening can be triggered by emotional stress, such as the death of a loved one, a break-up, or constant anxiety, it is also known as broken-heart syndrome.

Bloody Hell, she thought. So you CAN die of heartbreak. All through that night Lisa and Edward talked about the madness of love. Edward, with his passion for Shakespeare, talked at length about *A Midsummer Night's Dream*. He talked about the cruelty of Oberon, sprinkling the love juice on his wife Titania's eyes, so that she would fall for a donkey.

'Do you think Shakespeare was being filthy?' Lisa asked. 'You know, donkeys have a reputation for large members ... so Bottom, with his ass's head also, we have to believe, has a very large ...'

'Lisa ...' Edward shifted very uncomfortably. He did not like that sort of language. He had a puritanical streak, and disliked talking about sex and body parts. Lisa loved to tease him.

'And the thing about Bottom is that he just goes with it. He just doesn't consider that the queen of the fairies is out of his league, that he's punching above his weight. But love can be like that. One minute, one person has all the power, and the next minute it changes. Shakespeare understood this, didn't he?'

'Of course he did.' The little pocket edition of the play was by the bed. Edward flicked through it and found a quote:

'"The more you beat me, I will fawn on you. Use me but as your spaniel – spurn me, strike me, neglect me, lose me. Only give me leave, unworthy as I am, to follow you".'

He put down the book as he warmed to his theme, turning a marital crisis into an intellectual discussion.

'There's so much self-immolation when it comes to love. And self-hatred. Love can so easily turn to hate. Some Tudor philosopher – Giordano Bruno, was it? – actually said that hate's a kind of love. Obsession, that's all it is. The lunatic, the lover, and the stalker are of imagination all compact, they have such seething brains – that's what Shakespeare would have said if he was around today.'

She smiled as she plumped the pillows and straightened out the bed linen. That was the thing about Edward. He always understood. And, though it could be annoying that he couldn't stop sounding like a teacher even when they were talking in bed, he always had such comforting explanations for things.

But she had moments of perfect cruelty. Like Anna Karenina, who fucked Vronsky and then noticed her husband's ugly ears, she suddenly saw Edward's physical imperfections. His hair was going prematurely grey, and he was flat-footed. She'd never noticed this before. When she criticized his feet, he glared at her, and she thought for a moment that he was going to hit her. And yet he was still tender, loving. He held her in his arms. 'Darling, in the long run, it's a good thing to have your heart broken. It really is.'

PART THREE

Accusation

CHAPTER 17

Belinda Bullrush

Belinda Bullrush was something of a legend around Blagsford. A former ballerina, she lived in a houseboat on the Grand Union Canal with her cat, Matilda. Lisa met her at the only independent bookshop still standing, the Albion, which was run by a man called Dicky the Book Spiv. That wasn't his real name, but everyone called him Dicky.

After the end of the affair, Lisa was determined to get out of the house and off social media. She wandered around Blagsford looking for an independent bookshop. She set herself very strict rules about not buying new books online. She was a bit of a bore about it. Frankly, the Albion was an unprepossessing place, set back from the main road; its grimy windows tattooed in scrawled writing. But inside, it was heaven. Books were laddered in piles head-high, and there was a faded painted armoire housing fabulous china: teacups and saucers. Lisa was a snob about mugs. She never ever drank her coffee from a mug, so Dicky's paper-thin mismatched china was a revelation. With a practised eye, Lisa scanned the shelves. There was nothing sloppy about the bookseller's taste: a superb poetry section, serious modern fiction. The second-hand shelves were thoughtful; Firbank, Waugh, and Maugham rubbed shoulders with Barbara Pym and Muriel Spark. She spotted a dusty pile of dated and unloved Iris Murdochs.

Dicky was notoriously grumpy. On principle, he refused to install Wi-Fi. There was no way that his establishment was going to be a free home for Blagsford's crazy and needy. He'd heard the stories of students buying a cup of tea in the local café and staying all day to write up their essays, and go on Facebook. That was not going to happen in his cosy shop. He was not running a house for the homeless, for God's sake. He wanted to sell proper books. Anyway, he was a 'cash-only' kind of man. He was often away from the shop on nefarious business (he claimed he was doing 'walking tours', but nobody believed him), so the shop was managed by an itinerant group of single ladies and retired teachers.

The thing that Dicky fully failed to grasp was just how adored he was. He had the sweetest smile. When he smiled, it went all the way up to his eyes. Kind eyes. And God, Dicky was funny. He was very good friends with Belinda. He rather worshipped her, though he'd die before admitting it.

Lisa chose a vintage teacup with faded painted roses and a cracked saucer and asked the beautiful girl with the black, shiny hair if she could have a Lady Jane Grey (Earl Grey was so common). Lisa tried to spark up a conversation, telling the girl that she'd never noticed the bookshop before, and had felt nervous about entering.

The Beautiful Girl smiled, 'I felt the same thing. Dicky needs to do something about the front of shop. It doesn't know what it is. But this place is the heart of Blagsford.'

Lisa warmed to her. She was so natural. So at ease with herself. She had dirty fingernails. Ahh, she's a gardener, Lisa surmised. She must turn the conversation to gardens.

'I'm Belinda. Belinda Bullrush. I help Dicky out. He's very special. You have to pay cash. There's a machine outside the Co-op if you need cash.'

Lisa fumbled in her purse and extracted a note. 'I'll buy some books, too. Keep the money.'

'Thank you. I can see that you're very kind. I like that.'

And that was the beginning of one of the most important friendships of Lisa's life.

*   *   *

Belinda was not a gardener. Her fingernails were grubby because the only source of hot water on her boat was a woodburner, and she was forever lighting twigs and kindling. She didn't believe in firelighters: those were for wimps. Bee had strong, capable, workman-like hands. They were slightly at odds with the rest of her person, which was elegant and understated. Bee wore large, floppy hats. She was trying to disguise her loveliness, because she had a difficult relationship with beauty. She told Lisa that she bought her clothes from the local second-hand shop. For Lisa, with her snobbish attitude to clothes, Bee looked sensational. She wore cute, sexy tea dresses with ankle socks and brogues, and pulled it off. How does she do it, she wondered.

To her surprise, on only their second meeting, Lisa started crying.

'What's wrong? Please tell me, but only if you want to.'

'Belinda. I don't know you, and maybe that helps. I'm in love with someone who is not my husband. The affair is over, but I'm still in love with him.'

'OK. You're speaking to the right woman. I won't judge you. I have an extremely fluid attitude towards love and the intimate workings of the human heart. But I want to say one thing to you.'

'Please do.'

'Don't be sitting in the seat I'm in. I can tell you to follow your heart, but I'm not going to do that. I'm alone, and you're not. You've got to think about that.'

'I don't feel lucky. I feel wretched.'

'Well, if you need to unburden your grief, I'm here to listen. I'm not sure I'm ever going to give you advice, Lisa, I don't do that. Besides, I'm not sure you'd listen.'

'Yes, I would listen, but I wouldn't necessarily follow it.'

So they talked, and they talked. And they drank tea: lots of it. Every so often, Belinda would spot a customer and bully them into buying a book or a hot drink. She was fierce about protecting Dicky's interests. There was not much browsing when Belinda was in charge. She called it 'keeping a vigilant eye'. Every now and then Belinda would break into a pirouette. Her knee injury had put an end to a promising career as a ballerina, but she had retrained as a yoga and Pilates teacher. She was pencil-slim, with a waist like a wand, and small, pert breasts. Lisa thought she looked a cross between Virginia Woolf and Olive Oyl. She seemed to be from another space and time.

The floodgates opened, Lisa told Belinda about Sean and Emma, and how they were somehow intricately linked in her heart. As Lisa explained, she didn't need a psychotherapist to tell her that she fell in love with a doctor because she wanted a saviour for her daughter and for herself. Belinda seemed to understand completely. She was so very kind. And Lisa was badly in need of kindness.

*   *   *

Edward was in shock for the first few days after the revelation of Lisa's affair. He felt numb. Could think of nothing else. It was how he imagined a bereavement would be – the closest he had

144

ever come to that was the time his daughter had nearly died. He had never known his father, and his old mum was still going strong down in London, always complaining about her arthritis, but basking daily in the extraordinary rise of her son from his humble origins to the great school and then Oxford, and now his prestigious position as a headmaster.

'Do you want me to move out?' Lisa asked.

'Do you want to move out?'

She was infuriated by his way of answering a question with a question.

'No, I don't. Where would I go, and what about the children?'

'I thought you might like to go away for a while – maybe back to Liverpool – to sort yourself out, work out what you want to do.'

'I'm not the type to run away, Edward. You know that.'

They relapsed into stony silence. Lisa was the one to break it.

'Keep buggering on. And let's not take it out on the children.'

He couldn't resist a dig: 'How very good of you to think of them, as I'm sure you were when you were planning your dirty weekend in Amsterdam.'

Lisa blazed back: 'Just like you always put the children first. Never the school, the students, the teachers, the governors, the bloody Headmasters' Conference, the Chamberlain brand.'

She could see it was going to be a difficult summer.

*   *   *

Lisa knew that it was over. She was heartbroken and relieved at the same time. The butterflies in the stomach – those of love and those of guilt – vanished overnight. She lay awake, thinking of Sean lying awake beside his wife, who knew nothing. Did he kiss his wife's eyelids, as he had hers? How strange it was that she had wept in the arms of her husband, as he comforted her because her heart had been broken by the loss of another man with whom she was still crazily in love.

She must obey the rules. No texts. Twilence.

But she could not forbear to look at @AsIWalkedOut. There were two last tweets, written within minutes of her coded Graham Greene message.

LoveLaurieLee @AsIWalkedOut
She drove him to the brink of madness.

LoveLaurieLee @AsIWalkedOut
When the affair ended, Laurie typed her name over and over again. Night, night Lisa. Lisa Blaize. Lisa Blaize. Lisa, Lisa, Lisa.

*   *   *

The following night, unable to sleep, she went downstairs at the blue hour of four in the morning. When she tried to go to @AsIWalkedOut, she discovered that the account no longer existed.

CHAPTER 18

An Unexpected Letter

'Lisa, I've got something to tell you.' Edward was speaking with a tremor.

'Oh God, not again.' Last time it had been *I've got something to ask you*. She felt sick. How much more could she take? Was it Sean's wife? Someone who had seen them together? Sean himself?

'Lisa, I've had a letter. Would you be minded to be Lady Chamberlain?'

'What on earth do you mean?'

'You're not going to believe this. But this is a letter from Number 10.'

'Spit it out, Edward.'

'It says that the Prime Minister intends to recommend to the Queen that I should be knighted for services to Education, but before doing so, she wants to know whether I would be minded to accept.'

'Oh Edward, darling, I am so happy for you. It's well deserved. Such a reward for all you did at St Joseph's. Your mother will be so proud of you. I would be very, very minded to accept being Lady Chamberlain.'

He proudly showed her the citation: 'Edward Linford Chamberlain, for services to Education.'

'Darling, you mustn't tell a soul. It's top secret until the publication of the Birthday Honours List in mid-June. You must be discreet, darling.'

She sent a text:

> S, you'll never guess … please may we meet for coffee? You will laugh so much when I tell you.

No reply.

Another text:

> Well, if you're not going to reply I shall just tell you. I really AM going to be Lady C.

* * *

It was the best possible end to their first academic year at Blagsford and, for Lisa, a welcome distraction from heartbreak. They arranged a party, ostensibly to celebrate the end of the exam season and the news of a major boost to the school's finances as a result of the confirmed acceptances from a dozen Indonesian boys. Lisa specified on the invitation that the dress code was to be 'Gatsbyesque'. She knew this would aggravate the more boring members of the staffroom, with their ragged tweed and dowdy greys.

The Honours List was published on the morning of the party.

* * *

The less welcome letter came exactly a week later.

... I don't know how much attention you pay to Lisa's Twitter account, but if you have a look at her tweets over the past five or six months you will get a sense of what people are concerned about and why Lisa has become an object of ridicule, not just at Blagsford, but across the public school network more widely. You will be able to see that she comes across as almost pathologically vain and egotistical.

And on it went:

There is something not quite right about someone (unless they happen to be Jordan, aka Katie Price, writing for Heat magazine) who thinks it will be of interest to others to know that she always turns long-haul flights into a 'spa opportunity', and who even posts pictures of the lotions that she will be using to make her 'skin feel fab'. One of her tweets, an entirely typical one, reads, 'My dressmaker has just left (Yes, I did just say that!) and says he loves my 36, 24, 34 measurements. Yay.' It has become a standing joke in the Common Room and even among the pupils.

Lisa's tweets about her sparkly, high-heeled shoes, her bikini from the Elizabeth Hurley range (God help us), her designer dresses, her hair, her waterproof mascara, etc. etc. etc., ad nauseam, are absolutely relentless, and it's all pretty sad as far as the pupils are concerned (and indeed as far as most of us are concerned) because this is a woman in her forties who wishes to be taken seriously as a writer, and who in some sense represents our school.

The close-up picture Lisa posted of her face and her upper body in her new bikini (entitled 'my new bikini') would have been better kept private. It's not a flattering picture (face very

*lined and drawn, breasts flaccid and saggy, underarm stubble,
etc., let's be honest). She is every inch the spoilt young child
wanting to show off all the time, with tweets along the lines of
'Off to the theatre wearing my designer dress and sapphires
and waterproof mascara, yay!'*

*Staff, pupils, parents, and especially Old Blaggers like to
think of our alma mater as a distinguished academic
institution, a jewel in the crown of our great English public
school system. Anyone looking at Lisa's Twitter account would
find that difficult to believe.*

*There are rumours in the staffroom that she takes bribes
from wealthy parents wanting a place for their children. Who,
for instance, bought her the Indonesian sapphires? It wouldn't
have anything to do with the admission to Blagsford of a boy
named Widjuju, by any chance, would it? There were
indiscretions made about the knighthood, which, as we all
know, was supposed to be kept top secret until the
announcement.*

*Sorry I missed the party, but, Ed, I'm sure you had enough
of your cronies to flatter and flutter around you. I'm sure Lisa
was wearing one of her tight-fitting dresses, revealing her ample
breasts. Her vanity is astounding. She even tweeted holiday
pictures of her insect bites saying that 'even the sandflies find
her irresistible'.*

*I realize that this letter has taken on a bitter tone. It's
because I was one of your staunchest supporters when you
arrived here. I do feel so very disappointed, Edward. You and
Lisa need to take your responsibilities as representatives of the
school much more seriously.*

*I am writing this letter for your own good. Be warned. You
have become known as the Tony and Cherie Blair of Blagsford*

– the man on the make and the gobby Scouser. Is this really
how you want to be regarded? If you do not silence your vain
and vulgar wife, it is you who will feel the consequences when
the governors of the school are made aware of how she is
disgracing the venerable name of Blagsford.

   Anon (I'm too much of a coward to say who I am, but I
represent the views of a large number of people in Blagsford,
across the Headmasters' Conference, and, for that matter, in
your old stamping ground Oop North)

*   *   *

'Lisa, I've had a poisonous letter. It's unbelievably cruel. And very
funny. It claims to be from a member of staff. It's a vicious attack
on you. Of course, I don't believe a word of it. These idiots know
nothing about you.'

'Why do you say "about you", and not "about us"? Is the letter
aiming to hurt you or me? Is it about who you are and where
you've come from?'

'Probably me. First there was Airfaregate and now this. You're
my Achilles' heel. They know that.'

'Does it mention Sean?'

'No. Would you like to see it?'

'No, Edward, certainly not. I make it a rule not to read anonymous letters. People who write things like that are rarely "well"
people. And I don't want spiteful things sticking in my head. In
fact, I'm surprised that you read it, knowing that it was unsigned.
The person who did this wants to sow a seed of doubt in you.
Please don't read it again. Throw it away and forget about it. In
fact, just give it to me.'

'But they seem to know so much about you. I'm curious. It
reads to me like a bitchy gay, you know the type who hates

women. Well, there are lots of them in the world of teaching, so no clue there. Critical of your tweets, your grammar, your body. Digs at your Liverpool background. It even implies that I wrote your book for you.'

'Ah, Sir Edward Chamberlain, that purveyor of feminist fashion history. The man I met a year after my book was published. But I hate to see you so upset. Don't let them get to you. It doesn't bother me one bit. Is it someone jealous of the knighthood? How petty and unkind. Anyway, I'm not ashamed of being a Scouser and not having had a posh education.'

'Darling, perhaps you had better stop tweeting for a bit. Just let the dust settle.'

CHAPTER 19

Flattered and Followed

Father John Misty, who had once received a very unpleasant and completely unfounded anonymous letter himself, was not at all surprised by the turn of events. He asked to be filled in on every detail. Lisa told him that she hadn't read it and wasn't going to. But she repeated what Edward had told her.

 DM from @FrJohnMisty: Blaize, I've been thinking some more about that letter!

DM from @Lisa_Blaize: Oh have you, now, Sherlock. Do you think the bursar is in love with Edward? Or am I in love with the school gardener and his wife?

DM from @FrJohnMisty: You said that the person mentioned the word 'folk' in relation to your Gatsby Party. Well who would do that? Surely it's a very American expression. Or a Scottish one. So do you have an American or a Scottish teacher in the school?

DM from @Lisa_Blaize: One of each, but they're both men. You're on the wrong track: I know that this letter was written by a woman. The details about my clothes, my body, the bitchiness. It's not a man. I'm sure of it.

DM from @FrJohnMisty: I have, in my time, encountered bitchy men. Remember what I told you about the priests in Old Compton Street? But seriously, I'm worried about you. I don't like this business. I think you and Edward should call the police.

 DM from @Lisa_Blaize: That's a bit OTT. I think it's best ignored. I'm not giving it the oxygen of publicity.

Twitter: *what's happening?*

 Lisa Blaize @Lisa_Blaize
You won't silence me. Unfortunately for you, my courage arises at every attempt to intimidate me.

* * *

'Darling, remember what I said about Twitter? I think you should be careful. We do have enemies. Don't feed them ammunition. I've been thinking some more about that letter. If it is someone we know and not some troll who's decided to cross the line into the real world, then it's got to be someone from my past. The writer oscillates between calling me Edward and Ed. I was always Ed at JYA, but I'm Edward here at Blagsford. If they decided to impersonate a teacher, they'd have looked at the school website and seen the Headmaster's Welcome from Edward Chamberlain. But then as they warmed to their theme they inadvertently slipped back to Ed, which is how I was known in Oxford and when I taught down in Surrey.'

Lisa wasn't persuaded. This all seemed very tortuous. Why were they letting it get to them? 'Mightn't it be the other way round – someone from here who saw the old "Ed the Head" story in the Liverpool *Echo* – that's bound to be still online somewhere – and then they put in a few Eds deliberately, to lay a false trail?'

'I really don't think it's someone on the staff here,' said Edward, 'There's no real inner knowledge of the workings of a private school. It's all based on your Twitter, larded with a few details that anyone could have found online. I'm convinced that it's an outsider masquerading as a teacher at Blagsford. Lots of things just don't add up.'

Lisa was rinsing plates and glasses at the sink before loading them into the dishwasher. She raised a small chopping knife, pointing it melodramatically at her husband.

'Well, *darling*, I am not going to be silenced by some sad old troll who hides behind their laptop. The boys around school call them keyboard warriors. They are not warriors, they are cowards. Do you know, for me, the worst moment in *Pride and Prejudice* is when that ghastly fool, Mr Collins, intimates that if he marries spirited Elizabeth Bennett, he will silence her. Shut her up. Austen knows that this is the gravest sin a man can commit against a woman he professes to love. Edward, please don't attempt to silence me. I don't want to be married to Mr Collins.'

Edward grinned. 'As if I would, or could. I would never try. The problem is that the people here in Blagsford don't understand vivacity. Or that you're a cross-over girl. You love Wagner and Van Morrison, Henry James and Harry Potter. I don't want to change you. In ten years of marriage, Lisa, you have never bored me. Not once, not ever. And they don't see you as I do, how lovely you are in your silence. And I don't mean that in a Mr Collins way. I mean it in a Mr Knightley way. Now shut up and come to bed.'

*   *   *

Sticking to her rule about not contacting Sean, she relied more and more on her father confessor.

DM from @FrJohnMisty: Did it mention Sean?

DM from @Lisa_Blaize: No, Edward said not. That's the supreme irony. The letter attacks me for things I haven't done (as if I'd take a school bribe. I can afford my own bloody sapphires), and doesn't mention the one terrible thing that I have done.

DM from @FrJohnMisty: Fuck. I see what you mean. So is it someone who knows you?

DM from @Lisa_Blaize: Who knows? Probably not. It all seems based on my Twitter persona. And clearly someone with no sense of humour. And guess what? They used a second-class stamp. The shame.

DM from @FrJohnMisty: Now that's the first interesting thing you've said. Hmm: Vicious and tight. Must dash. Off to Compline. Love you, Blaize.

DM from @Lisa_Blaize: Love you too, father. And stop saying Fuck so much. You could get into a lot of trouble with your parishioners.

DM from @FrJohnMisty: Naw … they fucking love me … XXX

*　　*　　*

156

Edward was in the shower. Lisa was reading in bed. Her bedroom was a paean to Coco Chanel. Everything was black and cream. Her four-poster bed was hung with heavy cream silk drapes edged with black grosgrain ribbon. The carpet was cream wool, topped with an enormous black fur rug. She had invested in art deco furniture: a beautiful curved chair in the shape of a fan, a mirrored dressing table, and black silk lamps.

Suddenly, she called out: 'Edward, you don't think it could be Moira, after all these years. Finally wreaking her revenge?'

Edward came in, draped in a towel. 'Don't be absurd. Moira is happily remarried. She never gives us a second thought. You're barking up the wrong tree.'

But in the dark, small hours of the morning, he changed his mind: 'God, Lisa, I think you could be right. Moira's an editor, a stickler for grammar, just like the person who wrote the letter. Revenge is a dish best served cold. Moira would have loved to be Lady Chamberlain. And, do you know, as a Scot, she often used the word "folk". I thought she was so happily married. That she had moved on. That's the saddest thing.'

'Well, except that she won't really try to harm us. It's just words. But why would she especially attack *me*?'

'I don't know. She was always more angry with me than with you. But it's a possibility. To make me think I made the wrong choice, and that she would have been a more dignified Lady C? That you were always just some little social climber, and that you've finally got your way? And there's something else. It's something that Nick mentioned. When we were in Jakarta, he told me – to my astonishment – that she kept in touch with him after the divorce.'

'So?'

'He said that he thinks Moira is still bitter about never having had children. Apparently she tried for years with her new partner, but to no avail. It must have been hugely traumatic for her, especially when she heard that we had gone on to have two children. It's just so much easier for men than for women. Nick reckons that she thinks that you and I destroyed her chances of motherhood.'

'Hang on a minute. You always told me that she was the one who didn't want children. She only wanted them when you threatened to leave her. People want what they can't have. She had ample opportunity to have a child.'

'Well, she tried everything. But it didn't happen for her. Spare a moment to think how it must have hurt her.'

'But she took all your friends. You were *persona non grata* for years in and around that school down in Surrey. That was all her doing. You left her the house, provided for her.'

'Hell hath no fury. Revenge a dish best served cold. That's all I'm saying.'

*   *   *

'You might stop posting photographs, Lisa. Maybe leave that to Snapchat or Instagram.'

'I have stopped posting pictures, Edward. I stopped doing that in May.' There was no point after the end of the affair.

She tried to follow her husband's advice. She knew that the received wisdom was always to ignore online trolls and anonymous letter writers. But then she said to herself: I'll stop in my own time, not when I'm told to. In a flash of anger, she went to her keyboard. If the troll was going to come into the real world by writing anonymous letters, she'd get back at them in the Twittersphere.

Lisa Blaize @Lisa_Blaize

Dear Troll, I can afford to buy my own bloody sapphires.

Then she quickly deleted it. Don't give the cyberstalker what they want: your attention.

Surfing the net, she found a wonderfully acute description of trolling by an eleventh-century Sufi philosopher, Al-Ghazali. It amused her that he had anticipated our social media problems by a thousand years. She fired off a series of tweets.

Lisa Blaize @Lisa_Blaize

A thousand years ago, a Sufi philosopher called Al-Ghazali identified four types of Twitter troll. The first type is the worst.

Lisa Blaize @Lisa_Blaize

Al-Ghazali's Troll Type 1: Jealous haters. Advice: 'Depart from him and leave him with his disease.'

Lisa Blaize @Lisa_Blaize

Al-Ghazali's Troll Type 1, part 2: 'Of diseases which cannot be cured, the first is that which arises from envy and hate.'

Lisa Blaize @Lisa_Blaize

'Every time you answer him with the best or clearest answer, that only increases his rage and envy. And the way is not to attempt an answer.'

Lisa Blaize @Lisa_Blaize
'Envy eats up excellences as fire eats up wood.'
#Al-Ghazali.

For good measure, she added an equally prescient quote from Jane Austen, dripping with irony:

Lisa Blaize @Lisa_Blaize
'To flatter and follow others, without being flattered and followed in turn, is but a state of half enjoyment.'
#Persuasion

Lisa took great pleasure in this burst of tweets. She knew that she was taunting her troll, but she couldn't help herself. Her quotes got more retweets and 'favourites' than any of her previous posts.

CHAPTER 20
The Albion

The Albion Bookshop became a second home to Lisa. She usually cycled into town. Much as she adored her hot pink Fiat 500, it was always impossible to find a parking space in Blagsford, so she left it looking increasingly dusty and forlorn in the driveway outside Headmaster's House. She felt virtuous when she got on her bike. It was Tiffany Blue, with a basket on the front, and she called it Audrey.

Always one for nicknames, she loved calling Belinda Bullrush 'Bee'. She was a busy bee, always helping out, doing her private tuition and her stretching classes in an unassuming corner of the bookshop.

She relished the banter between Dicky and Bee. Dennis was crotchety about the school students, whereas Bee defended them to the hilt.

* * *

'Why do young people insist on carrying around rucksacks? What on earth do they keep in them? They come in here with those huge things on their backs, barging into things, like lost camels. Why don't they just use a sensible shoulder bag?'

'Because, Dicky, if you are a man, then you would automatically be categorized as "gay". Only gays carry shoulder bags. They're called "Man Bags", and no self-respecting man has one.'

* * *

'Young people just don't know what a book is these days. They used to walk in here and attach themselves to a book like a transition object, walk around for a while, put the book back down, then walk out. Now what they do is they walk in, walk around looking bewildered, and walk out, without even touching a book. They don't know what to do with books any more.'

'Well, the world they are in is a textbook world. Everything is served up to them inside boxes, already labelled. Your shop isn't very labelled, Dicky. It's rather blurry. They don't know where the tea room ends and where the bookshop begins. And you're not very good at labels, Dicky.'

* * *

'Dicky, do you have any cake? People keep asking for cake.'

'Oh, I can't keep abreast of cake at the moment … things are going to the dogs … I might have someone coming in with some vegan cake next week.'

'Oh Lordie, vegan cake? If you can organise *vegan* cake then you can organise cake, Dicky! Who wants *vegan* cake? That's a step too far.'

* * *

'Dicky, where do you get your lovely china teacups from?'

'My grandmother.'

'What was her name? I love old names.'

'I can't remember. I just know I got her teacups.'

* * *

They had no idea of how funny they were: like an old married couple. For the first time since meeting Sean, Lisa felt at home. Felt safe. She loved her conversations with Bee. When they had afternoon tea together, at the Albion, it was like being in the presence of Fanny Burney. Bee was observant, shrewd, and properly clever. She made the pompous Blagsford teachers look like errant fools.

Being a former ballerina gave her an especial interest in the body.

'Lisa, your great beauty lies in your child-like form and energy – that is what makes you so attractive. You have a beautiful youthfulness in your legs and knees, and the way you are in trousers and shorts – your boy persona. It's delightfully unconstructed. The way you move like a child still – it's rare – so embodied and gauche – ageless. Loveable. I don't know many women with that youth in their body movement. It's not about anything constructed or put on. It's the opposite of strutting. And that makes other people feel relaxed and embodied.'

Lisa hated compliments. They made her blush and feel awkward. It was not easy to take a compliment from a woman as beautifully made as Bee.

'I think women's bodies are much nicer than men's. But I'm not a "lezzer", as my friend Toby's v v funny 104-year-old grandma would say.'

'No Bee, I can see that you're not a lezzer.'

'You see, Dicky has very beautiful nostrils. Really, they are his best feature. He's always been rather vain about them. Do you know he calls us Sharon and Tracey?'

'Cheeky Bastard. I prefer to think of us as Charlotte Bartlett and Eleanor Lavish in Forster's *A Room with a View*. Do you see yourself as Miss Bartlett or Miss Lavish?'

'Oh I think I'm the lady writer, Miss Lavish. Would you like to borrow my Macintosh Square?'

Lisa squealed with laughter. Bee really got her.

'Bee, I've got to tell you something. Edward's received an anonymous letter about me.'

Bee was suspicious of Edward. She had bumped into the whole family while they were walking on Pig Hill. They had exchanged a few words. Edward, never good at small talk, had initiated a conversation about Wittgenstein and weather. Bee had made a hasty exit.

'He's intimidating. That huge brain and his lanky, angular body, like a Daumier caricature. He speaks in a very reverential manner.'

'He's not a reverend, he's a fucking knight of the realm. My Mr Knightley. Bee, don't be absurd. He's lovely. You've only met him that one time. I've never been intimidated by him. He has the most incredible sense of humour. He's very self-deprecating. You just need to get to know him.'

'Touché. Now tell me about the letter.'

So she did.

'And I'm scared – I've told you I'm psychic, and I've got a horrible feeling that this is only the beginning.'

* * *

And it was. The next letter was to her, alone.

Hi Lisa,
I look Edward up on Google now and again purely because
I'm interested in what goes on here in school and also in some
of the stuff he's saying about education, but the latter only from
an amateur perspective. Until the other day I had not looked
you up on Twitter although I know that a lot of people in school
do follow you either officially or unofficially (i.e. not necessarily
as dedicated 'Followers' as such).

I was aware that something unpleasant had happened to you a few weeks ago because people were saying at the time that you had tweeted things about a stalker or troll and a poisoned-pen letter, or something along those lines. People said you were exaggerating – but I can imagine how such a nasty experience can tip someone over the edge. I didn't look up what you had said at the time, and tried to keep clear of the whole thing. I have come to loathe certain aspects of Twitter and really do believe that it can bring out the worst in people. My daughter had a bruising experience on Facebook a couple of years ago which has strongly coloured my view of social media.

Having tried to steer clear of the whole business, I happened, in this last week of term, to see a long letter pinned to the main school noticeboard where everyone could see it. It was addressed to Edward, but was largely about you, and I immediately took it down because it was very personal in nature and it didn't seem right that it was in a public place. Evidently students had been reading it – there were comments scribbled in the margin and so on. Some of them very offensive. 'We all know the head loves his baby mama dripping with bling.' That kind of thing. I found it very painful reading.

I thought it must be the poisoned-pen letter you had reportedly received, though what it was doing in such a public place was a complete mystery to me. I wondered whether Edward had left it there as a way of shaming the person who had written it, but that seemed unlikely as I'm sure he wouldn't have wanted everyone to see the very cruel things that were said about you in the letter.

I haven't destroyed it because I don't feel it's my place to do so. I think I should probably just return it to you and Ed, though if by any chance you haven't seen this letter, I'm loth to send it to you because it is very hurtful. I did find myself looking you up on Twitter for the first time, just to see if you've read the poisoned-pen letter, and I discovered that its content does tally with some of the things you've posted, though many of the tweets quoted in the letter don't appear to be on Twitter now. I'm guessing you deleted them (understandably).

Anyhow, seeing your tweets for the first time did give me some insight into what all the fuss had been about and I hope you can forgive me for expressing some views about it because the impact of social media on our lives is something that's been troubling me for some time. I find myself getting drawn in to what everyone in school has been talking about.

I feel more than ever that Twitter is a pernicious influence on all of us and that we need to step back and reassess what we're trying to get out of it and what effect it's having on ourselves and others. You make some reference to a deranged 'Twitter stalker', and I'm not sure whether you mean by that the person/people who wrote the letter or someone who has been trolling you on Twitter.

I do think, though, that the idea of a Twitter stalker is a bit of a contradiction in terms because Twitter invites followers. I've been trying to grasp what the difference between a Twitter follower and a Twitter stalker would be. Stalking implies intruding into someone's private life, whereas people only put things on Twitter that they want people to read or see, presumably. Anything that people want to keep private they can keep private by not putting it on Twitter or Facebook or whatever. Your tweet of a quotation about a life in which one is not flattered and followed being only a half-life made me think. If people want to be flattered and followed on Twitter, they surely have to take the risk that not everyone will admire what

166

they see and read. But if they don't admire it, or if they disapprove of it, it doesn't necessarily mean that they are deranged nutters.

I believe we are sending our children damaging messages about the need to be 'flattered and followed' – it really is appalling that we're creating a society in which children, and many adults to boot, crave constant validation on social media. Surely the half-life is the one where you feel the need to be flattered and followed, not the one in which you are not flattered and followed. This compulsion to live one's life through the eyes of others is just crazy

I don't know who the stalkers and/or trolls were and I don't know who wrote the letter, but I can think of a few possibles as, sad to say, there is a lot of ill-feeling around at the moment. I've been here for a fair while, but sometimes I think this school is a nest of vipers.

*   *   *

'There's been another anonymous letter, Bee.'

'Oh Lordie, poor you. What is wrong with people? There's just so much Puckish intrigue in Blagsford.'

'It's a bit more serious than that, Bee,' Lisa protested. 'This is someone really trying to bring us down. I feel sick to my stomach. Edward's furious with me.'

'Did they invoke your Tweets, like last time?'

'Yes, so I guess you are going to tell me off for tweeting. That's what Edward keeps doing.'

'You know my feelings about Twitter,' said Belinda primly. 'Besides, I like old-fashioned letters on proper note-paper.'

'Well I bloody don't like old-fashioned letters. Look what they're doing to me.'

167

'Twitter is not the answer. It's a form of premature mental ejaculation. Why should any of us believe that we are intrinsically interesting? It's all part of this Me, Me, Me celebrity culture. I suppose in the world of social media we are all celebrities. Except that most of us are not. Twitter gets you followers, and Facebook finds you friends. But what is that all really about? Are they really your friends? And I'm sorry, but I think you're tweeting to keep some sort of contact with Sean. Direct Message him if you're still intent on contact.'

God, you couldn't get anything past Belinda. But Lisa wasn't going to admit to it. Furthermore, she would never DM Sean. Far too risky, as his wife could easily hack his account. An innocent-seeming tweet to the whole world was much safer than a DM or a text, which risked discovery. Lisa was surprised that Bee knew about DMs. She was always full of surprises. She might look and sound old-fashioned, but she was anything but.

'Bee, I like Twitter. People spend a long time creating the perfect tweet. I think it's a bit like a haiku. There's a discipline in making every syllable count, in expressing yourself in 140 characters. People who share your values retweet fascinating articles that I wouldn't have time to find. It's like being able to sit and have a chat with people who share an interest no matter where you are or how solitary your workspace. I hear about new exhibitions, calls for conference papers, how fashion is regarded in the media, refuting silly "news" pieces, especially on corsets, for example. Sharing professional opinions on dress history about exhibitions, films, TV shows, books. No wonder I love it.'

Bee was unimpressed.

'It's not real, Lisa. It's a substitute world for real friendships, real people, real communities. Twitter's just as full of fake friends as it is of fake news.'

'I disagree. I feel like it's a way to communicate with my female friends. Lots of us don't have the time for anything more than a quick tweet. It keeps us close, and women are so funny on Twitter. When I'm writing away on my computer, I love it when an amusing Tweet drops in. It's really entertaining, if you don't take it too seriously. You should try it.'

'No thanks. Lots of women get abused on Twitter, Lisa. Much more than men do. It gives damaged people a forum to bully and abuse women.'

'I know that. J. K. Rowling and Mary Beard get the most toxic Twitter abuse, but they keep on tweeting. And they put down their trolls with great skill and wit. And why should they be silenced? You're supposed to be the ardent feminist.'

'It's addictive, and they're giving the abusers what they most desire: attention.'

'And I suppose you think that's what I'm doing? But how else do I respond to an anonymous hater? I don't want them to think I'm weak, or that they've got to me.'

'But that's precisely what you're doing. Giving them oxygen, giving them air-time. Perhaps dignified silence is more powerful.'

That was the problem with Lisa Blaize. She didn't really do dignified silence. She had always been the one at school sticking up for the bullied kids. She would not allow herself to be intimidated. And she wanted revenge on the person who was hurting Edward. She changed the subject, partly because she knew that Bee was right: she was addicted to Twitter.

CHAPTER 21

'I'm Not a Troll'

Lisa knew it was another one. She wanted to throw it straight in the bin, but Edward insisted on donning a pair of gloves to avoid smudging any fingerprints, slitting it open with his antique paper knife, and poring over it for clues.

'Elementary,' he said, examining the postmarks. 'This has a second-class stamp and the one that came three days ago was first class. They were posted on the same day.'

It was indeed a continuation of the previous rant.

I'm going to get a little bit more personal now, at risk of you thinking you have a second deranged 'troll' or 'stalker', but I'm not a troll, not a stalker, and have no intention of looking at your tweets again. Twitter is an efficient way of promoting one's work and networking with people who share one's interests so I wouldn't want you to go running scared from it, but I do question the motive for, and wisdom of, some of the very personal things you share on Twitter. I don't know anyone else who does that in the same way and to the same extent. I find it very unusual (a more cynical person would say it is a bit weird!).

I have no envy of your life or Edward's life at all, Lisa, I genuinely don't; quite the reverse, in fact. I am extremely happy and fulfilled in my own life, but I think that Twitter is leading to a situation where people are living their lives through the eyes of others all the time and need constant validation and praise. We all of us need to question this. The people who use social media most effectively are those who have acute self-awareness and a really sharp wit. If you don't have those things, you can come a cropper and look self-obsessed and deeply insecure.

I think that the person who wrote the letter pinned to the noticeboard was out of order in many ways, especially when it came to comments about your physical appearance. I was reminded of the way that Mary Beard got so much criticism on Twitter. It's very mean to pick on anyone for the way they look, but in our misogynistic society middle-aged women are an easy target.

There are a lot of writers and other very successful people out there who only use Twitter for work-related matters, and who, no matter how successful, don't succumb to self-praise. Often, they get an agent to handle their Twitter account for them, thus avoiding the cringeworthy, attention-seeking that some people succumb to. The person who wrote the letter I found was complaining about a certain childish attention-seeking, and I wholly agree with that sentiment even though it was expressed in such an unrestrained way. The truth is, no one reading that letter could fail to see where the writer was coming from.

I didn't think I would end up joining the ranks of those who've been moaning about you on Twitter, Lisa, but there we are. I had to see your tweets at first hand to believe what everyone was saying. I'm not sure what to do with the letter I rescued from the noticeboard, because some of the comments scrawled on it might upset you. But I think I should probably return it to you and Ed. Either that or just destroy it.

Unlike the person who wrote the letter I found, I don't give a fig about Blagsford's reputation (it will survive all of us, of that we can be sure), but I do care about the damage Twitter is doing to us and our children.

I think we should all try to resist the whole egomania thing if only for the sake of the next generation and their mental health, as they are the ones not knowing what life was like growing up without Twitter and Facebook. You've got a following because teenage girls are interested in fashion, and I'm not going to deny that you've won yourself a bit of a reputation with your book and your Alexander McQueen piece in the paper. You can lead the way, Lisa, by behaving in a more grown-up fashion on Twitter. Admit you've been naïve, vain, self-centred, and a show-off, then you could help girls to feel they don't have to be under so much pressure from social media to be seen to have the perfect life. You might just be listened to if you made a public repentance. You like to represent yourself as a good Catholic girl, so go on, have a Road to Damascus moment.

Yours, a true well-wisher

*   *   *

'They're not very kind people.'

'Well, that's assuming it *is* a staff member. But you're probably right that no one comes to Blagsford in search of the milk of human kindness.'

'These last two letters, though …' He held them up, having retrieved the previous one, just to check that the typeface was indeed the same. He had read them both very slowly, twice.

Blimey, he thought, it goes on and on. I thought it was never going to end. Someone really is obsessed with her. He could understand that: they'd been married ten years, and he still couldn't keep his hands off her. But it was very important not to panic her. He must play it down. He summarized the main points, the general thrust. He was good at that kind of thing.

'I am staggered, I have to admit. I mean, the time it must have taken to write these two efforts. I wish I had that kind of spare time in my life. There is remarkable attention to detail. And to grammar. I must confess they are rather well written. Definitely someone educated, not your traditional spotty teenage troll in a darkened room. In fact, this latest letter is a textbook masterclass in deranged reasonableness.'

'I'm glad you admire their style. That hurts, Edward. How can you be so calm about it? I'm scared – are you saying that someone really put that first spiteful letter about me on the noticeboard?'

'No, Lisa. I'm not. Don't worry, I have my spies in the staffroom. And remember, as far as I can tell, everything in all these letters has been based on information that you have posted on Twitter. This person doesn't know you from Adam.'

'I'm not so sure. Did you say that they knew I'm Roman Catholic?'

'Don't you exchange frequent tweets with a holy father? You might just as well say that detail proves it's someone who doesn't know you, because they're assuming that your confessor is a Catholic when he's really an Anglo-Catholic.'

'And you say that it talks about middle-aged women. Maybe it is Moira.'

'No, it's not Moira. She's not a woman hater.'

'Yes, from your description of it, that first letter was steeped in misogyny.'

'And you saying so on Twitter has clearly riled the author into writing the second and third ones.'

'It's the misogyny that makes me think it really is a member of staff. You know how the masters treat women. I've heard how they talk about women. It's appalling. I don't like your staff. All boys' schools – they're hideous. Not because of the boys, but because the men in the staffroom have arrested development. They're just petulant schoolboys themselves.'

'That's just teachers, Lisa. You know what we're like. You were once one yourself. Too much time in the classroom. We're all socially dysfunctional.'

'Speak for yourself. That's why I got out. Because I didn't want to end up like those dried-up losers.'

Then she put it out of her mind. She washed her hair, applied a rose-scented face mask, and rubbed oil over her body. The one good thing about the end of the affair and then the letter was the weight she had lost. She couldn't eat when she was stressed. She'd also started jogging every day, instead of just when the mood took her. Running was the best antidote to Twitter and trolls and stalkers and not seeing Sean.

Lisa had always used clothes and make-up as armour, but now she stepped up her game. She couldn't quite shake the suspicion that the troll was a member of staff. If that was the case, she wouldn't let them see that they had got to her. Her weight loss was so extreme that she had to invest in a new wardrobe. She bought dresses by Chanel and McQueen. If she was going to be trolled by a disgruntled member of staff, she was going to look fabulous. She was going to age disgracefully.

CHAPTER 22

Malicious Communications

Dear Ms Blaize,

I am writing to you about your wonderful and informative book on fashion, which I bought last year and thoroughly enjoyed. Like you, I've always been fascinated by the relationship between fashion and feminism. In your book, you argue that in the late 18th century, women writers such as Mary Wollstonecraft, Mary Hays, and Mary Robinson (Hail the three Marys!) made powerful political statements about female fashion. How interesting that the chemise made fashionable by Mary Robinson in 1781 accorded women an unprecedented degree of liberation: physically and psychologically. I must say, it hadn't really occurred to me that without restrictive corsets and hoops, women were able to move about more freely: so obvious!

But those chemise dresses were so daring. You could see everything when it rained, and the flimsy fabric clung to every curve and line.

I hope you won't mind my saying that I once had a daughter who loved fashion. I thought of her when I read your book. Sadly, she died. She was suffering from anorexia nervosa, and she didn't make it. Ms Blaize, I implore you to stop posting selfies on social media. It gives such a bad example to young girls like my daughter. Girls today are under such a lot of

pressure to look a certain size, weight etc., they don't need
people like you adding to their misery ...

*   *   *

Fuck, she really got me there, thought Lisa as she carefully folded the letter and popped it into a clear plastic cover. Clever. She's upping her game.

'Edward, there's been another letter.'

'Why did you open it, I thought you said that you never read anonymous letters?'

'She invented a name and a fake address. I didn't realize what it was until I opened it. It began as a kind of fan letter about my book, then suddenly veered into abuse. But she wrote about a daughter who died of an eating disorder. Can you imagine faking a dead daughter? You'd have to be really sick to do that.'

'Well, what if it's genuine? It's by no means certain that it's the same person.'

'Edward, it is. I know it. Look at the address. No house number or road. God, she nearly had me there. She knows that I don't read anonymous letters because I said so on Twitter. She's desperate to get to me. To make sure that I read her vile invective.'

'Here, give it to me. Let's put it with the other ones. I think it's time to call the police. If you're right and it is a woman who is mentally ill, who knows what she'll do next?'

*   *   *

'Is there anyone who holds a grudge against you?' the young community police officer asked.

'Too many to list,' Lisa laughed.

'For example?' asked the policeman.

176

'Well, there's Lee the maintenance man, for a start – I fired his mother. He always looks at me as if he wants to kill me.'

'Lisa, don't be ridiculous,' said Edward. 'Lee can hardly string a sentence together – we're dealing here with someone highly educated, but with a psychotic streak.'

'We are looking for two things in cases like this. Blackmail and physical threat to your person. I can't see any evidence in these letters.'

'What about the claim that the sapphires were a bribe?'

'Possibly, sir, but we'd need a little more than that to make the case for forensic analysis – that sort of thing doesn't come cheap, you know, and, to be honest with you, our budgets are very stretched.'

Lisa liked this young policeman. He was sweet and kind, and took it all seriously. But he had, inadvertently, put himself in Edward's bad books. Edward had been playing catch with George when the officer arrived, asking for Sir Edward Chamberlain. The young man nodded at the baby, 'Your grandson, sir?'

'No, my son,' said Edward, curtly.

'Oh, well done, sir!' came the beaming reply.

Edward didn't know what was worse. Being thought of as his son's grandfather, or being congratulated for still having it in him to be a father. I'm not yet fifty, he thought. Has leadership aged me that much? Bloody cheek.

The policeman left his card and said that they should be in touch with him if matters escalated. 'If there is a persistent pattern, sir, madam, you might be able to invoke the Malicious Communications Act.'

'What's that?' Lisa asked.

'It prohibits people from sending or delivering letters or other articles for the purpose of causing distress or anxiety.'

'Our case exactly,' said Edward.

'But that would be a matter for your solicitor and the civil courts, not the police,' came the disappointing explanation.

Once he had left, Edward and Lisa discussed possible suspects. She was annoyed that she had thrown the most recent envelope into the fire before realizing that its contents were not a fan letter. The postmark on the first letter had, tantalizingly, been too faint to read. But on the second and third ones it was Birmingham. No great distance from Blagsford. That told in favour of the staffroom and against Moira – there was no way she would have travelled from Guildford all the way to Birmingham. If it had been her, she would have posted the letter from the anonymity of London, where she worked. It had to be someone local. Could it be a parent or someone in Blagsford town? Lisa hadn't moved in that world at all. Maybe she should start doing some digging.

CHAPTER 23

@FreddieSwings

DM from @Lisa_Blaize: Hi Freddie, it's Lisa Blaize here. So sorry again about the Bertie business. Don't suppose we could meet for a coffee at the Bean?

She hoped that Freddie Cole would think that she was going to offer advice about studying fashion, as a way of making up for having failed to save Bertie.

DM from @FreddieSwings: OK. When?

DM from @Lisa_Blaize: Tomorrow at 10.30?

DM from @FreddieSwings: OK.

Lisa made sure she was early, and ordered the coffees. Americano with hot milk on the side for Freddie, and an extra hot double espresso for herself. No pastries. Lisa could not be sure, but she suspected that Freddie had an eating disorder. So many Blagsford mums were on the spectrum. They definitely seemed to subscribe to Wallis Simpson's dictum that you can never be too rich or too thin, and yet their husbands were invariably fat and jowly. The thinner they got, the fatter their husbands became. Yuk. Edward had never lost his figure; tall and thin, he could eat what he liked and never put on an ounce of weight. In fact, he could do with a bit of weight on his face.

Freddie hurried in. She seemed always in a hurry. She was wearing her dark glasses, as usual. Lisa was anxious that Freddie would still be angry about Bertie's exclusion, but she seemed fine. She took a sip of her coffee, and launched in:

'Look, Lisa, to be honest, in the same position, I would have sacked Bertie. That boy is a nightmare, and always has been. Found a girl in his bed this morning. He found her on Tinder. He won't stay long at B. G. I don't know how we got him in there – state grammar school, and all that, not so susceptible to Daddy's offer of help towards a new sports hall.'

B. G. was the locals' name for Blagsford Grammar, the selective state school that had taken over the former premises of Blagsford when the ancient public school had moved to the edge of town.

'Thanks Freddie, that's so kind of you.'

'Real mixed demographic at the B. G. school gate. That's another good thing about Bertie's expulsion – not having to socialize with the ghastly yummy mummies. Not necessary at this age. I see enough of them at Euphoria. And there's this fantastic teacher called Mr Onions. All the kids rave about him. He's the first one to have got Bertie interested in his school work – shows what a waste of money Blagsford was.'

Lisa was really beginning to warm to Freddie. She was forthright.

'Oh, so do you belong to the gym? No wonder you have such a great body.'

'Thanks, Lisa. I first started going to get away from my husband. Then I realized that most of the women there were doing the same thing. It was also a great cover for my affair when I met Helen. God, those ghastly women. Up at 6.30 with their dumb-bells. That's what most of them are: dumb belles, with bad teeth from chucking up in the loos.'

Crikey, Lisa thought, I wouldn't like to get on the wrong side of Freddie. She was cutting. But hilarious, and very different to what she had expected.

'Are you happy with Helen?'

'Oh yes. I always knew I was gay. Most men loved it, loved the challenge. Once I met Helen, that was it for me.' Freddie lay her sunglasses on the table, and ran a perfectly manicured hand through her short blonde hair. God, she has amazing cheekbones, Lisa thought. She was really very, very pretty.

'So what can I do for you?'

'Well, I wanted to make sure that you were OK. I saw your ex shouting at you in the car park. And I wanted you to know that I tried everything.'

'Listen Lisa, you don't have to feel bad. It is what it is. How about you? I really do like your fashion column in *City & County*. And I love you on Twitter. You are so funny.'

'I'm OK. I've had a bit of trolling.' Lisa looked at Freddie carefully.

'Oh really. Well, that's to be expected if you're always online. And let's remember what that great sage Ricky Gervais says about trolls?'

Lisa raised a quizzical eyebrow. She was enjoying Freddie's company.

'Gervais tweeted something along the lines of this: Trolls don't hate you. They hate themselves. They're in pain and you getting upset is like their morphine. Don't administer. Enjoy the screams.'

*　　*　　*

 DM from @FreddieSwings: Thanks for the coffee, Lisa. You like your body and self. You don't present as a beauty queen, which is why you are as sexy as hell.

Lisa couldn't help blushing. She had never been bi-curious before. Not another Twitter flirtation. Time to consult Misty.

 DM from @Lisa_Blaize: Father, father, I need to confess.

 DM from @FrJohnMisty: what is it now, Blaize? I can't leave you alone for five minutes without you getting into trouble.

 DM from @Lisa_Blaize: I think I've got a girl-on-girl crush.

 DM from @FrJohnMisty: Isn't your life complicated enough already?

 DM from @FrJohnMisty: But I'm fine with this if I can join in and make it a threesome.

 DM from @Lisa_Blaize: I'm joking, lovely. But she did give me some good advice about not feeding the Troll.

DM from @FrJohnMisty: Good. Listen to it. And, by the way, I adore your blog. It's hilarious.

DM from @Lisa_Blaize: What blog?

CHAPTER 24

My Fabulous Life

Blog: https://lisablaizesite.wordpress.com

Welcome to My Fabulous Life

Hi there readers, time for my latest blog entry. Today it's all about the Headmaster's White Garden. Gosh I am so lucky to have my own White Garden, and a hunky School Gardener to tend it. Hope you like the pic below. The school-leavers look gorgeous in their fine clothes. The girls from our sister school so pretty in their ballgowns and the boys in their black tie. Last night was the Blagsford Ball. Drinks in the Headmaster's White Garden, and then dinner and dancing. Such fun.

My dress was McQueen, of course. White silk chiffon, cinched at the waist with a silver belt, and a thigh-skimming split. Metallic sandals by Christian Louboutin. Grabbed every diamond I could find, and was practically sparkling in the moonlight. Later that evening, Sir Edward covered my shoulders with a white fur stole (rabbit). We danced all night. I especially loved dancing with the gorgeous head boy. He could barely keep his eyes off me ... more anon ...

*　　*　　*

'My God, Edward. This cyberstalker is sick. How does she know that we have a White Garden?'

'Because, my sweet, silly darling, you keep tweeting pictures of the White Garden. And some jokes about the hunky head gardener. You're giving your stalker ammunition.'

'So how do you know that? Are *you* stalking me?'

'Not stalking. Just protecting. Checking everything's OK.'

'Censoring, you mean. Controlling.'

'No, love, waking you up. And are you still so sure it's a woman?'

'I know it is ... woman's intuition.'

'I'm not so sure.'

Edward told her that he had taken another good look at all her Twitter followers. That everyone from the head boy to Emma's teacher in primary school could see what she was tweeting. He thought she was making herself too vulnerable to the wrong sort of people.

'Perhaps it's time for a Twitter vacation?'

'OK, fair enough, I'll go quiet on Twitter for a bit and we can see what happens. But that stuff about dancing with the head boy ... what's all that about? That's a dangerous rumour to be circulating in such a tight-knit community. I know I once slapped and kissed a schoolboy, but that was a long time ago. God, Edward, maybe it's one of their mothers exacting revenge after all these years. What do you think?'

'I think that letters and blogs like these encourage paranoia and fear. You're letting it get to you. One moment you think it's Moira, and the next it's the poor mother of a boy you once slapped. How many enemies do you have?'

'Well, I probably have a lot. Edward, have you told the staffroom about this stalking business?'

'Not yet. I'm having a think.'

'But does anyone have a grudge against you? Against us? There's too much intimate detail in that blog for my liking.'

'Internet detail, not intimate.'

*   *   *

It had been such a crazy year that they had not booked a summer holiday. Indonesia had been enough as far as overseas travel was concerned, and Queenie was too young to put into kennels, so they went to the south coast for a week of English seaside air. It was such a tonic to be away from the claustrophobia and back-biting of Blagsford.

CHAPTER 25

#Lovelyme

'We're off for a staycation in Lyme,' Lisa had told Belinda Bullrush.

She was longing for Queenie to see the seaside. Lyme Regis was one of her favourite places in the world. Edward had never been there and she wanted him to know the place she loved so much. They booked a small apartment with a sea view. There was a secret passageway that led out from the flat via a fake front door onto the promenade, which the children especially loved.

They walked as far as the Cobb, then onto Monmouth Beach on the west side, where dogs were allowed all year. Queenie loved chasing the seagulls into the sea, and the children were happy with buckets and spades. It was a typical English seaside holiday, with salty fish and chips in newspaper, ice creams, and warm beer. Lisa loved to feel the sand between her toes. She helped George to pick shells, and they paddled in the turquoise water. Gosh, she must book George in for swimming lessons, she thought to herself.

As they walked back towards the Cobb, Queenie was yelping and barking happily at the birds and the waves. Then she began running around in circles. Lisa rummaged in her coat pocket for the requisite doggy bag. Shit, she'd forgotten to pack it. Edward, fastidious as ever, glanced expectantly. They mustn't soil this lovely beach.

'Oh God, I've forgotten the bag.'

'Lisa, how many times …?'

'I'm sorry. It's all the stress of packing for the holiday. I have some more at the apartment. Shall I run back?'

'No, we need to sort it now. We can get fined for this sort of behaviour.'

The children were playing in the sand, Emma, as always keeping a sharp eye on her baby brother.

'Don't you have a handkerchief, Edward? You always carry a handkerchief.'

'The handkerchief? It's one of my best linen handkerchiefs that my mother gave me. I'm not using that. I don't suppose you thought to bring baby wipes?'

'You barely notice your mother's existence. You never see her, so I don't know why you're suddenly so concerned about her handkerchief.'

Edward looked livid.

'What are you trying to say? That I'm ashamed of her?'

'Well you sometimes act like it'.

Lisa frantically searched her jeans' pocket and extracted a ragged tissue. Edward took it and began clearing up Queenie's mess. Oh God, it was getting everywhere, all over his perfectly manicured hands. Lisa cursed herself silently for not bringing baby wipes. Edward was furious.

'Give it here, and go and wash your hands in the sea.'

Lisa took the offering and ran off to find a bin. When she got back, Edward was drying his hands on his chinos. She could see he was still furious. He hated mess of any kind. Queenie was looking at him; the picture of innocence, and Lisa burst out laughing. She just couldn't help herself. Edward was not seeing the funny side.

'Why don't you make more of an effort to train this bloody dog? May I remind you that I was against this dog business until the children nagged and nagged and I gave in.'

'I'm sorry, it's my fault.' Lisa was really beginning to get the giggles, Edward looked so funny when he was angry.

She placed a hand on his arm. He took her hand and pulled her towards him, and, then, without a hint of what was to come, he put his hand around the top of her throat, and spoke softly: 'You fucking bitch.' It lasted the briefest of seconds, and he released his hand instantly.

'Lisa, I'm so sorry.'

'It's OK. It's fine.'

She made her way to the children, busy with their sandcastles. Queenie trotted after her, as she always did.

Edward, still shocked, joined the group.

'Who wants ice cream?'

* * *

Later, Lisa pondered the incident. Edward was clearly very angry. He'd seemed so calm, so unflappable when she had told him about Sean, but she realized that, deep down, he was shattered. How could she blame him? In a way, she respected his fury; it showed that he cared. But was it really her, Lisa Blaize, that he cared about, or was it his sense of self, his dignity? There had been tears in his eyes when he offered ice cream, but were they tears of self-pity? For that split second, she saw him as another person. She had felt something she had never ever felt before in Edward's presence; she had been frightened.

Neither one of them referred to the incident. She would bury it in the Lyme sand. Later that evening she took a long solitary walk on the Cobb. The sea always soothed her. Lovely

189

Lyme. When she got back, she took out her phone and posted a tweet.

Lisa Blaize @Lisa_Blaize
Beautiful sunny day at Lyme Regis. #Lovelyme.

Once she'd started, she couldn't stop. It wouldn't do any harm to post a few photos of herself on the Cobb, just to let Sean know that she was surviving. Liking her new hashtag 'LoveLyme', she appended it to each of them.

This brought out the trolls. It only took one to stumble across the picture before others responded in a chain reaction.

REPLY TO @Lisa_Blaize
U. R. A. Fox @1BigHorn
Lovely me? I'll second that, Lisa.

REPLY TO @1BigHorn
Night Prowler @Sniffer69
She looks like she needs a real seeing to.

REPLY TO @Sniffer69
Zwounder @rnxyzdm
I'd give her one too.

REPLY TO @1BigHorn & @Sniffer69
Teens Only @iLikeEmYoung
Scrawny old slapper, no thanks.

CHAPTER 26

Literary Ladies

Blog: https://lisablaizesite.wordpress.com

My Literary Pashurns

I was always a big reader. Right from being a very young girl, I was a big reader of the classics. And I mean big. That's because I was really, really clever, much cleverer than anyone realizes to this day, and I knew which writers to love. I loved the Brontes because of the language, the passion. I'll say it again: the LANGWIDGE, the PASHURN (I hope my Liverpool accent is coming through here, because it's such a big part of who I am). But my biggest passion is for fashion. Passion, fashion, get it?

The brilliant thing about fashion is that you can be passionate and intuitive. You don't have to worry about the nerdy stuff that makes you do well in exams. I'm a natural, you see, I can't be constrained by mindless rules. I always go with my gut instincts and don't bother listening to what those snobby academics have to say. That's why I loved Manchester and the one thing I don't love about my lovely husband is all that snobby Oxbridge stuff he was brought up with.

O, did I tell you that my biggest LITERARY PASHURN is for Jane Austen. She's so clever and funny, just like me. And she loved the seaside, just like me.

We couldn't get away for more than a week this summer. Sir Edward such a very important man, you know. So we just took the children to Lyme Regis for a week. I really do love Lyme, just like Jane, which is why I recently wrote Lovelyme in a hashtag. It turned out someone thought I meant Lovely me – as if, LOL!! They said they thought it must be a Freudian slip, the meanies. I mean, do I act as though I love myself? During our stay at Lyme I was very restrained and self-effacing. I only posted three photos of myself on Twitter, one of me in my Liz Hurley bikini which I absolutely love (it was just that I was photobombing the children, and not that I wanted everyone to see me in my bikini and pearls), and two of me in my blue halter-neck dress, which again had nothing to do with wanting people to see me in the dress both from the front and from the back. Each of those photos had a perfectly valid motive – the first one was to show that there's always time to drink fizz no matter how important you are, and the second was to show me saying goodbye to Lyme. Nothing to do with the dress at all, and nothing to do with the drop-dead gorgeous woman wearing it whose shoulders are broader than her husband's (I refuse to take any notice of those people who say I look like a cross between a tranny and a Cheshire housewife).

Goodness, I've just seen that it's cocktail hour, so I must dash. I'll be blogging again soon, so don't go away.

*   *   *

'Edward, this is identity theft. Isn't that against the law? There must be something we can do about it.'

'Apparently not, if that very immature young policeman who left us his card is to be trusted. I phoned him, and he told me that you can't stop someone setting up a blog in any particular name. I know you might find this hard to credit, but you're not the only Lisa Blaize in the world.'

Lisa thought this was harsh. Edward had coped extraordinarily well with the Sean business, but he couldn't resist the odd dig every now and then. He'd never been like that before. But he had the right.

* * *

Blog: https://lisablaizesite.wordpress.com

I Lurve Literary Ladies

I've been thinking about these literary types. They always go on about metaphors and symbols and the closed system of the text, whatever that is. They don't let readers read novels how they should be read: as if they were true. I mean, what's the point of creating a literary character who the readers can't treat as a real person? As a friend. Or as a bit like themselves. I like to think that characters in novels, and even in Shakespeare plays, are me. Lots of heroines in books remind me of me. It's a big part of who I am. Eustacia Vye, for instance. I so love her. I love her because she is passionate like me. I love Bathsheba, too, because she is a really passionate, clever woman like me, gobby yet smart, who feels oppressed, like I do, by having to express her passionate emotions in a language created by men. Scarlett O'Hara is another heroine who reminds me of me, which is why I said on Twitter that time that I was feeling very Scarlettish, LOL! The list goes on, really.

The thing I really can't stand about those literary types is their obsession with style. Who cares whether a book is well written or badly written? What matters is the passion of the author. That's why I only read the good reviews of my book about fashion, the ones that said I really got why some clothes are especially sexy (especially when worn by me, I said to myself when I read that!). I just ignored the bad ones which said that it was badly written and had too much cultural studies jargon (the thing is, I just had to put in that stuff for the stuffy academic critics – good thing Manchester taught me a few of the key phrases, male gaze, inscription of power, and all that).

Anyway, they were wrong, because Edward said that he thought it was very well written, and he should know, I mean he used to be a history teacher before he became a very glam and charismatic headmaster in both the public and the private sector, knighted for his work in turning round a sink school. O yes, Edward really appreciates my literary talent, but I guess that is mainly because he fancies me so much, LOL! He'll never dump me like he did Moira. TY, Edward. He finds me irresistible, maybe because I just am! As he observed in Jakarta, even the sandflies couldn't resist me. They were all over me as if I was a piece of shit, LOL! I know that Edward will never get bored of me, because I have 'infinite variety' like Cleopatra, and I make him hungry where I most satisfy! That's another thing I love: quoting things that remind me of me.

But hang on, what if Edward does dump me? Will I still be Lady C? What if he goes back to Moira? But I doubt he will. I mean, she's hardly a success. She's only a senior commissioning editor at Random Penguin, something that I could do in my sleep! In fact, I would get really bored in a job like that within two years because I'm too clever for it, just as I get bored of men within two years unless they happen to be a passport to a glam life, which luckily my darling Edward is, now that he's escaped from that shithole in Liverpool and picked up a knighthood. But I still worry sometimes (when I've had too many margaritas) that you will want to go back to Moira, EC. I fear you will do it out of low self-esteem and not being able to accept that I am ultimately much smarter and more attractive than you. Will Moira then become Lady C? And if I then marry Darren from Champneys, who did give me a lot of very special attention on my pampering weekend, will he become Lord D? I'm getting very confused. But I don't think I could bear it if one day my Ocado delivery man came and no one addressed me as your ladyship. I'd have to make myself some yummy pink Nigella Lawson ice cream (so love pink, hence my shiny pink Loubs for the Investiture). In fact, I think I'll go and make some now.

*   *   *

She turned to Misty for advice.

DM from @Lisa_Blaize: I saw the blogs.

DM from @FrJohnMisty: So crazy. Is it some old Blagger who's got a grudge against you? Quite funny, though. Gets your tone spot on. You are vain, Blaize.

DM from @Lisa_Blaize: I know, it's quite clever in its own way. But, once again, like the letters, it's all based on stuff about me that's out on the Internet.

 DM from @FrJohnMisty: So stop tweeting. Quit it. Just DM if you need to. Besides, it's all over with the Dr isn't it?

 DM from @Lisa_Blaize: Of course it is. But I suppose I just want him to know that I'm OK.

DM from @FrJohnMisty: Well you don't know that he's looking at your tweets. Is he still following you?

 DM from @Lisa_Blaize: Yes. And he favourites the odd tweet. But we're not in contact. I'm disciplining myself not to look at his tweets. I am not a cyberstalker.

 DM from @FrJohnMisty: I suppose it could be that lezzy mother. Do you remember that girl who had a crush on you at college? Started wearing the same clothes and dyed her hair like yours. You do seem to have this effect on people, Blaize. Sometimes you're too friendly. You need to protect yourself. Not let people in. Except me, of course.

DM from @Lisa_Blaize: I know. I make this mistake time and time again.

DM from @FrJohnMisty: Are you and Edward OK? He's always been insecure about you, for the obvious reason.

DM from @Lisa_Blaize: Yes, I think we're OK. He's been totally chilled about it. But I suppose that shouldn't surprise me. You know what they call him in the staffroom?

DM from @FrJohnMisty: No drama Obama?

DM from @Lisa_Blaize: You got it. You always get it.

DM from @FrJohnMisty: How about you? It's got to be affecting you.

DM from @Lisa_Blaize: I must admit I've got a few more wrinkles than I had before. Unlike Edward, with that fabulous skin of his. He snipes at me every now and then, but I'm OK with that, I deserve it. In a funny way, it's brought us closer together. What's even funnier, is he's become obsessed by Twitter. It's very addictive. You're right to say I should quit Twitter, but it's useful publicity.

DM from @FrJohnMisty: Don't lie to me. I know you too well. You're trying to keep some kind of contact with Dr Who. It's a slippery slope, Blaize. I bet he's still all over your Twitter. You are funny on Twitter, Blaize. That's been the problem with your stalker, they just don't get your sense of humour.

197

DM from @Lisa_Blaize: That's living in the south for you. No one in Blagsford gets my humour. They don't seem to understand irony. Twitter asks 'what's happening?' I tweet 'lost my glasses,' and then I get accused of being a narcissist.

 DM from @FrJohnMisty: Well you are. We all know that. I love people with big egos. They usually have a big ego because they're interesting. Shy people bore me.

 DM from @Lisa_Blaize: BTW you must follow Henry VIII, and Kermit. So hilarious. Miss you Misty.

DM from @FrJohnMisty: I love you.

CHAPTER 27

Hacked Off

Lisa needed a second opinion, so she asked Bee to meet at the Albion.

'Oh, you just missed Onions, again. He's dying to meet you. You'd get on really well.'

'Really, Bee, I'm beginning to think that Peter Onions is a figment of Blagsford's overactive imagination. I hear so much about him; he's a genius, he's a legend, he's the heart of this old town. He's the most inspirational teacher at Blagsford Grammar. Maybe Edward should try to hire him.'

'What's wrong, lovey? Sit down and tell me.'

'It's Edward. Do you think there's any possibility that Edward wrote the letters – and now these fake blogs?'

Bee stopped typing on her laptop and looked up.

'You're not seriously suggesting that Edward is your troll? OK, I'm going to say something very important. You must not go mad, Lisa. The idea that your distinguished husband is writing a fake fashion blog in your name is simply insane. This town has a way of turning even the most stable people into paranoid lunatics.'

'I'm not being paranoid; I just hacked into his email.'

Bee burst out laughing.

'Listen to yourself: you hacked into his email. Why?'

'I don't know. I just had the thought that maybe it was Edward all along. It was something that Sean said to me. Not directly, of course, but he hinted that perhaps I don't know my husband as well as I think I do.'

'He's probably right. Who really knows who the other is, and what they're capable of? But, in this case, I think you're wrong. Have you considered Sean's agenda, here? That he might have a reason to sow a seed of doubt in you? You might as well say that Sean is your troll.'

'But the emails. They were to his best friend, Nick, and it suggests that my husband's far more jealous than he's ever let on.'

'I'm not interested in hearing about this; they were confidential, and you hacked into them.'

'Well, it wasn't really hacking. I just happened to glance at the screen of his laptop and saw my name. Maybe he left his computer open deliberately, wanting me to see them, so that I could feel his anguish. That's it, Belinda, he *wanted* me to see them.'

'Far too Freudian – you're just making excuses. Lisa, listen to yourself. You're really losing it. You marched in saying that Edward might be the troll, and now you're saying he's wanting to share his pain with you.'

Lisa knew better than to continue this argument with Bee. She also felt deeply ashamed that she had looked at Edward's email. It was something that Sean had said to her, long ago, about how she was just a trophy for Edward, and that he didn't truly love her, or why else would he 'lock her away in a tower'? Sean would never do that. He would be her lover, her soulmate, her cook, her jester, but he would never lock her away. So, she had done the one thing she vowed never to do (like reading someone's diary): she had read personal, private emails that were not meant for her eyes.

*   *   *

200

The emails revealed that after he had found out about the affair, Edward, who always took pride in his self-control, had contained his emotions for a week. Then he had broken. He had been compelled to unburden himself to someone. But he hadn't wanted anyone in Blagsford to know that his marriage was in trouble. It would not have looked good. He had had his fill of salacious gossip in the staffroom when he had married Lisa at SJA. So he had turned to Nick, using his private email account, not the headmaster's, which his PA was all over.

One day, when he had been rushing off to a meeting, he had left his Gmail open on his laptop on the kitchen table. Lisa had come in, and before she knew what she was doing, she found herself working through a string of messages between Blagsford and Indonesia.

From: ELC1807@gmail.com
To: Nick.Staples@PasarMingguAcademy.co.id
Bloody hell, Nick, you were right. About Lisa having a faraway look and being glued to her phone when we were staying with you. She's been having an affair. With the bloody heart surgeon who saved Emma's life. How's that for medical ethics? I think she's completely in love with him. But I don't know how far they went – she swears they didn't fuck. But they were going to: he invited her to Amsterdam "for a conference". You know what it means to go to a foreign city with a woman – you've been doing it all your life. Just joking. But seriously, Nick, I'm totally devastated. I'm as much in love with my woman as I was the day when it began. And the thought of us breaking up – I can't bear it. Especially for the kids. I just don't know how it's happened. I try to give her everything. I thought she was so happy to get away from Liverpool. And that she'd never do anything to hurt the children. What have I done wrong? OK, it's been tough settling

into the new school, and maybe I've neglected her a bit. But why didn't she tell me she was unhappy? I'm perplexed in the extreme – but not jealous. What the hell am I going to do?

From: Nick.Staples@PasarMingguAcademy.co.id
To: ELC1807@gmail.com
What you're going to do, mate, is stay calm. Stay dignified like you always do. Let her feel the chill wind, but never, never, never shout at her. That'll just throw her into his arms. Tell me more about this heart guy. I bet he's married. If he is, you're going to be just fine. He'll be a serial philanderer (most surgeons are) and he'll run a mile now that you've found out. If he's not, you'll be fine as well – cos that would make him like me, not wanting to be tied down. You've always been a jammy sod, Ed – you caught her just in time. Would have been much more serious if she'd gone to Amsterdam. If that had happened, she'd be setting herself up in a fuck flat before you knew it. Keep me posted.

From: ELC1807@gmail.com
To: Nick.Staples@PasarMingguAcademy.co.id
Cold comfort, Nick.

From: Nick.Staples@PasarMingguAcademy.co.id
To: ELC1807@gmail.com
Here's comfort: Lisa has the strongest sense of family I've ever seen in a woman. Give her time. She's that much younger than you. Early onset mid-life crisis? She's always been precocious, your Lisa. Is she suddenly thinking that one day you'll be an old man and she'll have to change your colostomy bag and this is her last chance to trade you in for a younger, fitter model?

From: ELC1807@gmail.com

To: Nick.Staples@PasarMingguAcademy.co.id

This is not the time for banter. You've always been the one to keep my feet on the ground, stop me being pompous. But this is no time for joking. Maybe she does think I'm declining into the vale of years. I don't know.

From: Nick.Staples@PasarMingguAcademy.co.id

To: ELC1807@gmail.com

Are you talking? That's the most important thing.

From: ELC1807@gmail.com

To: Nick.Staples@PasarMingguAcademy.co.id

Oh yes, we never stop talking. The weird thing is that I know how she feels, and I don't feel angry. I feel sad for her. Her heart is broken. She looks so sad. She's cried in my arms over Sean. She told me that she hasn't crossed the line. But, come on. Does she expect me to believe that?

From: Nick.Staples@PasarMingguAcademy.co.id

To: ELC1807@gmail.com

Then again, you could have a revenge affair. There must be a whole queue of bluestocking headmistresses out there at those conferences, just waiting to be livened up by a man of your stature.

From: ELC1807@gmail.com

To: Nick.Staples@PasarMingguAcademy.co.id

I don't want a revenge affair. I want her to love me again.

From: Nick.Staples@PasarMingguAcademy.co.id

To: ELC1807@gmail.com

Then just make sure she respects you. Love her wisely, not too well.

*   *   *

There had been another exchange a couple of weeks later:

From: Nick.Staples@PasarMingguAcademy.co.id

To: ELC1807@gmail.com

How's it going, bro?

From: ELC1807@gmail.com

To: Nick.Staples@PasarMingguAcademy.co.id

I'm trying not to let her see it, but it's really getting to me. She's being evasive about how far they went. Swears blind they didn't do it, but won't look me in the eye and deny that they lay together. Says they were careful not to harm their marriages, their children. Naked in bed and not mean harm? I don't think so. I've just got this image in my head. Of him lying with her. On her.

From: Nick.Staples@PasarMingguAcademy.co.id

To: ELC1807@gmail.com

Ask yourself this, Edward: do you want to be divorced?

From: ELC1807@gmail.com

To: Nick.Staples@PasarMingguAcademy.co.id

No.

From: Nick.Staples@PasarMingguAcademy.co.id

To: ELC1807@gmail.com

Then do nothing for two years. I'll tell you where I got that tip. Do you remember that skinny girl Donatella at college? Her husband shagged around and she spent thousands on therapy before getting her answer with that simple question: do you want to be divorced? The answer was no, and now her marriage is back on track. So I'm your therapist and now you owe me a shedload of money! Or at least a few beers.

*   *   *

A few days later, Lisa was still ruminating on Belinda's ticking off. She felt terrible about her behaviour. Who was she becoming? Reading messages on the computer of the man she loved: that wasn't her. Belinda was right. Blagsford was tipping her over the edge.

Then a text pinged in from Freddie, asking if they could meet in the Blagsford wine bar. They had progressed from The Coffee Bean, and it was much more fun to chat over a glass of fizz. Lisa didn't mention the emails, but she told Freddie about the blogs. Freddie hooted when she heard about 'lovely me'.

'Freddie I promise you. I simply wrote #lovelyme. I didn't even twig that it spelt "lovely me".'

'Well, you are lovely, Lisa. Embrace it. You're very unself-conscious about your beauty. It's very … enticing.'

'Are you lezzing on me? You know I'm not one bit bi-curious.'

'Oh, I think you are. You're just afraid.' Freddie was wearing a micro-skirt, more of a belt than a skirt, and as she crossed her legs, she revealed a flash of silky underwear.

'Honestly, I have enough trouble with men. I don't need to complicate matters. I just can't see myself sucking on oysters.'

Freddie howled again. Lisa was so naughty, and yet somehow so innocent. She longed to corrupt her.

'Were you always glamorous, Fred? You always look so groomed, so perfect. So Audrey Hepburn. You seem to me be the kind of girl who grew up in a home with nail clippers and Sellotape on a holder. I always longed for that kind of home organization.'

'No, far from it. I was the dumpy girl who dressed like a student. Then I got a grip; lost weight, cut my hair short and got expensive highlights, went online and bagged a nice rich man. Simps.'

Lisa chuckled. She loved Freddie's candour. It was very un-Blagsford.

'Anyway, I'm feeling a bit jealous of this Belinda girl. Is she supplanting me in your affection?'

'Don't be silly. You should meet her. I think you'd get one another, but I'm not sure. She may be too clever for you.'

'Well thanks a bunch. I ought to feel insulted.'

'And she's quite proper and dignified, but not prim. She hates prim. She's very noble.'

Freddie filled Lisa's glass.

'I know I've slept with many, many men before my late flowering, but it was always on my own terms. I had my own rules, no married men, threesomes as long as everyone was happy, particularly the girl. That sort of thing.'

'Gosh, I'm such a prude. I've only ever slept with men I'm in love with, and I can count my lovers on one hand.'

'That's because every man you've ever met wants to marry you. That rarely happened to me. I had to go online to find a nice, safe husband who would provide. Look where that got me.'

'A jolly nice divorce settlement is what it got you, which is why you can settle the bill.'

'Of course, but I need the loo first. But I want to say one last thing to you. Have you ever really, properly considered that there are people out there who are very jealous of you? It's a mistake to underestimate the power of the green-eyed monster.'

Freddie got up and headed towards the Ladies. There was a large square pane of glass on the wine-bar floor revealing the wine cellar beneath. Freddie started dancing alone on the square in her miniskirt. It was a slow, sexy dance, asserting her sexual freedom. What a treat for the barman below, Lisa thought. But she felt a sudden stab of pity for Freddie.

* * *

Blog: https://lisablaizesite.wordpress.com

Loub Time!

Hi Fans, Lisa, Fashion Mistress here, well, I know all about being a mistress … giggle, giggle, but Reader, I married him!

Now what shall I write about today for all you cheap plebs who have to shop on the High Street whilst I shop designer: Chanel and McQueen doncha know! LOL. Oh lovely me. I do so love being me. As Chanel once said: 'Keep your heels, head and standards high' – well I certainly keep my heels high – Christine Laboutin being my heel of choice. You plebs will never get your filthy feet in a pair of Loubs anytime soon, so dream on. Head and standards … hmmm not sure.

Remember plebs that Chanel also said 'Elegance is being equally beautiful inside and outside'. So that's me sorted … LOL.

Now, must dash. Off to another exciting ball in the Big Smoke. Tonight, I'll be wearing Balmain in this season's ice tones (dove grey and silver), and, of course, my trusty sapphires. But I won't be wearing any lingerie: as Chanel said, 'It is always better to be slightly underdressed!'

CHAPTER 28

A Shed of One's Own

When she first came to Blagsford, Lisa felt trapped. She told Edward she had 'princess in the tower syndrome'. Living in Headmaster's House was like being in the middle of Piccadilly Circus. People came in and out, they never knocked on the door. Bianka's Hoover was permanently droning … a classic trick of cleaners, she knew. Keep the hoover on, and it looks like you're working. Edward's useless PA called Lisa a dozen times a day on some slight pretext. 'I'm not your bloody secretary, taking messages for you when you haven't told your PA where you are,' she told Edward. 'Close your study door, and ignore them,' he countered. He didn't understand. She could never close her door. It was a function of being a mother. Never turn your back on small children.

The claustrophobia of living in the goldfish bowl had been one of the things that had driven her into Sean's arms. If she wasn't careful, the same thing would happen again. She had to find a place where she could escape from the school and the family, so that she could work on her book.

The puppy was adorable, but she was making the problem worse, either yapping at the hordes of people pouring through the doors, or gazing at her with doleful eyes, nose twitching, appealing for a walk around the grounds and lake.

Lisa's ex-housekeeper Doris had a son called Lee who worked on the school's maintenance team. He was skinny, with peroxide hair that he dyed himself, parts of it far too yellow, urine-like. There were rumours that he'd once been inside for GBH. Queenie hated him. Every time Lisa walked her dog around the playing fields, she would run up to the students, tail wagging, but if she saw Lee, she would bark ferociously. Lee never once looked at Queenie, or Lisa, for that matter. He just stared straight ahead. He made her skin crawl. There was violence in every sinew, coldness in those dead fish-like eyes.

Prying eyes, that was what she hated about Blagsford.

That's it, Lisa thought as she walked Queenie around the grounds. I need a writer's shed. Somewhere close enough to the house if the children need me, but with enough space and quiet to get the work done. A she-shed.

She knew that there would certainly be a staff member or parent or, most likely, an Old Blagger with some objection to any kind of permanent structure, so Lisa decided on a shepherd's hut. It was on wheels, so planning permission was not required, and it could be wheeled away into the woods if anyone complained. She found one on eBay. A Cotswold green shepherd's hut, with a woodburning stove, and room for a desk and an armchair. It would be delivered in a few weeks.

Marie Antoinette, they'll all call me, she thought. Well, let them.

*   *   *

She and Edward had another row. They had never rowed before all the trolling and stalking business had started. The tormentor was doing more damage to the marriage than her affair had done.

'How dare that fucking troll parody my real blog in *City &
County*? It could cost me my commission. We've got to involve
the police again.'

Edward remained adamant: 'Don't give him oxygen by engag-
ing with him.' Edward remained convinced that it was a man.
Lisa was equally sure that the letters and blogs had all the hall-
marks of a female hand. The detailed attention to her clothes, her
body, her shoes. No, it was definitely a woman. Edward was
wrong.

Perhaps Edward was right however, about the troll giving up
if she just suffered in silence. She vowed to forget about the troll
and forget about Sean. But she was so discomposed by the fake
blog that she found herself unable to go on writing her real one
for the *City & County* website.

Every morning, she went for a run, and then she took her
laptop down to her brand-new shepherd's hut. Queenie was
thrilled and ran about the garden, chasing squirrels and crows. It
was endlessly amusing to watch the little puppy stalking the
birds, who seemed to taunt her, and then at the last-minute
swoop majestically into the air leaving Queenie looking utterly
bemused.

The hut was perfect. It was made of cedar wood, with a corrugated iron roof, which made the most delicious sound when the
rain came. Edward had asked the builder to drive it to the edge
of the lake, so she could see the swans and the heron, who was
her particular favourite. She taught herself how to light the
woodburner in the corner. The makers had thought of everything,
even a wooden peg holder for her coat.

Lisa set about sourcing the soft furnishings. She bought two
kilim rugs, and embroidered scatter cushions in soft greens and
pink for the sofa. She filled the log basket with tiny logs, installed

a battery hurricane lamp, and a Dickens bookcase. The last item remaining was a dog basket for Queenie. She had decided that she didn't need electricity. She would do it the old-fashioned way, with the woodburner, and candles. She wouldn't work there at night when it was dark, as she needed to be in the house with the children. It was her haven. She finally found a sense of peace that had eluded her since the move to Blagsford.

She longed to tell Sean, who had encouraged her to find a space to work. Writers need quiet and isolation, he had reminded her. You just need someone at the end of the working day to cook you delicious food and open the wine bottle. She missed his texts, his tweets terribly; his love and care, but she wanted to keep her promise to Edward. There would be no contact. Not on her part anyway.

With the summer sun blazing through its windows, the hut was so warm and cosy that Lisa dozed off, Queenie at her feet. In the days following her split with Sean, Lisa had found solace in the White Garden. It had helped heal her heartbreak. The roses were so fragrant, and so beautiful. She had asked the gardener to plant white lavender for ground cover, and in the hot summer days, she would fall asleep on a blanket on the grass, beneath the soporific lavender. Now she was preparing a winter haven.

Lisa was a sun-goddess and had always loathed the end of summer, but the shepherd's hut seemed to bring her closer to nature. She watched the rippled water of the lake, as the wind whipped across its silvery surface, and she made her peace with the rain.

When the hut had first arrived, she couldn't resist tweeting a photo of it. Sean would be pleased to know that she had at last found a room of her own, even though it was only seven feet by twelve.

*   *   *

Blog: https://lisablaizesite.wordpress.com

My Rusty Shed

Another fabulous day in the life of Lady C.

A sunny September day in lovely Blagsford, surrounded by my adoring fans. I so love an Indian summer. Wore my Indonesian sapphires to the New Staff Dinner for the beginning of the academic year. And a Chanel dress. How I love Chanel. So chic. While dressing, I danced to Freddie Mercury: Killer Queen … 'She keeps her Moët et Chandon in a pretty cabinet, let them eat cake she says, just like Marie Antoinette.'

The next day, I trotted off to my beautiful rusty corrugated-iron caravan to write my next best-selling fashion history. The Rusty Shed is my haven. It's decorated in such style, with lots of mirrors (just to bring in extra light, not to gaze at my reflection). I light my small, but perfectly formed (who does that remind you of? LOL), woodburning stove with the baby logs lovingly chopped by our wonderful (and sexy) School Gardener.

On my bookshelf I have several fashion books on Alexander McQueen and Coco Chanel. At my feet, as I write, lies my gorgeous Pomeranian puppy (called Queenie, obvs). Gosh it's so warm and cosy in my Rusty Shed.

PART FOUR

Expiation

CHAPTER 29

Honeytrap

'Well, that first year was certainly a baptism of fire,' said Edward to Lisa as she poured him a glass of cold white wine at the end of the first day of the new academic year. 'Let's hope this one brings a fresh start all round.'

They agreed that they had coped remarkably well with everything that had happened – the drugs business, the chickens, the affair, the anonymous letters, the blogs. In the face of Lisa's deceit, Edward had been admirable. He could not have fought better for the marriage. As a headmaster, he knew that there was always a reason for bad behaviour and that there were at least two sides to every story. He granted that he had made mistakes himself. In one of their rows during the summer, and of course there had been many, Lisa had said 'You took a mistress – the new school. So I needed someone else too.'

There was more than a grain of truth in this. He had indeed put the school before his wife. Returning to a public school was a kind of homecoming for him. He had failed to see how difficult it must have been for her to be in such an unfamiliar environment. Besides, Lisa was so much younger than him. Hadn't they often joked about him declining into the vale of years? And in those first months she had been friendless. Lessons had been learned on both sides.

He wasn't even angry with Sean. 'You're very loveable, who could blame him?' was all he would say. His policy was to downplay Sean. He wasn't important. He was the presenting problem. Lisa was, as Nick had gently suggested, having an early onset mid-life crisis. That was all.

Then there was Queenie. She was their chance to start afresh. Edward disliked all animals, especially dogs, so Lisa knew that the purchase of the puppy, just at the moment when the relationship with Sean was about to go to the next level, was a sign that Edward had realized something was wrong and made a real effort to win her back to him and their life at Blagsford.

As for her persecutor – she couldn't make up her mind as to whether the right term was stalker, troll, cyberbully, identity thief, pervert, or just plain nutter – the saving grace was that none of the letters or blogs revealed the slightest inkling that she had formed a deep connection with a married heart surgeon who had once treated her daughter. The persecutor clearly did not know what was really going on in her life. There was something rather delicious about being accused of everything apart from the one thing that she had genuine reason to feel guilty about.

*　　*　　*

Yum Yum: Naughty Boys

Hi folks, it's been a while since I blogged, so apologies. It's all happening here at Blagsford. You may have seen in the press the news about Naughty Boys dealing drugs. So bad. Well, my devoted husband gave them short shrift. Especially the leader of the pack. Let's call him … Boy A. Well, that's such a shame because I'd been paying a few night-time visits to his room. He's such a sweetie. And he likes sweets, chocolates, and biscuits. Need to give him that sugar high to keep him awake at night so that when I come to his room, and slowly undress …

*　　*　　*

Lisa slammed down the lid of her laptop. She debated whether or not to tell Edward that the blog was getting beyond a joke. Well, his one condition following the end of the affair was that there should be no more secrets. He was more relaxed than she had anticipated.

'Ignore it. We've agreed that it's most unlikely to be a staff member. And none of the boys would dare – they know that the IT manager could trace it back if it came off the school network. It's just some crank sitting alone in his room. Forget about it. Social media is full of these nutters.'

'But Edward, this person clearly knows about my history. That I once kissed a schoolboy, who was under my protection. This is really worrying. It's someone who knows me.'

'Darling, you're being paranoid. There's no mention of SJA. He's clearly just googled the school and found the drugs story

219

online. The scandal is not exactly new news, is it? That was last year's story. Resorting to that is a sign of desperation, I'd say. I bet you a nice meal in town that this will be the last blog. Though you do need to stay offline for a while. Please.'

'But I didn't tweet about the drugs. My stalker usually gleans her info from Twitter.'

'Not entirely. They must have read about the knighthood in an online newspaper. Just ignore it. Keep offline.'

'I don't want to keep offline. Why should my behaviour be controlled by this person? That means they've won. It's not as if I have a blue tick. I'm a nobody.'

'How many times do we have to have this conversation? Lisa, stop tweeting, just for a while. See what happens when there's nothing to write about. Stop giving him ammunition. Or is it that you still want to communicate with someone else?'

'Stop it, Edward. You know I don't. That's all over. You know that. But maybe my troll really is a staff member. After all, they all know about Bertie and the drugs bust. I can't have gossip around the school which says I've abused a boy. That is libel. The only way I can respond to this nutter is to go on Twitter, because I know she's all over my Twitter.'

'You're sounding hysterical.'

'Even if I tweet at four a.m. she's on it. Edward, you don't understand. Twitter is so immediate … there are millions of tweets per second. This troll goes on to my Twitter and pores over it. Most of my followers would never dream of doing that. They just see the latest tweet, and that's it. Someone else tweets, and it all moves on. I'm going to lay a trap.'

'What kind of trap?'

'Well. I'm going to tweet something – I don't know what exactly. I'll leave it up for a bit, and then I'll delete it, but if it comes up in a blog or a letter, then I know that I'm being stalked on Twitter.'

'But you know that already, which is why I want you to take a Twitter vacation. I think you should be careful. I've said it before and I'll say it again. You tweet as though you are sending a private text, but it goes to the whole world.'

'I know what I'm doing, Edward. You just don't understand social media in the way that I do.'

That evening she waited until very late before tweeting. Most people (well in this part of the world, anyway) would be in bed. She would send a tweet, leave it for a minute, and then press delete. If the tweet appeared in a letter or a blog entry, that would give her proof that the letter writer was a Twitter troll, not someone she knew. Then she would quit Twitter. But what to tweet? It would have to be something very specific, but not too much so. No, maybe innocuous would be better. A quotation. An insult aimed at Internet trolls. No, too obvious. What about a photo? It could be a risqué photo, and then quickly deleted. Yes, that was it.

Lisa searched for a jersey, finding a soft, grey cashmere with silver piping. Then she fished out a pair of sheer black hold-up stockings. That will get them going, Lisa grinned. She decided to take a long shower first. The jet of water streamed over her body. She liked the water hot, almost unbearably hot. The bathroom door opened a fraction, and then Queenie padded in. Queenie followed Lisa everywhere. If Lisa left the house, Queenie became melancholic and would lie on the sofa in the hallway until her mistress returned. Edward called it 'The Chaise of Expectation'. Queenie liked to lick the water from Lisa's legs when she came out of the shower. She sat patiently waiting whilst Lisa soaped herself. God, that puppy was so cute.

She roughly towel-dried her long, dark hair, wrapped herself in a soft white bath sheet and headed to the bedroom, Queenie trotting alongside. There was a full-length ivory-framed mirror in the bedroom. Lisa loved that mirror. It was so damn flattering. She put on a black bra, pale pink silk panties, and the stockings, and then the knit. She sat in front of the mirror, with her legs curled to one side, but outstretched. Her legs looked long, muscular and sexy, with just a hint of bare flesh above the stockings. If you looked really closely, you could glimpse the pale pink panties between her thighs. Her hair was tousled messily around her shoulders, but pushed back from her face. You could make out the contours of her large breasts underneath the knit.

She lifted up her hot-pink phone and snapped away. Click, click, click. Yes, that was fantastic. Perfect. The right mix of coy and sexy. That would really irk her troll. Lisa uploaded the photo onto Twitter, with a beating heart. She wrote a caption: Birthday Jumper. She didn't want anyone else to see it. How long should she leave it there? Five mins? Ten? It had to be up long enough for her troll to see it, but what if they were already in bed? What a waste of time. OK, then twenty minutes, she reasoned with herself. What if someone else saw it? The head teacher at the children's primary school? Some old Blagger who might make a complaint to the school? OK then, fifteen minutes. She went down to the kitchen.

Edward, who had been working late as usual, called out, 'Lisa, I'm going up to bed, are you coming?'

'Yes, I'm on my way.'

She deleted the tweet.

And then, as if in anticipation of a new resolution, she tweeted a quotation from the book she was reading. Until she got her proof one way or the other, she would tweet quotations instead of photographs and comments about her own life. Just enough of a Twitter presence to keep the troll nosing about her, but nothing that could be turned against her.

Lisa Blaize @Lisa_Blaize
But the rain is your ghost tonight. #EdnaStVincentMillay.

CHAPTER 30

The Mystery of the Missing Author

Irwin Schrodinger lived in the school with his black cat. There was no Mrs Schrodinger. Prior to the arrival of Queenie, Schrodinger's cat would sit all day on one of Lisa's garden chairs. This drove her mad. It stared at her like a green-eyed monster and left behind long black hairs, which made her eyes stream. She was allergic to cats, though fortunately not to dogs. One of the many improvements that Queenie brought to their lives was the exclusion of Schrodinger's cat from the White Garden.

Schrodinger himself was always polite to Lisa's face, but she knew that he was no friend. He was extremely clever and charming, but the chip on his shoulder was the size of the Rock of Gibraltar. Was it because he was Glaswegian, or because he was Jewish, or because he was working class? All three, probably. So what was he doing in a school full of braying public-school boys? In some respects, he reminded Lisa of Chuck. He was the kind of honest, blunt, plain speaker that was really anything but. Schrodinger seemed as out of place at Blagsford as American Chuck had at St Joseph's – Chuck had followed his heart when he had married Liverpudlian Milly, though it wasn't clear why he had chosen to stay there after they divorced. What, then, was the explanation for Socialist Schrodinger's presence at Blagsford?

Lisa guessed that he was there partly because it gave him a chance to moan about inequality while drawing a good salary, but

224

also because he genuinely loved teaching physics to a higher level than GCSE science, and there were more opportunities for that in a private school. There was no doubting his ability as a classroom teacher, or that the pupils adored him. Once he was on a roll, whether with the boys in the lab or at a staff meeting, everyone was mesmerized by his cruel wit, rendered all the more effective by the soft lilt of his Scottish accent, long since softened by his move away from the Glasgow tenements.

Unusually for a physics teacher, he was also the master who directed the Michaelmas Theatricals. The boys would do anything for him. It was a long-standing Blagsford tradition that a select group of boys moving up to the Lower Sixth would return to school a week early and begin rehearsals for a play, performed at the end of the second week of term.

He normally put on a comedy. The previous year, *Entertaining Mr Sloane* had been a huge hit. But he also loved his Shakespeare. For the new headmaster's first anniversary, he announced that it would be *Othello*. An extremely risky choice. Eyebrows were raised in the staffroom. But Schrodinger pulled it off. It was a very simple production. All the cast were dressed in black, except for Othello, who wore white. In between scenes, a punk song was played very loudly: 'I am the fly in the ointment.' It was an outstanding success. It was generally agreed to be Schrodinger's best show. Lisa loved it. It was the first school drama production that she had seen. She was disappointed that Schrodinger had not asked for her help in the wardrobe department. Even if they clashed, she still would have loved to offer help.

Still, she had work to do. She was finally making progress with her second book. *Lipstick and Lies* had been quite academic, and, though very well received, not exactly a bestseller. 'It's quite niche,' she had often found herself saying, defensively, at dinner parties (on the rare occasions when Edward's guests, the 'important parents' and 'influential Old Blaggers', deigned to ask her what she did). But the second book was going to be more middlebrow. This was her chance for a breakthrough to a much bigger audience.

Father Misty was determined to help her along. He knew that she needed the spur of a deadline to get some material into shape. So he arranged for her to present work-in-progress at a bookshop in his Leicester parish. 'To be honest, Blaize, they can't get any real authors to Leicester, so I offered them you,' he teased her.

The husband and wife team who ran the little independent bookshop were lovely. They had remortgaged their house to fund the business, and Father Misty was devoted to them.

She was to stay with Misty in the vicarage (seventies, redbrick, not exactly a perk of the job). Though the plan was for her to talk about her new book, they also hoped to sell a few copies of *Lipstick and Lies*. The talk was advertised as being about Alexander McQueen. There was a lot more interest in him following his death by closet. Misty met her at the station, happy as ever to see her.

'Blaize, how the hell are you? If you think I'm going to call you Lady Chamberlain, you can fuck off. Are all those Blagsford fuckers curtseying to you yet?'

'As if. Gorgeous to see you. How's my godson?'

'Can't wait to see you. Hoping you have presents. But first, we'll pop into the bookshop, I've got something to show you. You'll think it's hilarious.'

On the way from the station, Misty filled her in with the fortunes of the bookshop. The owners, Eliza and Benedict, had persuaded a local businessman to sponsor their literary evenings.

So Benedict had splashed out on a huge banner listing all the authors who were to be doing talks that autumn.

'Cost him a fortune, but he's over the moon with it. It's outside Sainsbury's, so let's have a look.'

They drove up to the supermarket, and there was Benedict's banner. It was huge, with ten author pictures and their names listed underneath.

'Fantastic author pic, Blaize. You look really good for fifty.'

'Very funny. Remind me not to invite you to my fortieth.'

Father John Misty was on a roll.

'The only trouble with that as a piece of publicity is that the names are all together at the bottom. You can't tell who's who. A lot of people tonight are going to be disappointed that you're not that old bat.' He pointed to a picture of another author, who had the look of being well past her prime.

'Thank you, dear sexist pig.'

'Ha ha. It's so good of you to come. I know how busy you are. Thanks, sweetie.'

'I wouldn't miss this gig for the world. Has Benedict got the salt and vinegar crisps in?'

'Yeah, and the crappy wine. Have I told you how much I love you?'

'Yes. You always do.'

Lisa's talk went down a storm, though she only sold six copies of *Lipstick*. Still, the evening was a boost, and she went home the next day determined to spend as much time as she could in her shepherd's hut, finishing the second book.

It was the first time she had left Queenie overnight. She couldn't believe how much she missed her. Her coal-black eyes and white fur. That 'I want a walk' look with her head cocked on one side. It was like leaving a baby behind.

As soon as she approached the door, Queenie began yelping. She threw herself onto Lisa, licking and jumping and rolling over to be tickled. The children ran down and laughed at Queenie's crazed jumping about. They told her how Queenie had slept on the Chaise of Expectation all night, waiting for her to come home. They had all missed her. George especially, who hugged her tightly.

'If Daddy snores, you can come into my bed tonight,' he whispered.

'OK, that's a deal.'

Lisa heard a loud pop as a champagne cork was upended. Crikey, I should go away more often if I get this sort of homecoming, she thought. Edward handed her a cold glass of fizz.

'I frosted your glass in the freezer, just the way you like it.'

'Thanks, lovey. I had a great time, but it's good to be home.'

Lisa's mobile phone rang. It was Misty.

'I've just walked through the door. What's up? You missing me, already?'

Edward couldn't hear Misty, but he saw Lisa's face whiten.

'God, you must be joking. How weird. What does Benedict think? OK, yes, send me the article when it comes out. Or I could look it up online. Thanks for letting me know.'

'What is it, darling?'

Lisa took a large gulp of her fizz.

'Bit of a long story, but the bookshop man had this enormous banner with all the author photos on, advertising the season's talks. It was hanging on a fence outside Sainsbury's. Huge great thing, made of plastic. Well, Misty just told me that someone has cut me out. My face isn't there. Just a huge hole. It's going to make the local news. How strange.'

Edward was already at his laptop.

'My God, look at this. "Mystery of the Missing Author": you've hit the big time, Lady Chamberlain. Breaking News on the Home page of the *Leicester Mercury*.'

'Apparently Benedict the lovely bookshop man is very upset about it. Mind you, he spent a lot of money on that banner. Who on earth would cut me out, and why? Do I have enemies in Leicester too?'

'Well, unless John Misty is playing a double game and is really your frenemy, I'd say it's some lad who couldn't resist a picture of a gorgeous girl. I wouldn't worry about it. It's quite amusing, really. It will be on his bedroom wall. And it'll give your man's author talks some great publicity – he probably cut it out himself just to get the story in the news.'

'It's very kind of you to say so, but I'm not some teenager's fantasy of a gorgeous girl – I'm a mother of two in my late thirties.'

'You don't look it.'

'Bit weird though, given everything else that has been happening lately. You don't think it's related to the troll, do you?'

'No, I don't. It's all gone really quiet on that front. No more letters, and I checked before you came home – nothing new on your fake blog. I think they've given up. It's what I told you: ignore and they'll move on to someone else.'

'We'll see. And all quiet on the school front?'

'Yup. Things have really settled down. People don't like change, but they're getting used to us. It's all working out fine. The only complaint was that Queenie is chasing Schrodinger's precious cat. I had to apologize. I've got to be nice to him since the play was such a success. It's made up for last year's sulk when I made him stand down as head of sixth form.'

Lisa took the dog for a walk to show that she wasn't going to apologize for the new member of their family. The fresh autumnal evening air and the dog trotting behind her, then veering off to chase a squirrel or a bird, helped her to erase from her mind the image of a man cutting around her face with enormous blunt scissors.

She posted her ritual tweet before bed. All through the first half of the year, it had been something for Sean. Now it was just a quotation.

 Lisa Blaize @Lisa_Blaize
You know, we can all be discarded quite easily.
#McQueen.

CHAPTER 31

The Evening Shift

Dicky and Belinda were having one of their talks, while Lisa was pretending to work. Belinda was discussing a dance colleague's recent breakdown as she sorted the bookshelves with Dicky.

'Polly's a divided self, Dicky. She gave up ballroom dancing, and her body and mind collapsed. Someone saw her in the antiques market clutching a disco glitterball.'

'I never liked her. You invested far too much in her. And it didn't work. You ought to try to look after yourself, Belinda. Can you stick *Heart of Darkness* next to *The Manly Art of Knitting?*'

'Dicky, where's the logic in that?'

'That's the point. I like mixing things up a bit. It adds a degree of the unexpected, the bizarre. And it keeps me from dying of boredom. Imagine Onions' face when he spots the knitting book with the camp cowboy on the jacket cover snuggled up to Conrad. He's bound to make a complaint.'

Belinda giggled. Peter Onions was the cleverest man in Blagsford. He had a love/hate relationship with Dicky, who loved to wind him up.

'Anyway, back to poor Polly. You have to be embodied, otherwise you turn in on yourself. She always craved male attention; the male gaze. All those sequins turned her mad. Oh how people suffer! Dicky, I've just finished Walpole's *Vanessa*, and thought:

Why are you torturing yourself you silly girl?! I'm just so exhausted by this autistic culture. It's such nonsense.'

'You see, Belinda, whenever I feel sad I just go and buy myself some more china.'

Lisa was really loving their banter, but she forced herself to concentrate on her work. She had to admit that her heart was no longer in her long-planned book about the art of dressmaking as a route to freedom for downtrodden women. Inspired as she had been by the Venetian women prisoners and their tailor's workshop, the seed sewn on her honeymoon now seemed as far away as the honeymoon itself. She was hatching a new idea – something more commercial, less self-righteous. But it was early days for that. For now, it was heaven to eavesdrop on Bee and Dicky. She'd pay good money to listen to these two in conversation.

Belinda executed a perfect pirouette as she whirled down to Modern Fiction, but she spotted a malingerer hovering over Classics and came to a halt, feet at First Position.

'Please may I help you, sir? Cash only. Hole in the Wall outside the Co-op.'

'Just browsing', he replied sheepishly.

'Browsing,' she echoed in her best Mary Poppins' voice.

With a despairing backward glance at Lisa, he bolted out of the Albion, leaving Belinda and Lisa helpless with laughter.

'Oi, Sharon and Tracey, what are you two laughing at?' Dicky loved to tease Lisa, especially since she had become Lady Chamberlain.

'It's Bee, she's outrageous. You're not going to have any customers if you keep leaving her in charge.'

'Well maybe I'll leave you holding the keys, and see if you have more success. By the way, that man was staring at you Lisa, I think you'd be great for business. Especially if you keep wearing those high heels.'

Belinda glared at Dicky. She did not approve of that sort of talk. Lisa, conversely, rather liked a man who noticed a woman's shoes. She crossed her slim legs, revealing just an inch of stocking top, whilst Dicky smiled appreciatively. It was true about Dicky; he really did have very attractive nostrils.

'I'll mind the shop for you if you're stuck. You know I would. But not during the day, as that's when I work best. I could do a couple of evening shifts for you.'

*   *   *

The Albion was hosting a poetry evening for three local writers. Lisa and Belinda were helping out. They laid out the chairs, moved the tables back, and poured the wine. A handful of people turned up, the lights were lowered, and the programme began. The first poet, a young, blonde woman with a beautiful sonorous voice, began reading. There was not a sound. She held everyone in the room spellbound as she read a poem that turned a memory of trauma into a thing of beauty.

This is it, Lisa thought. This is what is real. This is happiness. Words always had the power to soothe, to console, to inspire. Poetry had always been her favourite genre. She loved the intensity and the concentration of the language, the way that a word or a phrase could unexpectedly resonate – touch something deep inside. Keats, Donne, George Herbert, Katherine Phillips were her favourites. Lisa always kept stacks of poetry books beside her bed, so that if she were stressed about Emma or work, she could take succour. Now here was this brave girl, standing in front of her, baring her soul, sharing her stories and her grace.

Lisa had offered to lock up the shop. Dicky was racing off to see an old friend for a pint, and Belinda had left early to feed Onions' cat. Onions had taken off to the country for half-term, so, once again, Lisa had missed her opportunity to meet him. He always supported the Albion poetry evenings. Yet another of his legendary talents was that he was himself a published poet of distinction. It was such a shame that she kept missing him.

Once everyone had finally left, Lisa began clearing the wine glasses. The tables could be left until the morning. She turned off all the lights, including the switch for the twinkly fairy lights that lined the ceiling squares. In the darkened room, she was even more aware of the smell of the books, musty, mildewed, and the stench of red wine. It was deathly quiet. So dark. She tiptoed over to the old piano that Dicky had just had re-tuned, and played a few bars of 'Moonlight Sonata' just to break the eerie silence. My God, it was a pre-war Bechstein. On the top of the piano were piles of shabby paperbacks, and a stack of jazz CDs. She hadn't played for a while, and she was definitely rusty, her fingers not stretching as well as they should. It felt strange playing to an empty, now cold, shop, very strange. Was she trying to prove to herself that she wasn't frightened? She closed the lid of the piano and slid the stool underneath.

Maybe she should just check the loo, before she locked up? Lisa crept towards the back of the shop. What a shame that she had left her mobile at home, and couldn't use the torch app. The loo was on the left and the kitchen on the right. The kitchen was plunged in darkness, but she could see a hazy light coming from the direction of the loo. It was probably the glow from an outdoor lamppost, but she felt that she should double-check, just in case.

Her high heels clicked against the wooden floorboards. They gave her confidence. The *tip-tap tip-tap* of heel against wood. She should treat herself to piano lessons. She had been a promising student, but only had a cheap Argos keyboard with which to practise. So little time when she had children and a home to run. Her thoughts meandered to her family. Dearest Edward, her sweet children, her little dog.

Her meditations were suddenly interrupted by the creak of a door. It must be coming from outside. Then, as she made her way to the back of the shop, she saw that the loo door was closed, and there was a dull, yellowish light shining from underneath it … was there someone in there? There couldn't be. Why didn't they make a noise, or make themselves heard when she was playing the piano? Should she knock, or wait for the loo to flush, or should she run? She gave it a few seconds and then pushed the door gently to see whether it was locked. No, it was giving way. It was OK. No one was there. Someone had left the light on. She loved Dicky's loo, the walls embellished with different literary quotations. She smiled, switched off the light, felt for the keys, and turned.

And there he was, standing in the doorway of the kitchen.

CHAPTER 32

Hit and Run

'I swear to God, Bee, I was terrified.'

'I'm not surprised. Lordie, I wish I hadn't left you, but you know how Onions feels about Cecil. He's his world. I once forgot to feed Cecil, and Onions didn't speak to me for three months. I'll never make that mistake again. And Cecil is so cold. He shows not a morsel of gratitude ...'

'Bee, concentrate. I'm telling you. Schrodinger was in the kitchen, in the pitch black, staring at me. I thought he might have had a knife.'

'Well, he clearly didn't, because you wouldn't be sitting here with me in the Albion bookshop, drinking tea.'

'Of course he didn't have a knife. He was looking for his bloody cat. What IS it with Blagsford and cats? I'm not a cat person, Bee. They're so selfish. Look at Queenie. Now, there's loyalty for you, always a jaunty tail wagging, and always a morning lick to wake you up.'

Belinda looked at her darkly.

'That's enough of that kind of talk. Now you're the one going off-piste. Maybe Schrodinger WAS just looking for his cat. God knows, Matilda is always wandering off into my neighbour's boat. She's pathologically disloyal.'

'OK, but a mile from the school?'

'They've just published some research using GPS trackers, showing that cats often wander two miles from home,' said Belinda with a knowledgeable twinkle in her eye.

'But the way he was looking at me. It was dark, and quiet. He could have murdered me.'

'So what did he say?'

'That he liked my piano-playing. That he didn't know that I was musical. Weirdo.'

'Lordie.'

'Anyway, I saw him out and locked the shop, and we actually cycled back to school together. I wasn't going to let him see that he had spooked me.'

'Did you tell Edward?'

'Of course. He thought it was hilarious, and said I should take up the piano again. Sometimes, he really misses the point.'

'Keep an eye on Schrodinger, Lisa. And tell Dicky. He won't like the thought of a man lingering in his shop, and he's very fond of you.'

'Is he? How does one ever tell. Grumpy sod. Not a word of thanks for shutting up shop.'

'That's just his way. Don't mind him. He never shows gratitude to me, but then for my birthday he gave me a first edition of *Tender is the Night*. I looked it up on Abebooks, and it's worth at least £600. It made me feel awful. I don't help him for money or for favours. I do it because I love him, and I love the Albion. I worry that *Tender* will get damp in the boat.'

'I know you do,' Lisa said, soothingly. Bee sometimes got one in her bonnet when she talked about money, because she hated money and greed and unkindness. Lisa sometimes thought Belinda would be happiest if everyone went back to bartering.

'Leave *Tender* here. I'll look after it. Bee …'

'Yes.'

'You're a really good friend. I need friends in Blagsford. I miss my friend Jan, and John Misty. I miss all my sisters. I'm a girl's girl, Bee.'

'I know.'

*   *   *

And then he texted.

> Hi Lisa. How are you?

> I'm fine. What a surprise!

> What's the news?

> Well, apart from someone cutting out and stealing a large photo of me, I'm doing OK.

> Yeah. I saw that article you posted on Twitter. I just happened to be in the area and couldn't resist!!!!

> LOL. I had my suspicions.

> Call me if you need me.

238

> TY. Nice to hear from you.

Lisa was puzzled. She had no idea why Sean had suddenly contacted her. It was against the rules that they had set for themselves, but she couldn't bring herself to ask him to desist. She felt a stab of happiness in her heart when his name flashed up on the screen. But it saddened her, too. She had got used to being without him. She sent a DM to Misty, who was not amused.

DM from @FrJohnMisty: Thin end of the wedge, Blaize. Don't do it.

DM from @Lisa_Blaize: What have I done?

DM from @FrJohnMisty: Well, you answered him. Have you told Edward?

DM from @Lisa_Blaize: Not yet.

DM from @FrJohnMisty: Well you must. I told you that if anything new comes in, you must tell Edward. It's only fair.

DM from @Lisa_Blaize: I know. OK. I'll tell him. But why has he contacted me now? At this moment?

DM from @FrJohnMisty: You don't think it was him who took the banner photo?

DM from @Lisa_Blaize: No, of course not. He was joking. He always jokes. Like you. Any news on picture thief?

 DM from @FrJohnMisty: No, nothing. Benedict is loving all the fuss though. There was another article about it this week, saying that you had taken it well, and saw the funny side. I still think it's a bit sinister.

 DM from @Lisa_Blaize: Me too. Anyway, got to dash. Speak soon. Love you.

 DM from @FrJohnMisty: Be good, Blaize. And do tell Edward about the texts.

*   *   *

'Mummy, I've got something to tell you.'

It was little George.

'What is it, darling? You can tell me anything. Are you in trouble at school?'

'No, it's worse than that. You're going to be really angry with me.'

'Well you won't know until you tell me. I'm never angry with you, George.'

His brown eyes filled with tears, glittered like diamonds.

'It was me. I did it.'

'Did what?'

'I killed the chickens. Emma said it was my turn and I forgot to put them in, and I was too scared to tell you. I'm sorry, Mummy. It was all my fault.'

Lisa breathed. She pulled him into her arms.

'George, it's fine. They were just chickens. They were rubbish layers, anyway, and they were encouraging rats. It's OK. I was going to get rid of them. But I'm glad you told me. You must always tell me about things on your mind. And here was I thinking you'd bitten a girl in the playground!'

George laughed. Lisa sniffed his hair, her baby. So beloved, so sensitive. She was relieved though. She hated the thought that someone had taken out their dislike of her on her hens. It was just a mistake. Poor George.

*   *   *

Edward smiled when she told him.

'I told you that it was just a coincidence. You mustn't let these letters and blogs make you paranoid. Otherwise they've won.'

'I know. You're right. It was so silly of me.'

'The staff like you, darling. Look at the turn out for the Gatsby party. They know that your position here is a difficult one. And they all gave you a big round of applause when I said that you didn't choose to be first lady, you've taken on a role that you didn't ask for, and made it your own.'

'Schrodinger was a no-show. I just think some of them have such an old-fashioned notion of the role of a headmaster's wife – they expect me to shut my mouth and give tea parties, instead of being myself, let alone having my own life, my own career.'

'Well, quite a few couldn't make it. Don't read anything into it, Lisa.'

'OK. I'm taking the dog for a last walk.'

Lisa walked around the lake in the dark night with Queenie at her heels. She didn't bother with a lead and collar. Queenie was such a good puppy, she would run a few yards forward and then stop and turn her head, waiting for Lisa. They would walk past the tennis courts and the cricket nets, and then back towards the house via the lake.

It was a cold, foggy evening in Blagsford. The autumn trees were black skeletons; the huge weeping willow dipped its gnarled branches into the lake's shallows. There was no one else about. Trees were noisy at night, branches crackled, leaves swooshed. Then out of the lake, Lisa saw a large, luminous white shape looming towards them … *hisssssss*. Queenie took one look and bolted.

'Queenie. It's only the swan. Come back. It's OK.'

The fog had thickened, and Lisa could barely see in front of her, but she could smell the earth, dank and rich.

'Queenie … Queenie.'

It wasn't like her dog to go so far ahead. She had been hissed at by the swan before now. Maybe she was frightened of the fog. It was pretty spooky. Lisa walked quickly past the lake, her writing hut, and onto the lawn. She was starting to panic. She couldn't see Queenie. She started to run.

Beyond the lake there was a private, secluded road. The gate should have been shut tightly, but she saw that it was wide open. She carried on calling for Queenie, her voice becoming panicked and shrill. Then she saw it. A flash of white, a glare of orange and the screech of wheels. She pulled out her phone, stabbed a number into it and screamed for Edward. 'Quick, come down, It's the dog. Hurry.'

Edward would make it right. All would be well. Lisa hurried to the road, but the car had long gone. Deadly silent. Then she heard Edward shouting her name, and shouting for Queenie. He was at her side in a flash, but they could see nothing in the dark and fog. Lisa was screaming Queenie's name over and over again.

Maybe she's run onto the sports field. It's so dark. So cold. She doesn't like to be far from me. She'll be frightened.

'Your phone, Edward. Turn on the torch.'

They could see nothing. Edward fumbled with the button that activated the torch.

The beam from their phones shone around the bushes, not reaching the open fields beyond the road. Edward was shouting Queenie's name.

'There. What's that over there?'

Then they saw her – a white blob lying in a ditch on the side of the road. So small. There was a sudden moment of calm. Then Edward had her in his arms, his blue shirt was stained with blood. He carried her to Lisa.

'Edward, I need to call the vet.'

He shook his head.

'It's too late.'

*　　*　　*

They buried her in the garden. Lisa didn't know how one could feel so much pain over an animal. How could it be possible? Her life had been so brief. They had barely known her. But in a short time, she had brought so much love. The driver hadn't even stopped.

Most people in the school were shocked. An announcement was made in assembly. The schoolchildren had loved to see Queenie running around the grounds, chasing squirrels. On more than one occasion, Queenie had interrupted one of Edward's important managerial meetings, which always helped to relieve the tension. The senior management team had come to love her. Even Schrodinger had sent his condolences, despite the fact he was no doubt relieved that his cat could now reoccupy the garden chair. The Chamberlain children were devastated. George blamed the swan. He was the one who had frightened her into bolting.

Lisa was hit the hardest. Queenie had loved her the most, especially as they were together in the daytime when the children were at school, and Edward at work. Lisa felt choked with grief. It felt worse than almost losing Emma, than losing Sean. Queenie was a symbol of all she had lost. She wanted out.

'Edward, we need to leave. Can't you apply for a new job? I hate Blagsford. Everything has gone wrong for us since we came here.'

'But I really love this job. Every day is different. I don't want to leave. They treat me really well, and the primary school is fantastic for the kids – they're sure to get into the grammar. I don't want to move them. You're still upset about Queenie. Just give it a bit more time.'

'First the chickens, and then Queenie. What next? Will they poison my coffee?'

'Don't be melodramatic. George forgot to lock the chickens away, and Queenie bolted because the swan frightened her. These things happen.'

'But the driver of the car. We never found her. She never came forward. It was a woman driving that car. I think it was Bertie's mum.'

'Lisa, you can't make accusations like that. You're being absurd.'

'It was her car. Typical Chelsea tractor. Another one of those revolting blondes. She killed my dog because you busted her druggy son. Who next, Edward? Who next?'

CHAPTER 33

Blaze

She buried herself in her work. She was on fire with her idea for something more commercial. At last the words were flowing. The shepherd's hut was a perfect sanctuary, away from the goldfish bowl. Every morning, she lit the woodburning stove and then sat at her desk working on the new book. The nights were drawing in, but the woodburner worked like a dream. It was so easy to doze off.

The absence of Internet in the hut was a blessing, and the work flourished. She still missed Sean. To comfort herself she read a biography of Laurie Lee, just to feel close to him. She read about the meeting on the beach with Lorna Garman, and then the obsessive relationship that ensued. Lisa was becoming obsessed with Lorna. What did she have that made men so crazy about her? First Laurie Lee, then Lucien Freud.

Lorna was rich, glamorous, and married. According to her daughter, she was utterly 'wild and rampant'. Those who met her spoke about her feline grace. She was a tiger, a lynx. Freud painted her in an ocelot coat, confirming the image. Laurie Lee and Freud found her irresistible. She broke their hearts, and returned to her husband, becoming a fervent convert to Roman Catholicism.

Lorna's husband, a kind and gentle intellectual, was nine years older than his wife. He knew about the affair, but turned a blind eye in the hope that she would get Laurie out of her system. In time, she would return to him. The daughter she had by Laurie Lee said: 'She was nature herself: savage, wild, romantic and without guilt.'

Lee rented a green caravan close to where Lorna lived with her husband and children. Lorna would drive her chocolate-brown Bentley to the green caravan, bearing gifts: a tambourine, armfuls of flowers (lilacs, red roses, orchids, and lilies), sweet cakes, wine, paintings, music (Beethoven's *Spring Sonata*), rabbit, mushrooms, bananas, honey, eggs, books and poetry. She wore a green dress with a long line of seductive buttons down the front. Laurie Lee would play his violin in the candlelight, whilst Lorna (a gifted cook) prepared salmon and potatoes. They made love, over and over again. He wrote about her, over and over again.

Lisa pondered too about the horrors of love. Lorna and Laurie's affair was as tortured as it was passionate. That kind of love can't last. Laurie knew that. He knew that the illicit nature of the affair exacerbated its magic.

Lisa was drifting off to sleep, his beautiful words, quoted in the biography, entered her dream.

> *Her movements under me are a deft delight and for the first*
> *time in my life I experience the true measure and grace of*
> *love.*
> *Her mouth is like a lamp. She takes off some of her clothes*
> *and slips into the bed beside me.*
> *She is extremely ripe and soft yet strong under one's thighs.*
> *Her hair is sweet-smelling. I swim in her mouth and her nails*
> *in my flesh are like a bitter wind.*
> *It is a paradox that the best way to preserve the thrill and*
> *intensity of love is to put as much distance between myself*
> *and the beloved ...*

The wind and rain whipped around and rocked the green hut. A storm raged, but, inside, the lovers felt secure in the warm shadows of the caravan. Lisa was dreaming of making love, but was it with Edward or with Sean? She felt so sleepy, so content, so cocooned. A warm rush of air coursed through her body. It was all so peaceful. Why could she hear shouting?

*   *   *

She felt a cold blast of air, as a tall figure loomed in front of her and dragged her out of the shed onto the grass. In a haze, she saw figures running towards the lake, with buckets, and others sprinting with fire extinguishers. Where's the fire, she thought? Then she saw black smoke billowing out of the hut.

The head of maintenance picked her up and carried her away from the hut. She was freezing, and started to shiver uncontrollably. Edward was shouting instructions, and was also on his phone. A siren wailed in the distance.

'Come via the back entrance and past the lake, that's quickest,' she could hear him say. He was very calm.

Someone put a blanket around her shoulders, and she watched, helplessly, as the school gardener sprayed a fire extinguisher inside the hut. There was foam everywhere, over her eighteenth-century century blue velvet chair, her antique desk, her beautiful Georgian prints.

'Get my book, my notebooks,' she cried. 'That's all that matters.'

A fire engine screeched down the path and onto the lawn. There must have been eight of them. But they couldn't put out the fire. The fireball was trapped between the back of the stove's fireplate and the corrugated iron of the outside of the hut. Two firemen began spraying underneath the hut, desperately trying to get to the fire. Inside, the back wall was being ripped to shreds. They were coming at it from both angles, and then they finally had it under control.

'You were lucky,' the chief officer said later. 'In five minutes the whole hut would have exploded. It was like a tinderbox in there. It took nine extinguishers to put it out. I will have to fill out a form about this. This could have been a terrible tragedy.'

Lisa did not feel lucky right at that moment. She surveyed the damage. The men's filthy boots had ruined her rugs, vases and glasses were smashed, the furniture blackened and stinking of smoke. The water damage was almost as bad as that from the smoke. The only things unscathed were her notebooks, which Edward had saved. Behind the stove she saw the remnants of the back wall. It had peeled away like paper. There appeared to be white cotton wool between the charred wooden struts behind. She took out her phone and took photographs of the damage.

'Sheep's wool,' the fire officer confirmed. 'For insulation. Made our job a lot harder, but it probably did slow down the fire. You need to get onto the manufacturer. That stove was not safe. And it did not comply with fire regulations. Can you tell us what happened?'

'Officer, my wife is in shock. Could we leave it for a bit? She's freezing.'

'Of course, anyway, I need to check everything over for our report. Go and have a cuppa, and we'll speak to you soon. You were very lucky, though. Your guys here did a great job.'

Back at the house, Edward told Lisa how he had glanced out of his study window to see smoke billowing out of the hut. He had been about to go to London for a consultation at the Department of Education, so it was a miracle that he saw this just before he was due to leave to catch the train.

Lisa was white with shock.

'I was asleep. I could have been killed by the smoke fumes. That's not the way I want to go, Edward. Someone just finding a charred slipper like poor Zelda Fitzgerald. That's my worst nightmare. I just don't understand how it caught fire.'

'They'll get to the bottom of it. Sounds as if it could have been a fault with the woodburner. It's only stuff, darling. You're safe, and I rescued your notebooks. That's all that matters. All the work you've done on the new book. It's all there. It's all going to be fine. We're insured.'

'But I won't feel the same about it, Edward. It will take ages to make right. It's a shell.'

'Well, we can buy a new one. Leave it with me. I will sort it out. Darling, I need to cancel my meeting. Give me a moment.'

Lisa turned on her laptop. She plugged her phone into her computer and uploaded a photograph of her burnt-out hut to Twitter. She wrote a caption:

Lisa Blaize @Lisa_Blaize
How many firemen does it take to put out a fire in a shepherd's hut? 8 of them, judging by today.

Almost as soon as she pressed send, a text pinged into her phone, making her jump.

OMG, Lisa, it's me. I just saw your tweet. Are you OK?

DM from @FrJohnMisty: What the fuck happened today?

249

DM from @Lisa_Blaize: Hut caught fire.

DM from @FrJohnMisty: That is not funny. Arson?

DM from @Lisa_Blaize: No, faulty woodburner.

DM from @FrJohnMisty: I think you should get out of Blagsford. Why did Edward bring you? I blame him for all your stress.

DM from @Lisa_Blaize: Don't. He's a saint. He's married to me, after all. Things have settled. It's just a coincidence.

DM from @FrJohnMisty: And the dog? What about him?

DM from @Lisa_Blaize: HER! Well, I did suspect a couple of people who have a grudge against me. But there's nothing I can do to prove it. I'm OK. The blogger has gone quiet. And the Blaggers seem to have calmed down. In fact, the staff have been really nice to me. Even the Glaswegian seems to have a smile for me.

DM from @FrJohnMisty: What about the Doc?

DM from @Lisa_Blaize: Surgeon. He sent me a text after the fire. He saw my photo on Twitter.

DM from @FrJohnMisty: Told you he's still stalking you on Twitter. I'm uncomfortable about this. I'm not going to lie. I pray for you every night.

 DM from @Lisa_Blaize: Good. Someone needs to keep an eye on me. Don't worry. I'm fine!

 DM from @FrJohnMisty: F.I.N.E? Fucked-up, In-denial, Not-happy and Evasive. That's what we clergy think to ourselves when someone describes themselves as Fine. #Justsaying

 DM from @Lisa_Blaize: Stop worrying. I'm going now. I love you.

 DM from @FrJohnMisty: Hmmm.

CHAPTER 34
Suspicion

'We've got to work this out,' said Lisa. 'My life's in danger. Someone in the school has tried to kill me.'

Edward sighed, but she interrupted him before he could start his usual spiel of 'It was all an accident, you're reading too much into coincidences, becoming paranoid – you should be happy because there haven't been any more letters or fake blogs.'

'Edward, if you love me, you'll use that huge brain of yours. You're always telling the students that you can learn about the present from studying the past. Social mobility through education in Tudor times and in ours, all that stuff you're always banging on about when you have to defend your rather old-fashioned ideas about learning. Think of Blagsford as a Tudor court. How would Shakespeare tell the story?'

'Hmmm. I suppose the play's *Othello*.'

'*Othello?*'

'*Othello*. Iago has a professional motive and a sexual one. He's in love with Desdemona. And half in love with Othello. His love turns to hatred very quickly.'

Edward mused for a moment. '"He hath a daily beauty in his life that makes me ugly."'

'What?'

'You remember, that thing he says about Cassio. It's the key to Iago's character. He can't bear beauty or happiness because he's so miserable.'

'OK, so you're saying it's someone who is miserable. What else is driving Iago?'

'Being passed over for preferment.'

'Preferment?'

'Promotion.' Edward paused again. Then he and Lisa spoke at the same instant: 'Schrodinger.'

He had taken the lead in the grumbling about Lisa's business-class airfare to Indonesia. He had been head of sixth form under Camps. A key role. There were rumours that he had been the first to go to the governors with the news that it was Headmaster Camps who had cocked up and taught *Hamlet* when it had been the previous year's A level text. Some said that Schrodinger was a left-wing idealist who wanted the school to be run by a staffroom collective; others that he had been intending to throw his hat into the ring to succeed Camps; still others that he simply liked making trouble for authority figures.

Edward had not judged him. But he had insisted that, if he was to improve the Oxbridge success rate, the head of sixth form would have to be someone who knew the system, who could match pupils to colleges, and groom boys for the dreaded interviews. Not a clever but chippy physicist from Glasgow.

So one of his first acts had been to remove Schrodinger from his senior administrative role and return him to full-time classroom teaching (and directing the play). 'That's where you're so brilliant, Irwin. I've never met a better physics teacher in all my years in education.' Edward wanted his own wing men in the key leadership roles. He had even toyed with the idea of trying to persuade Chuck to come to Blagsford – after all, with the failure of his marriage, the man from South Carolina had no particular reason to stay in the north of England.

'Schrodinger as our Iago?' said Lisa, not convinced, but not unconvinced. 'You know him better than I do, and I admit that he doesn't seem to like me, but I just don't think he's got it in him. Irwin's a bit of a sad stick, but he's not evil. Unless you're exaggerating to punish me for what happened with Sean, some of the stuff in these letters sounds seriously disturbing. Schrodinger's not a madman.'

'Well, nor is Iago. There's something about the smallness of Iago's schemes, their pointlessness, their domestic scale, that makes him so despicable. Maybe Schrodinger wants to drive a wedge between us. He wants to sow the seed of doubt. That's the reality of evil. It's banal, and not all glamorous. There are lots of Iagos in this world. We all know one or two. Wreaking their cruelties in small places, close to home.'

She paused, then said triumphantly: 'That's why he chose *Othello* for the play this term!'

*   *   *

 DM from @Lisa_Blaize: We might have worked it out.

 DM from @FrJohnMisty: Tell, Blaize.

 DM from @Lisa_Blaize: Disaffected physics teacher.

DM from @FrJohnMisty: Plausible. Fat, gay, misogynist?

DM from @Lisa_Blaize: All three.

DM from @FrJohnMisty: Bingo.

*   *   *

Lisa was determined to share her discovery with Bee, whose judgement she trusted implicitly, but on her way to the Albion she got a shock. She was cycling past the Blagsford library, when she saw a blonde girl in her bubble-gum pink Fiat. What the hell is she doing in my car? Lisa thought. Then, with a sharp stab of recognition, she realized that the driver was Freddie. She'd recognize that face anywhere. Fox-face, with those pointed features. Though it was clear that Freddie had grown out her short crop to a shoulder-length bob. How odd that Freddie would buy exactly the same car. Had she finally ditched the Chelsea tractor? For a second, she allowed herself to think that Freddie had ditched the white car because she had killed Queenie. But, no, that was Schrodinger.

Bee took a dim view of Lisa's detective work.

'You're becoming paranoid. That's what Blagsford does to people.'

'I'm not paranoid. And what does that mean?'

'When someone is paranoid they are over full with unreconciled parts of themselves; that is to say parts that are not properly integrated; false selves and broken, or not properly fitted self-parts. Blagsford attracts unfinished people, not planed down,

255

sanded off, dusted down. So many people I meet here feel like half begun projects.'

'Am I like that, Bee?'

'No. You're too sure of yourself. Too honest about your own failings. But you have to be careful, because paranoia is an atmosphere. Largely an atmosphere to *one's self* – what Sartre calls "bad faith" – then that atmosphere spreads – as atmosphere always does. Atmosphere is not containable. It contaminates. There is deep emptiness at the heart of that mode of being.'

'So you think Schrodinger is innocent?'

'I don't know.'

'But what about Freddie? Might she have bought the pink Fiat so the dog can't be nailed on her?'

'I don't think so. Maybe she just admires your style'.

'The next thing you know, she'll be riding around on a Tiffany blue bike called Audrey.'

'It's not all about you, Lisa!'

'I know that. But it's bloody awful to be in this position. Waiting for the next thing to happen. OK, I need to relax.'

Bee pulled down a volume from the fiction bookshelf.

'Read some Barbara Pym. You'll love her. Perfect antidote to the stresses and strains of modern life. The cashpoint's out of cash, so you'll have to write Dicky an IOU.'

'How is Dicky? Haven't see him for a while. Is he still doing his tours?'

'Yes, but he needs a sabbatical. He wants to write a novel. He has first-class honours from Oxford, you know.'

'No, I didn't. He's one of the few people around here who doesn't boast about his academic credentials. A bit like that Onions you always talk about: another unsung literary genius in Bee's Academy of the Underrated.'

'Dicky is a genius,' said Bee firmly, 'and so is Onions. They're a dying breed. There's too much mediocrity in Blagsford. And Dicky is very sexually reconciled. He embraces his feminine side. He's been promoting a book called the *Manly Art of Knitting*. It has a cowboy on the jacket cover.'

Lisa chuckled and popped Pym into her handbag. She could always rely on Bee's good sense and quirky humour. From now on she was going to forget about Twitter and trolls, and focus on her marriage and children.

*   *   *

HokeyCokey @charlieboy
Whats going down @Lisa_Blaize. I saw ur pic u looked hot in your bikini. U still not follow me.

Lisa Blaize @Lisa_Blaize
Why are you messaging me @charlieboy?

HokeyCokey @charlieboy
id date u. u so fit.

Lisa Blaize @Lisa_Blaize
Well, I'm afraid I don't date schoolboys.

Having ended the conversation, Lisa typed Freddie's name into the Twitter search box. She was still feeling suspicious about the pink Fiat business. Freddie's tweets were usually amusing. Freddie was obsessed with a lesbian site called pink velvet sofa. God knows what her son thought about her retweeting all that stuff. Lisa saw at once that Freddie had changed her profile picture. She had dyed her hair brunette. She looked so different with brown hair, almost unrecognizable. Lisa called Edward.

'Come and look at this. It's Freddie. She's grown her hair and dyed it brown. She looks like me. First the car, and now this.'

'She looks so different. It suits her. Blonde women often age badly. Maybe she just wanted a change.'

'She wants to be me, Edward. I still think it's her. I always thought that the letters and blogs were written by a woman, not a man. Schrodinger's a red herring. We got that wrong.'

'Darling, I don't think so. I have something to tell you. I caught Schrodinger red-handed about to pin up a picture of you on the school noticeboard.'

'What?'

'I asked him to hand it over. It was a doctored picture of you with someone else's naked body and the Twitter blue bird perched on your shoulder. It's quite sexy, actually.'

'For God's sake, Edward. That's such an inappropriate comment to make. What did you say to him? Are you going to fire him?'

'I don't think I can. He swore blind that he was taking it down. That one of the boys pinned it up as a joke. But he refused to name the boy. What can I say? I can't call him a liar.'

'Who do you think saw it? How long had it been there?'

'I'm not sure. Probably not very long. It might have been a schoolboy prank, but I think he was lying to me. He went bright pink when I caught him. Blushing is always a sign of guilt. His body betrayed him.'

Lisa's thoughts flashed back to Sean. He often blushed in her presence. The back of his neck would go all red. She called it his 'Lisa Rash'. Gosh, she hadn't thought about Sean for ages. She must be getting over him.

'Well, I'm not so sure. The evidence is pointing to Freddie. She's in love with me. I'm sure of it. She's always trying to seduce me. Remember the flash of underwear and the sexy dance?'

'Lisa, she has a girlfriend. Why would she want another one? And she knows that you're heterosexual. It doesn't make sense. Besides, imitation is the greatest form of flattery. You should be pleased.'

'Well, I'm not. It's creepy. Her new hairstyle and her pink Fiat. She's another Missy Robinson. Remember when she started dressing the same as me? And that time she "accidentally" spilt red wine on my white dress?' Lisa shuddered at the memory. 'I'm going to confront Freddie. I'm not putting up with this.'

Lisa turned back to her laptop and DMed.

DM from @Lisa_Blaize: you free for a drink this week?

DM from @FreddieSwings: Anytime. Name the day.

*   *   *

One of the school ushers brought bad news the next morning, that Doris's son Lee had been arrested for ABH; he'd bottled another man in a pub and had been taken away in handcuffs. Doris was devastated and refusing to come into work. Lisa had never liked Lee, and Doris had not forgiven her for firing her, but she immediately went online and ordered a large bunch of flowers to send to Doris. Whatever else she was, Doris was a mother, and a devoted one at that. She typed in message to Doris:

Sorry to hear your news. Thinking of you. Looking forward to
welcoming you back when you're ready. Love, the
Chamberlains.

*   *   *

On the way to meet Freddie, Lisa bumped into one of Doris's friends, Brenda, in the quad. She asked after Doris, and told Brenda to pass on a message: that if Doris needed anything, she need only ask. Brenda raised a quizzical eyebrow, but assured Lisa (whom she insisted on calling Lady Chamberlain) that she would pass the message on.

Schrodinger was collecting his post from the office and nodded his head towards her in a curt greeting. Lisa looked him straight in the eye, and he blushed a deep red. She wished him good morning, and hurried through the gate, where she unlocked Audrey and tossed her bag into the bike's front basket.

They were meeting at The Coffee Bean. Lisa wanted to keep a clear head for this confrontation. Lisa ordered Freddie's Americano with hot milk on the side and her own extra hot double espresso. She secured a table in the corner of the shop. She felt nervous. She picked up her phone and saw a text from Bee wishing her good luck.

'Hi Lisa. You're looking amazing, as always.'

Freddie was looking very glamorous, in a tight black sweater and black jeans. She sat down beside Lisa, and pulled the coffee towards her.

'Freddie, you look so different as a brunette. It suits you. But it will take some getting used to.'

Privately, Lisa thought the dark hair drained Freddie. She needed to add a few highlights to break up the colour.

'Thanks, Lisa. I was getting so grey, and felt I needed a change. I'll probably go back to blonde, as it seems to be growing back ginger. Not quite sure I'm ready to be Rita Hayworth.'

'Did you come in your new Fiat?'

Freddie blushed.

'Sorry, I'm such a copycat. I love hot pink, and when I saw your car I just had to have one. I got fed up with trying to park the Range Rover in town. You don't mind, do you?'

Freddie smiled, such a smile of warmth and friendliness, that Lisa felt temporarily off guard.

'Guess what? Helena and I are getting married! Will you come to the hen night?'

Freddie's happiness radiated from her. It wasn't simply that she was glowing, she exuded deep contentment and tranquillity too. How could Lisa have suspected her friend? She took her hand and pressed it.

'Freddie, you deserve this happiness. You do. Congratulations! I am very happy for you. For you both. Are you each wearing a wedding dress? Vera Wang?'

Freddie hooted.

'No, it's going to be a very small affair. Helen's wearing some floral thing, it's a bit hideous to be honest. I might go for something simple by DVF. Haven't decided yet. I'd love you to come, but no upstaging the brides, please. Anyway, what did you want to say to me?'

Lisa smiled. 'Nothing. I just wanted to see you.'

CHAPTER 35

Christmas Market

When Lisa got back, she found Edward in his study on the phone. He raised his finger to his lips to shush her. It was clearly an important call. It was probably about the Lee situation. Poor Edward. It was one thing after another in this school of his. She ran upstairs and switched on the kettle. She'd make him a nice, strong coffee.

But it was not about Lee.

Milly, Chuck's estranged wife, had called Edward. She told him the awful news that Chuck had been diagnosed with tongue cancer. And it had metastasized. Stage Four. It was not looking good. Milly said that Chuck was in good spirits. He was at home, on indefinite leave from SJA. He had asked Milly to make the phone calls, so that he didn't have to endure the pity. He was a proud man.

'I've told him to stay off the Internet. He keeps googling his prognosis, and it's making him feel worse. He's made some Internet buddies that are going through a similar thing, but I'm not sure that's wise.'

'I bet SJA's struggling without him – he was such a great Deputy, you know, Milly. Who's filling in for him? Has Missy Robinson seized her moment?'

'No, she left a while ago – got a deputy headship in Birmingham. I think Chuck said that the new head's brought in someone from outside.'

Edward told Milly about the fire and the dog. It had been ages since they had spoken. After the divorce, Lisa and Edward had inevitably kept more in contact with Chuck than Milly. He realized how much he missed her. She was so no-nonsense.

'Chuck will be upset to hear about Lisa. Sounds like a lucky escape. Thank heavens you were there and got her out in the nick of time. How did it start, Ed?'

'The theory at the moment is a faulty woodburner. She's had a bad time of it, Milly. Anonymous letters, trolling blogs, then the dog, and now this.'

'What do you mean?'

'Oh, some nutter has been sending anonymous letters, based on things she's said on Twitter, and then writing a phony blog pretending to be her. It's quite unpleasant really. Really catty, bitchy stuff. Very personal.'

'Heavens, how sad. You know, Ed, in my experience, people who do that sort of thing are usually not very well.'

'I know, but it's hard getting that through to her. She's becoming paranoid. The latest is that she thinks that the fire was an arson attack. It's nonsense, of course. But that's the thing about these trolls, they can really get to you – especially if you've got a vivid imagination, like Lisa.'

'Well yes, that's one of the downsides of the Internet. People think that they can say anything. It's that thing of not being face to face. People can be so cruel. Ordinary, reasonable people, who wouldn't hurt a fly, become monsters.'

'Anyway, Milly, this is all nothing compared with what Chuck is going through. Does he want visitors?'

'God, no. He's in complete denial. It's one of the stages. But I'll keep you posted, Ed.'

*   *   *

263

Lisa was upset to hear about Chuck. She felt bad that they had lost touch. He had been a loyal friend in the early days of Lisa and Edward's courtship. He had never taken Moira's side in the way that all of Edward's Guildford friends had. He had always looked out for Lisa. Had always made her laugh, with his ribald jokes and teasing. Lisa had come to value honesty and plain-speaking more than ever, given the two-faced backbiting at Blagsford. Say what you like about Chuck, he always spoke his mind and told you what he thought to your face.

Lisa had been surprised to receive Sean's text after the fire. She had wondered if he still stalked her on Twitter, and this latest text rather suggested that he hadn't entirely lost the habit. It was sweet of him to be concerned. She had texted back a light-hearted message saying that she was OK, and making a joke of the 'blaize'. But there was something else that was worrying her.

He had sent another text in which he mentioned her 'Birthday Jumper'. He told her that he had looked at some erotic pictures in his time, but that 'Birthday Jumper' was the sexiest. He clearly did not realize that she had deleted the photo after ten minutes. And why was he looking at her tweets after midnight? She decided not to tell Edward about the latest text exchange.

It was almost a year since their affair had begun, and she had moved on. You can never reheat a soufflé. It was over, and that was best for all concerned. She was putting Sean on the back-burner. Not that he would ever harm her. Not a hair on her head. He was just making sure that she was happy. Poor old Chuck, though. She ought to make contact with him. Why do bad things happen to good people?

*   *   *

On the anniversary of the day when she had bumped into Sean in the Coffee Bean and signed up for Twitter, she decided to take Emma on a mum and daughter trip to Stratford-upon-Avon. It would take her mind off her 'flinglet', as she was now trying to call it, in order to remind herself that it had never really got off the ground.

She had heard that there was a fantastic evening Christmas market on the streets, and that the Christmas lights were beautiful.

It was cold. Lisa dressed herself in black jeans, and a warm black Helmut Lang jersey, and boots. Emma, who was going through a phase of wanting to look like Mummy, put on black leggings, a black polo neck, and a black coat. Her light brown hair was like a halo around her sweet face. On the drive there, they chatted about Christmas, and school, and friends. Lisa switched on Classic FM, so they could sing along with the Christmas carols.

The market was great. There was a stall selling the most beautiful German tree decorations. Lisa, always extravagant, bought lots. She loved Christmas, and they always had five trees in the house – one in the hallway, one in the dining room for Christmas dinner, one in the drawing room with the presents under it, and a little one in each of the children's bedrooms. Two of the decorations had 'Emma' and 'George' carved on them. Perfect. They bought churros to dip in hot chocolate, and listened to the carol singers. Then she stopped still. The carol singers came from a Downs' Syndrome organization, raising money for the families. The children were dressed in scarves, and woolly hats, singing their hearts out. It was the most beautiful thing she had ever seen. Her eyes filled with hot tears. Her aunt had Downs. Lisa had spent a lot of time with her, growing up, and she adored her, like everyone else in her family. Her aunt had not spent one day in care, ever. The family had looked after her like a queen, even after her mother and father had died. Lisa could not drag herself away. 'Look, Em,' she whispered, 'isn't that the most gorgeous thing you've ever heard?'

But Emma wasn't there. Lisa looked around to see what stall her daughter was looking at. She couldn't see her. Don't panic. It's OK, she will be here somewhere. It's Christmas time, the safest time to bring children out at night. She called her name, and then called again. Nothing. Lisa started to shout for her daughter. People were staring at her.

'I'm sorry, but I can't see my daughter. She was here just a second ago.'

Lisa's vision was blurred. It was as if time was standing still. She walked quickly down Bridge Street, and onto the main promenade. Maybe Emma had wandered down towards the huge Christmas tree in the Memorial Garden. Lisa broke into a run. As she approached the bridge over the Avon, she scoured around. Fuck, why was Emma wearing black? Why had she let her wear black? She saw what looked like a halo of bright brown hair. She approached the bridge and then couldn't believe her eyes; hundreds of boy scouts streamed across the bridge in her direction. She couldn't move. It was like being in a horror movie. No, this could not be happening. Hurry up, hurry up. Now she was screaming, and a man approached her.

'I've lost my daughter. Please help me. She's only nine. She was holding my hand, and then I stopped to watch the singers, and she was gone.'

'God! Tell me what she's wearing? What does she look like?'

'Like me. She's dressed exactly like me.'

Lots of people were trying to help. Someone called the police.

266

Lisa was crying now. 'Help me. Help me. She takes medication. I need to find her. Has someone taken her?'

Lisa thought her heart would burst in her chest. Someone's got her. Emma would never disappear like that. She's too sensible. She needed to call Edward, but she couldn't find her phone in her bag. It must have slipped out in the car.

By now, Lisa was almost at the car park on the recreation ground on the far side of the river. She needed to find her phone. She ran and ran, where had she parked? Every car looked the same. Then she saw her shocking pink Fiat 500. But where were her car keys? Who cares? She never locked the doors to her car.

Then she saw. Emma. She was sitting in the front seat, shivering.

'Mummy, Mummy, I lost you, so I came back to the car. Why are you crying?'

Lisa grabbed her and pulled her close: 'God, I thought I'd lost you. Good girl, good girl. You did the right thing. Come with me, Em.'

She ran back to the nice man who had looked so concerned.

'I've found her. She made her way back to the car. Thank you for helping me.'

'No problem. She does look just like you. Happy Christmas.'

CHAPTER 36

'What You Know, You Know'

Lisa was glad that she could tell Edward after the event, in the knowledge that there was a happy ending. Thank God she had left her phone in the car and not rung him in a panic. He looked horrified when she told him, particularly when she described that terrible moment when the boy scouts filled the bridge, blocking her way.

Emma couldn't see what the fuss was about.

'Stop kissing me, Mummy. I'm fine. I'm here.'

After the children were tucked into bed, Edward poured Lisa a glass of cold Chardonnay. They sat by the fire. Neither spoke. Kind, kind eyes, Lisa thought. Never a word of reproach nor criticism.

'Edward, for just one minute I thought ...'

'Don't say it. It's OK, it's all over.'

'It was the very worst thing that has ever happened to me in my life. I now know the true meaning of fear.'

But she felt calm. The first time she had felt at peace since the move to Blagsford. So much had happened since the day that the letter had dropped through the door. But she had survived. They had survived. Her family. Her love.

Now all that mattered was giving the children a Christmas to remember.

*   *   *

There was another surprise to come. This time for Edward. Lisa had arranged, secretly, for Edward's mother to come to Blagsford for Christmas. She knew that she was taking a risk, and that he might be furious with her. Edward wasn't close to his mother. And he hated surprises. He liked always being in control. But she had done it. It had been a while since the children had spent time with their grandmother.

But Edward was always capable of surprising her. When Shirley walked through the door, he let out a gasp and pulled her into his arms. The children, who were in on the secret, giggled, whilst waiting expectantly for GramMa's presents.

'Happy Christmas, Edward,' said Lisa. She was thrilled to see mother and son together. They were so physically alike. He turned to his wife, his eyes watery, one arm around his mother's wide shoulders.

'You're so kind, Lisa. Thank you. Thank you. Sometimes a boy needs his ma.'

Shirley laughed, exactly Edward's laugh, hearty and deep. Then she reached out for the children and held them close. Lisa looked on, and felt a rush of contentment. Family. It was all about family. She would never risk breaking this again. If the golden bowl was a little cracked and tarnished, it could be mended and made stronger.

*   *   *

All through the festivities, GramMa held the children spellbound with stories of Edward's childhood and how he was transformed by his scholarship to the great school. The memories came back to him, and made him determined to deliver on his plan of giving inner-city kids the chance of a Blagsford education.

269

On New Year's Day, Edward drove his mother to the station in Blagsford. When he got home, he told Lisa that he was signing up for Facebook.

'Really? I thought you were always telling your boys to get off Facebook.'

'It's because of Ma – she says that all the extended family Facebook each other. It'll be my way of keeping in touch with my roots.'

When he came to bed that night, he told Lisa that, on setting up his account, he'd not been able to resist seeing if his ex-wife Moira was on Facebook.

'I found her so easily – she seems really happy. She's married her new partner, and they've adopted a little Chinese girl.'

Chuck had not been so lucky. Two days after Christmas, Milly phoned to tell them the news. Chuck had clung on so that they had one last Christmas together. He had died at four a.m. on Boxing Day morning. It was so desperately sad. Milly was being very strong.

She asked them to the funeral. Would Edward do a reading, as he was such a close friend? They had separated, but Milly was doing everything that a bereaved wife would do. She was magnificent. She told them that Chuck had accepted death with great fortitude and good humour. He was a brave soldier, she said. Never complained. Just got on with it. Milly talked too about her lost baby. It had broken them. Chuck had never been the same. It had changed him irrevocably. In her own way, Milly was asking their forgiveness for Chuck having stopped sending Christmas and birthday presents to his godson George. He had made such a good start in performing that duty, but after just two years, he couldn't bear to see the Chamberlains with their children. It was easier to stop sending presents and cards.

Edward prepared a beautiful reading for the funeral. Shakespeare: 'Golden lads and girls all must, as chimney-sweepers come to dust.' Lisa was in tears. She was so moved to see how many people had turned up to pay their respects. Chuck was so popular. His many acts of kindness were shared, his naughty sense of humour, his grief over his son, his sorrow at being too ill to attend the investiture for the MBE that his estranged but still beloved wife Emilia had won for her charity work as chief executive of the Warrington Women's Refuge, awarded in the Birthday Honours list the previous summer.

Edward whispered to Lisa at this point in the eulogy: 'I had no idea Milly was in the same Honours List as me – to be honest, I never looked as far down as the MBEs.'

It was so strange being back with the SJA crowd. Lisa felt like a completely different person. Everyone was so friendly. Happy to see them. Asking after the children. Congratulating Edward on his knighthood. Lisa spent most of the time with Jan. She had missed her old friend. She apologized to Jan for her neglect.

'The problem is you don't go on Twitter, Jan. That's all I have time for with two kids.'

'And you're hopeless on email. And you're always losing your phones and changing your number. We could do old-fashioned letters on snail mail.'

Even Missy, who had come back from Birmingham, was polite. Now that she had her promotion, she seemed more secure, less frosty. To Lisa's surprise, Missy asked to see pictures of the children on her phone, and seemed genuinely interested in their welfare.

Lisa barely had time to catch up with Milly. But as they were leaving, she made sure she said a few words and gave her a hug.

271

'Lisa, thank you for coming. Chuck often talked about you in his final months. And wait, I've got something for you. He gave me this envelope before he died. I have no idea what it is, but he insisted that I give it to you.'

Lisa took the brown envelope. She opened it in the car. There was nothing in it but a sheet of A4 with a colour printout of a photograph.

*   *   *

So it had been Chuck. He had stalked her on Twitter, written those vile letters, posted those nasty blogs. He might even have been @charlieboy, too. He had wanted to drive a wedge between Lisa and Edward for reasons of his own, reasons which would never be fully explained.

'From this time forth he never will speak word,' said Edward, remembering *Othello*. Then he added: '"Haply for I am black." You can take the boy out of South Carolina, but you can't take South Carolina out of the boy.'

Lisa's mouth dropped open. 'Chuck never said anything racist.'

'Not to our face. But not everyone's as colour-blind as you, my darling.'

*   *   *

Chuck had downloaded Birthday Jumper and printed it out. But none of those other incidents – Queenie, the shed, Emma – were anything to do with him. By then, he was ill, and the letters and blogs had stopped coming. The disasters were just coincidences, the kind of bad things that happen to us all at some time in our lives. It all made sense, but it was so sad.

They were silent for most of the journey south, in shock. It was dark and very cold by the time they got home. Lisa went

272

straight to the children's bedrooms, kissed their sleeping fore-heads, and tucked them tightly under their duvets.

She went downstairs. Edward had a glass of wine waiting ready for her. They talked, deep into the night.

'Edward, it's the banality of it all. That's what's so depressing.'

'What do you mean?'

'He had no reason to do it.'

'Hang on a minute, now you think about it, there could be many reasons. I got the headship at SJA when he didn't. And he only found that out in the newspaper – the bloody governors didn't have the courtesy to tell him. Then, for all we know, he might have got the idea that I wrote a lukewarm reference for him when he tried for the post a second time after I left.'

'Come on, that's no reason to get at *me*.'

'His marriage broke up and ours survived. He lost his child and ours survived. It's all making sense. And I did always wonder whether he fancied you. He was always staring at you.'

'That might be because he hated me.'

'Or me. God, I've just remembered something. I forgot to thank him in my leaving speech.'

'So?'

'Banality, as you say – maybe that one little thing tipped him over the edge.'

'Such a tiny thing. To go to such spite after all that kindness – you know, that time when Em was in hospital.'

'Then me getting the knighthood and Milly just a lousy MBE. That was the last straw. I did wonder why he never wrote to congratulate me. And he knew he was ill by then. He had nothing to lose, and the chemo was probably frying his brain.'

Edward opened another bottle, as he warmed to his theme, convinced that he had found all the answers. Then he checked himself. It didn't quite all add up.

'Lisa, one thing surprises me. I can see that he stalked you on Twitter and wrote the anonymous letters. He wanted to destroy our marriage. But the blog. That puzzles me. It doesn't feel like him. And the voice sounded different.'

Lisa stopped him in his tracks, before he could suggest that maybe the blog was by someone else. They weren't going to go down this road now. No more paranoia. What they knew, they knew.

They decided that they would tell no one. Least of all Milly. She had never really known her husband, and what he was capable of, but there was nothing to be gained by enlightening her now. Wives very often don't know what their husbands are capable of. Ignorance really is bliss.

At least the Chamberlains had their answers. No more looking over their shoulders in the school grounds. Although she felt bad about all the innocent people she had suspected, Lisa felt content. No one had really got hurt. But she felt particularly guilty about Schrodinger.

Sean seemed to be doing well. He had stopped tweeting, and had joined Facebook, and had been posting lovely photographs of his family. There was no contact with Lisa, and she wanted it that way. She had truly loved him. But it would never have lasted between them. All she wanted to know was that he was happy. He would always be loved. He was that kind of man. The heart surgeon with the enormous heart.

She had allowed herself a last tweet of the 'meant for Sean' variety.

Lisa Blaize @Lisa_Blaize
She wanted to build her life again on the firm ground of
ordinary pleasures; her children, the garden ...
#LornaGarman

CHAPTER 37

Launch

The burden was lifted. Lisa was back in the swing of things. She rebooted her blog and her column for *City & County*. She wrote like a demon. And just over a year later, as winter turned to spring, she finally published her second book.

It was a biography of Elsa Schiaparelli, who in her time had been as famous as Coco Chanel, but whose fame had not endured so well. She had not already been the subject of a dozen biographies. She was especially known for her knits, and for inventing the wrap dress. She had a fantastic sense of colour. It was one of Schiaparelli's firsts in this area that gave Lisa her title. The biography was called *Shocking: Elsa Schiaparelli and the Invention of Pink*.

Edward, so proud, wanted to throw a lavish celebration, but Lisa wouldn't hear of it. She wanted a small, intimate party in the Albion. Dicky was delighted, and promised to clean the shop. Bee, knowing better, brought her Marigolds and got to work a couple of hours before the party began.

Lisa had invited Schrodinger, mainly to assuage her guilt about suspecting him of being the troll. She had also invited Sean and his wife. She knew that he wouldn't come, but she wanted him to know that he was welcome. Sean didn't text or DM or email. He sent a beautiful, hand-written letter. He told her that he was well, and that he was happy, that he often thought of her, that he would never regret a single minute of their relationship. He made her laugh when he wrote that he had finally met a patient who had survived a Takotsubo heart attack. He could always make her smile. Then he wrote something that made her cry, warm sobs that splashed onto the pages.

You are a remarkable woman, Lisa. I don't think I've ever met anyone as loved as you. You're so warm, so full of life and love and laughter, so giving and selfless. You're a free spirit and Edward knows and understands this, that you need space and a degree of freedom to thrive and be truly happy. I regret nothing, and am so happy that you came into my life.

There would always be a tiny part of her heart that belonged to Sean, the doctor who had saved her daughter, and helped to mend her own heart, and then broken it. Edward was right. She was a better person for having had her heart broken. She folded the letter. It was time to get ready for the party.

*   *   *

Dicky had paid for the piano to be tuned. He and Bee had hung tiny fairy lights across the ceiling, and there were jam jars full of spring flowers; paper-white narcissi, blue grape hyacinth, and late-flowering snowdrops.

They were to drink pink champagne, and Lisa had ordered tiny pink fairy cakes embellished with lobsters. Dicky was delighted to showcase his china plates, but was pretending to be grumpy, complaining about potential breakages. His shop was full, and that made him happy, though he would never admit to it.

Lisa was wearing a Schiaparelli hot pink strapless gown of flowing crêpe de Chine teamed with silver strappy sandals (Lucy

Choi, a better cobbler than Jimmy Choo, in her opinion). Copies of *Shocking* were stacked in huge piles on tables covered in pink silk. Edward's launch present was a pink Montblanc fountain pen for signing.

After the speeches, the guests mingled, sipping their pink fizz. Freddie and Helen, the newly-weds, chatted with Bee, and Lisa could see her publisher, Annabelle, talking to Dicky, and looking rather admiringly at his handsome nostrils. Edward was deep in conversation with Schrodinger. There were others, too. Jan and Milly had come from Liverpool, and there was a good turn-out from the Blagsford staff. To her surprise, many of the students had come along. Best of all, John Misty was there. Her oldest, dearest friend.

He took her aside: 'Blaize, I told you all those years ago that if you lost weight and got yourself some decent clothes, you'd do OK. Now look at you!'

'Fuck off, Misty. How very dare you come along to a launch party about the fashion industry wearing a dog collar and a black dress?'

'And no knickers. Do you want a quick flash? No, I thought not. I'm so proud to be your friend, Blaize. Have I told you how much I love you?'

'You always do, Misty.'

'And you never say it back.'

'I love you, John.'

They chatted briefly about Sean, and Chuck.

'The thing is, Misty, I was too busy for real friends, using Twitter as a substitute for the real thing. I was lonely. But I was too stubborn to make new friends in Blagsford, tarring everyone with the same brush. I look around now, and everyone I love is in this bookshop. Well, almost everyone.'

278

Her eye caught Schrodinger, who was staring at her. She excused herself and approached him.

'Thanks for coming.'

He was clutching a copy of *Shocking*. As she spoke, he blushed to almost the same hot pink as the jacket cover.

'Lisa, Edward just told me about the anonymous letters, the trolling, the fake blogs. God, what you must have been through. It's appalling.'

'It's OK. It's all over now.'

'That time when Edward saw me with the naked picture of you. I was taking it down. I didn't want you to be humiliated. I always looked out for you.'

He blushed again as he spoke, and Lisa finally understood.

'I'm sorry. I thought it was you. I thought you hated me. I got it all wrong.'

'I could never hate you. But why didn't you just ask me, and I would have told you the truth?'

'I do believe it, and I ask thy pardon.'

Schrodinger took her proffered hand and raised it to his lips.

'Just one thing, though,' he said. 'The real reason I came tonight is that I'm a massive fan of Father John Misty and I saw his name on the message board of your Paperless Post invitation. But I've just met him and he's only a bloody priest.' Lisa cracked up.

Strains of Cole Porter tinkled from the piano, and the guests gathered around. Dicky began softly singing 'I Get a Kick Out of You'. Bee was buzzing around, lighting tea candles, graceful and beautiful as ever. Dearest Bee, so full of love. Lisa looked about for Onions, who had promised to make an appearance. She was finally about to meet the famous genius.

279

Edward took her hand. 'Time for us to go. I promised to read to the children. And I promised to phone my mum. We'll help clear up in the morning. Let's go quietly.'

'Yes,' said Lisa, 'and I need to feed the baby.'

As they left in the pink Fiat, Lisa saw a grey-haired man in a long tweed coat walking into the Albion. She saw Bee squeal with delight and throw her arms around him, whilst Dicky glared. It was Onions.

*   *   *

The next morning, her editor rang to thank Lisa for the party, and for introducing her to Dicky. Annabelle and Dicky had clicked, and Dicky had told her about his unpublished novel, *Guys and Dolly Birds*. Annabelle had loved the sound of it, and Dicky had promised to send her the manuscript. Lisa was delighted. Then they chatted about *Shocking*.

'Tweet all the coverage to your followers, every mention helps,' Annabelle told her.

There were good reviews, and interviews on the radio, and even a brief television appearance on Midlands Today. The book – lavishly illustrated, so a great coffee-table present for the style-conscious reader – squeezed into the non-fiction bestseller list. Lisa was thrilled. Before she knew it, she was being interviewed for the cover story of the glossy *Style* magazine of the *Sunday Times*.

Lisa tweeted the news that she was in the Top Ten, together with a message telling her followers to look out for the forthcoming interview. The paper had sent a photographer, who caught her on a bright spring day in the White Garden, looking relaxed and happy, purposeful and professional, and just a tiny bit sexy.

The following Sunday, the picture filled the front cover of the magazine, along with the caption 'Meet the New Face of Fashion History'. She was on her way. A bestselling author, in the public eye.

EPILOGUE

Ratby, Leicester

He was thrilled when he bought his new home after his divorce. It was a two double-bedroom terraced house on a newly developed estate in Ratby, just 4.9 miles from Leicester. It was situated just off the A46, with easy access to the M1 and M69. He was pleased to note, when he got the house particulars, that close by was a Co-op, various small local shops, including a well-stocked newsagent, and a good choice of public houses. He liked a pint after a hard day's work.

The house had gas central heating, double-glazing, a fitted kitchen with hob and extractor fan, and a small, fully enclosed rear garden. The fence was nice and high, with solid panels. Real cosy. Just what he needed after the wife left. There was also a parking slot for his red Skoda. Neighbours nice enough, kept themselves to themselves. He liked it like that.

He spent most of his time in his bedroom on his computer. Easy just to fall into bed when he felt tired. The bedroom was a bit messy. A clothes maiden and a few plastic laundry baskets of unwashed shirts lay behind his swivel chair. He had a nice IKEA desk, though. Plenty of space for his computer and printer. He absolutely loved Halo 3.

The man was bald, slightly overweight, and in his forties. He was dressed in a bottle-green zipped jumper and jeans, with the belt unbuckled. He had spotless hands and neatly cut fingernails.

He wore a watch with a leather strap. His glasses were gold-rimmed. He was clean-shaven.

The bedroom was painted a shade of yellow clotted cream, and adorning the walls were pictures of women. They were mainly celebrities, cut out from magazines or downloaded from the Internet and fixed with Blu-Tack. Every inch of wall space was covered. Cameron Diaz, Angelina Jolie, Holly Willoughby. Gary Brandon liked a classy girl. No Katie Price or Cheryl for him.

In pride of place, over his double bed, was a large photograph that had been cut out of a plastic banner.

He went to his desk. He switched on his computer and entered his password. The Dell Ultra-Sharp 34-inch curved monitor flickered slowly to light and said '*Welcome, Gary Brandon*'. It then revealed a screensaver of Charlize Theron on a South African beach, clad only in a diaphanous black kaftan, curling between her thighs and exposing her ample buttocks. He liked a back view.

He looked down at the colour supplement on his desk. Not his usual hunting ground, he would be the first to admit. He smiled.

He had been waiting for a chance to meet the girl on his wall. It had been dark when he had seen the banner outside Sainsbury's and swiftly slit around her face with his Stanley knife. He didn't bother to try to find out who she was. He just liked having her above him on the bed, that face, that hair, as if she was about to come down on him.

But when he had gone to the newsagent that morning to get his *Sun on Sunday* (he only bought it out of nostalgia for the pre-Internet days when he had to rely on top-shelf magazines and *The News of the World*), he had spotted the face on the front of the colour magazine. 'Going upmarket this week, sir?' said the

Asian newsagent as he handed over the cash. He made a point of not answering.

Now he had her name. He opened Twitter, and typed it into the search box. Up it popped, the thing he needed. So easy these days. Her Twitter handle and profile.

@Lisa_Blaize

Fashion historian and author of bestseller
*Shocking: Elsa Schiaparelli and The Invention
of Pink*. Married with three fantabulous
children. Special interest in textiles
and lingerie.

Halo Guy @1972Halo
@Lisa_Blaize. Hello Lisa.

Acknowledgements

Lisa and Sean owe their knowledge of the affair between Laurie Lee and Lorna Garman to Cressida Connolly, *The Rare and the Beautiful: The Lives of the Garmans* (Harper Perennial, 2010) and Valerie Grove, *The Life and Loves of Laurie Lee* (André Deutsch, 1983). As Lee's authorized biographer, Grove had access to his unpublished diaries, from which she quotes but without specific references. Sean's quotations on pp. 92, 119, 123, 124, 129 and 246 are from longer diary extracts quoted by Grove on pp. 166, 171, 80–81, 121–30 and 81–82 of *The Life and Loves of Laurie Lee*. The quotation on p. 128 attributed to Alexander McQueen was on the wall of the V&A's exhibition *Alexander McQueen: Savage Beauty* (2015).

The author is grateful to her loyal editor Arabella Pike, for allowing her to dip her toe in the murky waters of fiction and to Susan Watt for hands-on editing with scrupulous attention to detail and many bright ideas.

Huge thanks to Hilary Davidson for fashion advice. And to the malicious communicator for some (very) raw material.